A Time For Grace

LAURA BILLINGHAM

FIRST EDITION

All characters and events in this publication, other than those clearly in the public domain, are fictitious and any resemblance to real persons, living or dead, is purely coincidental.

All rights reserved.

GREEN CAT BOOKS

www.green-cat.co

CONTENTS

ACKNOWLEDGEMENTS

I'd like to thank my partner, Grey, for supporting me (working to pay the bills!) whilst I dropped out of the rat race to focus on writing and building a business I could run from home. Big thanks also to Green Cat Books for believing in this novel and the talented Pixie Drew for bringing Grace and Ysabella to life on the cover of this book.

CHAPTER 1 – The Unhappy Start

With tears streaming down her face, Grace flung open her car door, slamming it shut as soon as she was in and hitting the lock button. Her left breast was tender where the oafish bloke at the party she had so hurriedly departed had seen fit to squeeze and pinch as she was dancing, and her mouth felt bruised from forced kisses.

Dashing her hand across her eyes, leaving a streak of black mascara over her nose in the process, Grace fired up the engine. *That's it, celibacy for me!* Even as she thought it, a part of her was saying, *don't be silly, woman, somewhere out there is the man for you - you just haven't found him yet.*

Arriving back at the tiny flat above a bookshop in Wilmslow, she parked her ancient Mini in the allocated spot in the yard and ran up the metal steps to her door. It was good to be home, and with a sigh she kicked off her shoes and switched on the electric kettle; tea and toast sounded like a good idea right now - that and snuggling up in bed with her books. Finally, ensconced in bed with a plate of toast dripping with butter and a huge mug of tea, Grace felt able to relax...it had been a hell of a day, actually, a hell of a year, and she desperately needed a change of scene. Funds being low meant that was highly unlikely to happen anytime soon so, she told herself, *better just get on with it, girl!*

Munching on her toast she began to run the events of the past year over in her head; it had started out well, after excellent results in the second year of her midwifery degree she had started the third year all guns

1

blazing and was thoroughly enjoying the work, both the practical and the theory. No matter how many births she witnessed and assisted in she was sure she would never ever get over how moving the event was for all concerned. It had been a relatively late decision to take a degree in midwifery, made when she was 23 after a string of dead-end jobs, but it had most definitely been the right one. Then, just before Christmas, had come the news that her father had been diagnosed with pancreatic cancer. It was a particularly aggressive type and he had died at the beginning of February; her world and that of her mother's had fallen apart for he had been the linchpin of the family. Her mother simply hadn't coped and took an overdose of pills and vodka in early April, leaving Grace effectively without family aged 25. *Well, not strictly true*, she thought, thinking fondly of her eccentric uncle Ray in his rambling old house in the Cotswolds.

The one person she had hoped would support and be there for her, her boyfriend Dave, had sadly proven himself to be incapable of being anything other than a self-centred little boy; rather than allow her to lean on him, he had seemed to expect that his life would go on as normal, that she would cook, clean and generally look after him as she had over the two years they had been together. Eventually Grace had had to throw him out for the sake of whatever sanity she had left.

Given all the stress she found herself under her studies had suffered and eventually the university had agreed to let her defer the third year and start afresh in the new academic year. This reprise allowed her to concentrate on settling her parent's affairs, which was messy and not much of a financial legacy, and then buy the little flat she now called home. Now, in mid-July, she found herself at rather a loose end and longing for the new term to re-commence so she had something to occupy her mind.

Thinking of Uncle Ray as she had been led Grace to wonder if he may fancy some company, for a while. She'd always loved her childhood visits to his beautiful, large but rather ramshackle home and realised it was probably several years since she had last made the trip. Of course, he'd been at the funerals and had told her then to visit when she felt ready. Resolving to phone him in the morning she turned off the bedside light and snuggled down under the duvet. Before long she was sound asleep, somehow the idea of doing *something,* even so small a thing as ring her uncle, felt like an achievement and Grace had always needed to 'achieve' in some way or another.

The following morning after a long, hot shower, strong coffee and cereal, Grace ferreted around in one of the many remaining unpacked boxes in her minute spare room looking for the old address book which contained her uncle's phone number. After a few minutes she shouted triumphantly, "Gotcha!" and sat cross legged on the floor, mobile phone in hand, flipping the pages until she came to 'Uncle Ray', then in brackets (Raymond Minter). His name had always made her giggle as a child and she remembered being rather glad that she bore her father's surname rather than her mother's. One-handed she touched the numbers on the screen of her smart phone and saved the entry, *better than relying on an old book* she thought before hitting the dial key. The connection was quickly made, and Grace heard the

3

sound which confirmed the ancient telephone at Uncle Ray's; if it was the one she remembered and, as he **never** got rid of anything unless it was broken, it was a fair bet it was, was ringing loudly in the echoey old hallway.

Several rings later a breathless and gruff voice answered somewhat peremptorily, "Yes. Who is this?"

Grace had to giggle, Uncle Ray was famed for hating anything technological, hence not updating to a new telephone, and indeed had only been persuaded to have a line installed because his wife, now dead many years, was ill.

"Uncle Ray, it's Gracie," that being his preferred version of her name, "I was wondering if I could take you up on your suggestion to visit, perhaps stay a few weeks, I need a change of scenery."

"Gracie, Gracie," his deep voice boomed back down the line, "how are you, my dear?" He sounded full of smiles now he knew who was calling him, and Grace imagined him in one of his tatty old cardigans running his hand through his thick grey hair, causing it to stand on end in a rather disreputable way. "Of course you must come, and stay as long as you want. I'll sort out a room for you today if you like? Your old room overlooking the garden?"

Grace grinned. She loved the room he mentioned, the leaded mullioned windows were probably fitted with their original glass, a greenish colour, very thick and slightly textured, which caused a rippling water effect in the room when the sun shone through. The wallpaper was faded roses and the white cast iron bed frame looked like it belonged to another time, (which it most probably did). It was shabby in what would, in certain circles, be termed chic and had been Grace's room of choice whenever she visited as a child. "That would be perfect, Uncle Ray," she said, adding, "is tomorrow too soon for me to come?"

"Today, tomorrow, the sooner the better, my child," was the response, "I have worried about you up there all alone. You need to be around family, my dear, and as I'm the only family you have left you should be here!"

This was said with such authority that Grace felt almost like the small child of old whom he would admonish to 'eat your greens', 'brush your teeth', 'get to sleep'.

"Yes, Uncle," she said meekly, "I have a few things to sort out here first and then I shall set off to you early tomorrow morning, should be with you by lunchtime. Will that be OK?"

"It certainly will, Gracie, and I look forward to spending time with you, my favourite niece."

"Your only niece," she chided.

"So definitely my favourite then!" Gracie could hear the warmth of a smile in his voice, it would be good to be with someone who cared for her.

For the rest of the day Grace was occupied with tidying the flat, packing for her trip and sorting out the payment of a few bills. Around midday she took a break and a

5

popped out to her local coffee bar for a foaming cappuccino and a panini; there was very little by way of food at home and it seemed pointless buying stuff when she was setting off early in the morning. Feeling refreshed she walked slowly back to the flat, paper bag containing a lemon muffin, a ham sandwich and a packet of crisps (her evening meal) in hand, lost in thought; the events of the previous night were still fresh in her mind and she shuddered as she remembered the drunken man who had groped her.

Since the split with Dave, she'd had very little contact with members of the opposite sex (her fellow midwifery students being exclusively female - although there was a male student in the year below) and going to the party had supposedly been her re-introduction to the world of dating, drinking, dancing and generally having fun. *Fun!?* she exclaimed internally, *I'd have had more fun staying at home and sticking needles in my eyes!*

It hadn't started well, she had turned up at the prescribed time, bottle of red wine in hand, to find everyone except the host was apparently in the local pub. Not wanting to drink as she was driving, Grace chose to stay and make desultory small talk with the host, someone she scarcely knew. It was excruciating, and the relief felt by both of them when the other guests finally began to drift in from their sojourn in the pub was palpable. Having spent a couple of hours already imbibing their body weight in alcohol, most of the guests, students in the main, who had chosen not to go home over the summer break, were more than halfway to being very drunk and Grace felt distinctly out of place;

not only was she sober, she was also several years older than most of them.

The 'groping git', as she mentally christened him, had suddenly appeared at her side as she was dancing with a couple of girls from her course. He'd broken into the middle of the group and begun gyrating and grinding his hips against one of the girls before turning his attention to Grace.

"Cmhere, sschweetheart," he'd slurred before launching himself at her, grabbing her boob as he did so and attempting to place a wet kiss on her lips.

Wrenching herself away, at some cost to her breast, Grace had managed to initially repel his advances with humour, but he simply wouldn't take no for an answer and had managed to pin her against a wall where he assaulted her boobs again and forced his tongue into her mouth in a parody of a kiss. Struggling wildly, she'd kneed him very firmly in the groin and slapped his face - hard - before snatching up her handbag and bolting for the door.

As she fled she heard him shout, "Bitch. You wanted it!" The attack on such a sensitive area of *his* anatomy apparently having restored his ability to speak coherently.

That thought made Grace giggle a little as she ascended the steps to her door, *funny what a knee in the bollocks does to a bloke!* she reflected, but what was it about her personally that appeared to attract men who only wanted to get in her knickers? She wasn't overtly flirtatious, never gave off 'I'm available' signals, well at least she didn't think she did, and she never dressed too provocatively. What Grace couldn't see, would never recognise, was the sparkle in her eyes, the tilt of her head and her shapely body...she didn't need plunging necklines, high heels or a face full of make up; sex appeal simply oozed from her pores and males responded, mistaking her innate sensuality for overt sexuality. Men simply misinterpreted her and were often taken aback by her negative reactions. Some would become abusive, some merely retreated abashed, but few were ever strong enough to stick around and discover the real Grace Barnes. Consequently, when Dave, good looking and charming, had appeared and seemed to want more than sex, Grace had been so surprised she had effectively just given in. It turned out he'd been after a mother/cook/cleaner and not a lover; in fact, eventually she had come to the conclusion that he was a closet gay. When he had then been such a useless lump after her parents passed away, it had been easy to kick him into touch. He'd protested of course and professed undying love, but her mind was made up and out he went.

"Someday your prince will come, Gracie," she said out loud as she turned the key and entered the flat, "you've just got to hope you recognise him!"

The rest of the day found Grace in a reflective mood, normally a glass-half-full person she began to feel rather miserable; just for once she would have liked someone to be there for her, someone to hold her tight and tell her everything would be alright but, as one of life's natural born copers, it was usually her that propped up others and somewhere along the line she had forgotten how to let someone look after her.

"Snap out of it, you mardy bugger," she remonstrated with herself, "life's a bitch and then you die! Make the most of what you have girl, there are no second chances." Finally, grinning at herself because she'd found herself speaking aloud, Grace retreated to bed looking forward to heading off to Gloucestershire on the morrow.

Chapter 2 - On Her Way

With a quick breakfast eaten, pots washed and car packed, Grace toured the flat making sure all was in order and everything other than the fridge freezer was unplugged. Her spirits had lifted considerably since the previous evening and now she was looking forward to spending a few weeks with her uncle, a few weeks of doing very little other than read in his lovely garden and eat and drink things she hadn't made or bought herself.

By 7 a.m she was on her way, any later than that and she would have become snarled up in the rush hour traffic on the M56, but at that time of day it didn't take her long to join the M6 heading south towards Birmingham. Grace turned up the volume on the CD player she had paid to have fitted to her pre-CD days Mini and sang along to Nerina Pellot as she tootled along, no point in trying to exceed the speed limit in this particular car so she may as well just enjoy the journey and get there in one piece.

Eleven o'clock saw her in a service station, enjoying (well drinking) coffee from a cardboard cup, she had briefly considered a muffin to accompany it until she saw the price...£3.50! She'd wait until she got to Uncle Ray's before eating anything. His, or rather his housekeeper's, carrot cake was delicious - as indeed were all her other baked goods and Grace found herself salivating at the thought. Checking the directions she had hastily scribbled in her notebook she decided she would arrive in Duntisbourne Abbots within an hour or so - as long as she didn't miss the junction for the A417, something she had done in the past and which had then entirely thrown her; 'directionally challenged', as she freely admitted she was! Friends had asked her many times why she didn't use the satnav facility on her phone, given her propensity for getting lost and she finally admitted that the simple answer was she couldn't work out how to use it and so stuck to the tried and tested method of looking at a roadmap. She also thought satnavs exceptionally annoying and having an excellent memory found it far easier to retain the road numbers in her head - which was fine on shorter journeys but a tad more trying on cross country jaunts.

A little more than an hour later, thankfully she hadn't missed the exit this time, Grace turned down the narrow little lane which led to her uncle's house. As she negotiated the final bend the house came into view, soft purple wisteria covered mellow stone walls and the panes of glass in the leaded windows caught and reflected the bright midday sunshine. She sighed, it truly was a beautiful house, most of it built in the 17th century and little changed except for a relatively new extension to the rear of the property which housed a modern kitchen, well 1950's modern anyway...Ray's wife had insisted that if she was going to live there she wanted 'all mod cons'. Grace couldn't really remember her Auntie Maud, she had been only 3 when she had passed away; to her the house had always been just Uncle Ray's and it didn't seem to alter from one visit to the next - Uncle Ray appeared almost stuck in a time warp and other than maintenance had really done nothing to the house since Maud died.

Parking her car on the gravel drive to the side of the house, Grace got out and stretched - she rather liked driving but there was no denying that her little Mini was cramped, even for someone who barely scraped 5'5". The front door swung open and Uncle Ray bounded across the front of the house to greet her, dressed, as per usual, in a pair of worn brown corduroy trousers, checked shirt and a voluminous cardigan complete with leather patches to the elbows.

"Gracie, Gracie, Gracie," he boomed, enfolding her in his arms and crushing her against his bony chest, "it's so good to see you my dear. Let me look at you." Pulling away from her he eyed her critically, "You're too thin, Gracie, and you look tired, come on, let's get you inside and Mrs Parkes can start to feed you up...coffee and walnut cake today - my favourite. We'll bring your belongings in later."

Grace grinned at her uncle, something about him had always reminded her of an over exuberant Afghan Hound, his floppy hair - prone to standing on end after one of his hands through hair sessions – oversized cardigans and general tendency to dress entirely in shades of beige and brown, adding to the overall effect. "I've been dreaming of one of Mrs Parkes cakes since I stopped for coffee in a service station. It's great to be here Uncle Ray."

Arm draped around her shoulder Uncle Ray guided her into the house, bees were humming busily in the wisteria and the perfume from the gillyflowers and sweet peas in the cottage-style front garden was heady. Grace felt the tension she had carried within her since the death of her parents begin to dissipate, it WAS good to be here.

The hallway of the old house was, as usual, cool and dark with that indefinable but undeniably 'old' smell. The ancient telephone was still in its accustomed spot on the hall stand and a selection of coats and jackets, all in varying shades of brown, hung on an old-fashioned coat stand which was surmounted by a tatty leather hat in the style of Indiana Jones - Uncle Ray's headgear of choice in inclement weather. Rooms led off either side of the wide hallway and the old oak staircase hugged the left hand wall as it made its stately progress to the upper floor. Grace and Uncle Ray continued to the very rear of the house where what once had been the original 'kitchen' had been split into a formal dining room one side and on the other access to the 'new' extended room with modern plumbing. Uncle Ray may have given in and allowed for the construction of this extension but his will had prevailed with regards to the fitting out of the room, no 1950's melamine in here, instead solid oak units had been built and the original large fireplace retained. Any appliances, other than the Aga, were hidden away in a separate utility area. It was a beautiful homely room and right now smelled quite delightfully of freshly brewed coffee and newly baked cake...Grace's mouth watered.

Mrs Parkes turned around as they entered the room and bustled over to Grace, chivvying her to take a seat at the scrubbed wooden table and plying her with a huge chunk of cake and a mug filled to the brim with an aromatic coffee.

"Miss Grace", she intoned, "it's always a pleasure to have someone other than your uncle to cook for!"

Grace smiled, she knew the woman was fiercely loyal to her uncle and had worked for him since before Grace herself was born.

"Now, now," retorted Uncle Ray, "there's Adam too these days and he eats like the proverbial horse!"

"Adam?" Grace raised an eyebrow in question.

"He's a conservationist and historian, helping me to research both this house and our family, Gracie. Comes here a couple of days a week and Mrs Parkes spoils him rotten."

The eponymous Mrs Parkes, Grace had no idea of her Christian name as she had never actually heard anyone call her anything other than Mrs Parkes, nodded. "It's lovely to have someone other than Mr Minter to feed...someone who actually notices the food before wolfing it down!"

That there was a great deal of affection between employer and employee was very evident; in some ways they were more like a long married couple than housekeeper and boss, but Grace knew Mrs Parkes lived in the village with her husband who acted as rector for the local church, which was visible from the house, and had raised a couple of sons who were now providing her with a brood of grandchildren.

"Mr Adam is about your age, Miss Grace," Mrs Parkes added, a speculative gleam in her eye, "perhaps you should arrange to take him out and about whilst you're down here, show him the area as it were. You know the place quite well by now and I'm sure he'd appreciate being escorted by someone as pretty as you." Subtlety was not one of Mrs Parkes' strong points and Grace couldn't help but laugh at the blatant attempt at matchmaking.

"I'm sure Uncle Ray is keeping him very busy with his research, Mrs Parkes, and I wouldn't want to be the one to take him away from that," was her noncommittal response, but she could tell from the look in the housekeeper's eyes that this was a topic which would be re-visited - and soon.

Uncle Ray, meanwhile, was also looking at Grace and he joined the conversation with, "You know, Gracie, you could do worse than someone like Adam, he's a fine young man, he'd look after you like a man should."

"Uncle Ray!" exclaimed Grace, "You're as bad as she is. I've not even met the man and you're both trying to marry us off. Honestly!"

Uncle Ray had the good sense to look abashed, "Sorry, Gracie, but you have had such a torrid year, I only want to see you happy, love."

Grace smiled, "I know, Uncle...but I'm really not sure a relationship is what I need right now. Not that I'm not very interested in meeting this paragon of manliness though! Now can I please just enjoy this delicious cake?"

The cake *was* delicious and having not eaten since breakfast Grace was ravenous; the generous slice barely touched the sides and a laughing Mrs Parkes cut her another large piece. "Nice to see you haven't lost your appetite, Miss Grace...how on earth do you manage to stay so skinny?"

Grace grinned and after swallowing the last bite of cake replied, "It's a gift, Mrs Parke, perhaps it will catch up with me when I'm middle-aged."

The three of them passed a pleasant half hour or so in desultory chat as the coffee was drunk and cups replenished a couple of times, before Grace declared she needed to use the bathroom and unpack her belongings. Uncle Ray offered to collect her bags from the car whilst she availed herself of the downstairs toilet and Mrs Parkes informed her that lunch would be ready at 1.30...adding, "If you still have room that is!"

By the time Grace had used the cloakroom and made her way upstairs to her usual room, Uncle Ray had already carried her single small suitcase and soft holdall from the car and deposited them on the bed. He was looking out of the open window at the pretty front garden of the house but turned when she entered the room.

"Gracie my sweet, I'll leave you in peace for a while, you must be sleepy after the drive. It's still an hour until lunch so you have time for a nap if you like, I'll call you when Mrs Parkes is ready to serve." He crossed the room and gave her a quick hug before exiting the door which he closed quietly behind him.

Grace took a deep inhalation, breathing in the smells of the familiar room; floor polish, the heady perfume of sweet peas which were jammed into a small vase on the dressing table, freshly laundered bedding and the clean fresh air of the countryside. She did feel tired, so after removing her belongings from the bed, she laid down atop the white crocheted bedspread and within seconds she was asleep. Dreams came quickly to her, a dark-haired man with piercing blue eyes, flower-filled meadows and a castle on a hill.

The distant sound of her name being called roused Grace from her slumber. Stretching luxuriantly, she yawned and rubbed her eyes, it had been ages since she had fallen asleep so quickly and even longer since she had managed to sleep during the day. Swinging her legs over the side of the bed she sat up, the last vestiges of dreams receded and try as she might she couldn't recall anything other than a vague feeling of loss and sadness.

Finally, fully awake, she headed back to the kitchen where Mrs Parkes had laid the large table with place settings for two and was in the process of placing various dishes containing salads, cold meats and a selection of homemade breads. Spotting Grace she smiled, "As it's such a warm day and you ate so much cake, I thought a light lunch was in order. I've a meat pie ready for your supper, just needs putting in the oven, and there's new potatoes and green beans to go with it."

"Mrs Parkes, you are an absolute treasure," said Grace, "I wish I could take you back to Wilmslow with me! Not that there's room in my place to swing a cat, leave alone justify having a housekeeper."

Mrs Parkes smiled and produced a jug of freshly made lemonade clinking with ice cubes - the old fashioned still variety, not the chemical laden fizzy drink - and proceeded to pour a large glass for Grace which she put on the table with the rest of the repast.

"Right," she said, "time for me to go, I don't usually come in on a Tuesday but in honour of your visit Mr Minter asked me to pop in. I've written the instructions for heating the pie on here," she indicated a slip of paper she'd pinned to the cork notice board near the door, "and I presume you know how to cook the potatoes and beans?" This last was said somewhat dubiously, in Mrs Parkes world, everyone but her was useless in the kitchen.

Grace stifled a grin, "Thanks, Mrs Parkes, I'm sure we'll manage between us. I'll cover up any of the leftovers from lunch and put them in the fridge, shall I?"

"If you would, Miss Grace, there should be enough for sandwiches tomorrow. Oh, don't put any bread in the fridge, pop it in here," she pointed to the large earthenware bread bin, "it keeps it better."

Uncle Ray ambled into the kitchen at that point and shooed her off home, "Off you go, Mrs Parkes, and thank you so much for all this," he waved his hand at the table, "we'll see you Thursday, yes?"

"That you will, Mr Minter. Grace knows what's for your supper and there'll be left over meat and salad for lunch tomorrow. You'll have to fend for yourself for tomorrow's supper, unless you want me to come in and do something for you?"

"We'll manage!" Grace and her uncle exclaimed simultaneously.

Over lunch uncle and niece chatted about the tumultuous year Grace had suffered. Talking about the sudden deaths of both her parents brought the feelings of grief back; a grief she hadn't really expressed openly in the immediate aftermath of either death, too busy initially with comforting her mother and then, following her suicide, the small matter of coroners, solicitors and estate agents. Now, in the relaxed atmosphere of the beautiful old house and in the presence of her loving uncle she finally let go and the tears came. Uncle Ray led her to the old settle near the Aga, sat her down and held her in his arms as she sobbed and shook in paroxysms of grief. He said little, making instead the kind of simple reassuring noises one makes when a baby needs comfort. He knew she needed to unleash all the hidden sadness before she would be able to move on with her life; until this moment she had been functioning on autopilot, he knew her well enough to recognise this fact and also, a little wryly, he admitted to himself that it's how he had been following the death of his beloved Maud.

It was some time before Grace managed to control the tears and neither of them noticed the tall dark man who had appeared at the open kitchen door. Adam had arrived shortly after they had moved to the settle and for a few moments had stood at the doorway acutely aware that he was intruding on an intensely personal moment. Awkward as he felt however, and he did feel like an intruder, he found he couldn't take his eyes away from the young woman sobbing so heartbrokenly in Ray

19

Minter's arms. She appeared slight and slender, yet curvaceous and womanly at the same time; dark wavy, almost curly hair, fell around her face and although he couldn't see her eyes he knew, KNEW, they were of a deep hazel brown. Adam shook himself, this wasn't right, he'd come, at his employer's behest, to meet the niece, Grace -whom he presumed was this distraught young woman - but it wasn't fair to impose himself at this juncture. He found it hard to tear himself away however, every fibre of his being was urging him to rush in, take the woman in his own arms and tell everything would be alright now. 'Get a grip, man' he scolded himself as he finally turned and walked swiftly back towards the village.

When the sobbing eventually turned into sniffles and then finally ceased altogether, Grace heaved a huge sigh. Where on earth had that come from? She wasn't normally prone to such hysterics, usually managing to keep a lid on her emotions in fact.

"That's better," her uncle said, then, as if reading her mind, "it doesn't do to keep such pain inside. Does things to your head, you know!" He gave her a final hug and then stood up, "I think YOU could do with a cup of tea, young lady."

"And some of that coffee and walnut cake?" Grace asked tremulously. "All that crying's made me hungry." She smiled, a wobbly watery effort, but a smile nonetheless and her uncle beamed back.

 "Now that sounds like an excellent idea."

He busied himself making a pot of tea and cutting slabs of cake for the pair of them whilst Grace, excusing herself, made her way to the cloakroom just off the hallway. Viewing her blotched and tear-stained reflection in the mirror, she grimaced and filled the sink with cold water which she proceeded to splash onto her face. After patting her face dry and thoroughly blowing her nose she felt better, she honestly hadn't realised just how much emotion she had been holding inside and it felt good to finally begin to expunge at least some of the sadness.

Back in the kitchen Uncle Ray had placed the teapot, cups and a bottle of milk on the table together with the two plates of cake. "Mrs Parkes would go mad if she saw me using the milk straight from the bottle," he grinned as Grace walked in, "very particular about using a jug she is, but I just think it makes more washing up!"

"I'll wash up, Uncle Ray," offered Grace, "it's the least I can do. Sorry I blubbed so much, I seem to have soaked your shirt!"

There was indeed a large damp patch on the front of his shirt where Grace had rested her head as she cried, complete with streaks of mascara.

"You needed to let it all out, Gracie, it's a family trait you know, strong in the face of adversity!"

The phone in the hall began to ring at that moment so he excused himself to answer it. Grace wrapped her hands around the mug of tea and pondered on his words; he was right, her mother had rarely shown much by way of emotional weakness, that is until her father had died. It was probably the fact that up to that point her mum had seemed capable of dealing with anything which had made her collapse and subsequent suicide seem so shocking. Grace realised she hadn't dared let out her own emotions in case she should crumble as spectacularly as her mother. Bizarrely, to Grace anyway, the explosion of tears DID seem to have helped, it was cathartic to let go of all that pent-up emotion.

"That was Adam," said Uncle Ray, re-entering the kitchen and breaking her reverie, "I had asked him over to join us after lunch, but it seems something has cropped up and he can't make it. You'll meet him on Friday instead, as tomorrow he works elsewhere and on Thursday he and I have a meeting in Bath. You'll be OK for the day, won't you Gracie?" He thought it best not to mention that Adam had borne witness to her tears, he knew how proud and self-contained Grace was and how appalled she would be to know that a stranger had seen her so out of control. The more he got to know Adam Davenport the more impressed he was by the man; steadfast, loyal, intelligent and now he had shown a compassionate side. *Careful, Ray*, he counselled himself, *Gracie won't appreciate match-making even though he'd be bloody perfect for her!*

"I'll be fine on Thursday, Uncy Ray," smiled Grace, using the pet name she had employed as a small child. "In fact I was thinking of popping over to see Jenny, remember her? She used to live in the village when I visited as a kid and we became good friends. We've kept in touch and she's married now, lives in Cirencester and just had a baby. I'll give her a ring later, I'm sure Thursday will work for her."

Ray was relieved, if truth be known he had felt guilty about leaving her alone after he had pestered so long for her to visit, but the trip on Thursday to a specialist in Medieval French history had been arranged for ages, Adam and he hoped it would cast light on the family's origins in France and how and when the family had ended up in the UK.

"What would you like to do tomorrow, Gracie?" Ray asked her. Grace swallowed a mouthful of cake, took a large glug of her tea, and replied, "As little as possible! Mooch around the house, read a little, sit in the garden if the weather holds...really, I just need space to get my head straight again...well as straight as my head will ever get!" she grinned widely at the last statement. "Thursday I'll go and see Jenny and Friday you want me to meet the enigmatic Adam, so it would be great to just relax tomorrow...unless you had something planned of course."

"Nothing planned, no. I wanted to see what kind of shape you were in before dragging you into my social whirl," Uncle Ray quipped. "Perhaps you may be interested in taking a look at some of the family tree stuff I've uncovered...we go way back you know. Adam has helped me track an ancestor back to France and on Thursday we're meeting with a Medieval specialist who apparently has some intriguing clues to help us go even further back in time and further south in France!"

His enthusiasm was infectious and Grace found herself agreeing to take a look at the work done to date. "But not right now," she stated firmly, "all that crying has worn me out, I really need to sit quietly for a time, read a book or watch something on TV...just to let my brain calm down a bit."

Ray seemed a tad crestfallen, but only briefly, and led her into the cosy den which had once been a separate dining room but had for years been taken over as a place to relax on the squashy leather sofa he had installed.

"The telly's old," he said, somewhat needlessly as it was self-evidently not a new model, "but it works, and there's some videos you may like," he pointed to a pile of VHS tapes and the video player under the TV...the advent of DVD's obviously not yet having merited him changing the equipment.

Grace gave him a hug, "Thanks Uncle Ray, you're a gem. I'll just do that washing up and then come back and watch one of those films."

"There's a dishwasher now," he informed her, "Mrs Parkes insisted...but I never know how to work the damn thing! It's next to the sink, hidden behind a cupboard door."

"Well you load it up and I'll set it going once we've had supper," said Grace, sinking into the sofa and looking at the spines of the videos; she thought she had spotted **Pride and Prejudice**, the TV series, not the Keira Knightley film, and a few hours with Colin Firth sounded very therapeutic. Uncle Ray trundled off leaving her snuggled down on the sofa, video in the player and remote control in her hand. When he returned a couple of hours later it was to find her curled up fast asleep and, with her tousled hair and sleep-flushed face, looking years younger than her actual 26. He smiled gently to himself, Maud and he had longed for children but it wasn't to be, instead he thought of Grace as his surrogate daughter and the paternal urge to protect her, vulnerable as she currently seemed, was overwhelming. Debating whether to wake her, he eventually decided to just let her be; it would appear that she had been running on empty for months, rest was what she needed and there was no point rousing her from such a deep slumber.

When Grace finally did awaken, some three hours later, she was initially confused as to where she was; the TV was still on but showing a blank screen as the video had run to the end and then re-wound itself and the only noise was the soft hiss from the screen and the sweet sound of bird song. As she came fully to her senses she remembered where she was...Uncle Ray's. *Jeez* she thought, *how long have I been asleep this time?* However long it had been she actually felt better than she had done for many months, as if the weight she had been carrying around for so long had finally been lifted and she could look to the future. It had been the right thing coming here, the wonderful old house and the love of her uncle had already worked wonders on her bruised and battered psyche and she felt ready to take on the world again. She fast forwarded the video to the last point she recalled watching, after all she couldn't miss the wet-from-the-lake Mr Darcy!

Uncle Ray joined her a little later, and they watched together for a while before adjourning to the kitchen where Grace instructed her uncle on the intricacies of hob and oven, it being obvious that his usual evening meal was one Mrs Parkes plated for him to reheat in the microwave - a surprisingly modern piece of equipment but one which, for a change, he seemed remarkably adept at using. By the time the meal was prepared, eaten, the kitchen cleared and the dishwasher loaded and running it was almost 10pm and Ray was quite obviously flagging, so Grace suggested they both head to bed. Despite her impromptu naps earlier in the day she felt rather worn out herself and the idea of snuggling under the covers with a novel from the selection in the house's tiny library, really just an odd shaped room lined floor to ceiling with an eclectic array of books which Ray had collected over the years, was more than a little appealing.

Uncle Ray headed up first after hugging Grace tightly to him and murmuring, "I'm glad you're here, Gracie, this is your home you know, girly, or will be one day."

He loped up the stairs leaving Grace stunned...had he just intimated that he was leaving the old house to her? Shrugging her shoulders, that was a question for another day, Grace entered the small library room and selected a paperback novel by Philippa Gregory (a historical tale seemed fitting to her surroundings) before returning to the kitchen to pour a glass of milk. The milk was drunk but only a chapter of the book read before Grace once again succumbed to sleep. She dreamt again of the blue-eyed man and a place of vast stone walls and lofty views over a river sparkling in the sunlight.

Chapter 3 – The History Lesson

The sound of bird song greeted Grace as she awoke the next day; the morning sunshine through the greenish glass in the windows, which she had left unhindered by the floral curtains, cast a watery glow around the room and engendered in Grace feelings of immense contentment and of 'belonging'. Judging by the stillness in the house it was obviously very early and a quick check at her mobile phone confirmed this, 5.30. Her initial temptation was to remain where she was and sleep some more but her mind simply wouldn't be still and finally, after tossing and turning for a few minutes, she decided to get up and make tea and toast. She rummaged around in her case and extracted a lightweight robe and a pair of towelling slippers in a plastic wrap, which she had 'accidentally' put in her bag after a visit to a spa, and, donning the items she set off downstairs via the bathroom.

The old house was creaking its way into the day, the way old buildings do, but otherwise it was immensely peaceful and felt so very welcoming. Once in the kitchen, Grace cut a couple of slices of Mrs Parkes sourdough loaf and stuck it into the electric toaster she discovered hiding in one of the cupboards. Toast slathered with butter and a cup of tea made, she decided it would be nice to sit in the garden, so she exited via the kitchen door and took a seat on the bench which rested against the wall. Although early in the day it was warm and promised to get warmer, bees buzzed busily in the wisteria and a couple of colourful butterflies played chase across the garden. The birds chirruped, whistled and sang their morning greetings and Grace did an

27

internal *ahhhh* - for the first time in a long time it felt good - no great - to be alive.

The toasted sourdough was delicious, helped in no small measure by the generous application of creamy butter and Grace ate it rapidly, the fresh, clean air making her feel even hungrier than she usually did. As she contemplated further slices she heard Uncle Ray enter the kitchen, so she popped her head around the still open back door to say hello. Her poor uncle nearly had apoplexy not having expected her to be up and moving, but soon recovered and joined her in the sunshine with his own tea and toast, whilst Grace tucked into seconds.

"I never expected you to be such an early bird, Gracie," said Ray, "when you used to come here as a teenager we had all on to get you out of bed by midday."

Grace grinned, "Times have changed," she retorted, "these days I have shifts to cope with, early mornings and late nights. Plus, I seem to need less sleep AND I did have more than my allotted shut-eye over the course of yesterday. It's also a gorgeous day and I didn't want to waste it."

"So, what shall we do with this gorgeous day then, Gracie? I really would like you to have a look at some of the research Adam and I have done, it's your family and I think you will be interested, BUT I understand if you would rather sit outside and enjoy the sunshine." His words said one thing but his demeanour another; it was obvious he wanted her to share in the research, so Grace suggested a kind of compromise.

"You have some garden furniture in the shed, don't you?" she asked, gesturing to the ramshackle construction further down the garden. "At least you used to, I remember it. Why don't we bring that out and then we can sit at a table in the sun when you show me what you discovered."

"Sounds like a plan, Gracie!" he exclaimed, already halfway to the shed.

Within 10 minutes the two of them had carted the wooden furniture, a little cobwebbed and dusty but otherwise perfectly serviceable, up to the paved area outside the kitchen and installed the slightly mildewed parasol into the hole in the middle of the octagonal table. The pair of them were dirty and dishevelled as a result of their exertions and Grace couldn't help but laugh at the mohican-like quiff Uncle Ray had developed and the cobweb hanging rather fetchingly from his left ear.

"You are a scruff, Uncle Ray," she giggled, "what Mum used to call a muck magnet!" She paused momentarily as she absorbed the fact that she had just recounted a memory of her mother without the overwhelming sadness she had encountered on every other occasion since her death. "Come here and let me get rid of that cobweb," she added.

He succumbed to her ministrations without demur, even allowing her to flatten down the errant hair, then stood back and admired their handiwork. "You know, I haven't had this furniture out for years, didn't seem worth it with just me to use it." He looked rather forlorn and Grace realised he'd probably been lonely for years, ever since

29

Aunt Maud died in fact, it made her feel rather sad and not a little guilty for not visiting him more often. "Still, we'll get some use out of it now you're here, provided the weather holds of course."

Grace hugged him and said, "Even if it rains...there's the parasol," opening the item up to demonstrate, only to end up in gales of laughter as the damn thing, when fully opened, was full of holes - probably inflicted by mice judging from the amount of them and their raggedy edges.

Ray joined in her laughter, "Perhaps I should buy a new one, this is neither use nor ornament is it?!"

Once past their joint giggling fit at the threadbare parasol, the pair of them decided to head back inside to shower and dress, agreeing to meet back outside within the hour.

Grace ran up the stairs and made her way to the bathroom nearest her room, the plumbing was temperamental at the best of times, but that bathroom was fitted with an electric shower which was generally more reliable in producing a supply of hot water than was the old boiler. Freshly showered and dressed in a t-shirt and shorts she pulled a comb through her hair and decided to let it dry naturally in the warm sunshine; she glanced briefly at her make up bag and then thought *sod it*, choosing instead to simply apply a moisturiser. *Uncle Ray can have the 'au natural' me*, she smiled to herself. Just as she was about to set off back to the garden her mobile phone beeped once, indicating that a text message had arrived. A quick glance showed the sender to be Dave and the message was deleted unread, he'd sent regular texts begging to move back in and it was getting tiresome. He'd had to resort to sleeping on a mate's sofa since she had booted him out as he had no job and very little obvious intention in getting one; it was time he learned to stand on his own two feet and she had absolutely no desire to see him, let alone share a bed with him.

By the time Grace had reached the garden, Uncle Ray had made a pot of tea for them both and was in the process of sorting through a large box of papers, selecting and rejecting documents and placing the ones he deemed important in a pile on top of the table.

"Can I help?" asked Grace.

"No, no, it's OK," Ray responded, "You don't need, nor probably want, to see ALL of this," he indicated the box, "so I'm just trying to pull out the most interesting stuff."

Grace settled onto one of the chairs and helped herself to a cup of tea whilst he continued the search and find mission. After a few minutes he announced, "This should do," and put the box onto the ground beside him.

They chatted for a while about this and that, and then, after arranging the selected papers into some kind of order, Uncle Ray began to give a potted history of their family.

Despite herself, Grace did find she was drawn into the story and she gazed with fascination at the complex family tree Ray presented to her. It was apparent that an incredible amount of work had gone into tracing the various branches, presumably Adam had a great deal to do with it as the research was meticulous and the facts clearly presented - in a fashion quite unlike Ray Minter's scatter gun approach. Theirs was not a large family, each generation seeming to have produced only a limited number of children, but it must have required immense dedication to track people back through not only history, but, as Grace realised, geography. Her antecedents appeared to have arrived in the UK sometime in the early 15th Century but the family tree, and Uncle Ray's dialogue, indicated an origin somewhere in France.

"This is as far as we've got so far," Ray said, pointing to a name on the tree. "He suddenly pops up in some records from Brittany dated early 14th century. The name 'Bastier' is Occitan we think, and we can't work out how a Breton trader would have such a surname. That's why Adam and I are off to Bath tomorrow, a specialist there has found the same name in other records from even earlier and we want to see if there's a link."

"Bastier," Grace murmured, "I'm sure I've heard that name before."

Ray glanced at her in surprise. Her voice sounded almost dreamlike, distant, quite unlike her usual tone; she looked lost in thought as if focussing inwards, her eyes gazing sightlessly into the distance. Suddenly she seemed to shrug herself into the present again.

"No idea why I thought I knew the name," she laughed, "but just for a moment it was as if I'd heard it spoken before, a long time ago. Must be imagination working over time!"

Uncle Ray laughed back, "It's all the talk of the past, got you momentarily daydreaming I suspect. Perhaps it's the lack of nourishment, it is past lunch o'clock you know."

Grace pulled her phone from a pocket. "So it is! Wow, time has just flown by. Let's go and find out what goodies we have left from yesterday."

Some 30 minutes later they were back out in the sunshine, the table now bearing a selection of cold meats, cheeses, breads and fruit and a fresh pot of tea. Uncle Ray surveyed the food set out in front of them.

"I think I shall treat you to a meal in the pub tonight," he said, "nice as all this is, I don't want more cold cuts for supper!"

Grace giggled, "We could cook something," she admonished him, "I checked and there's plenty of stuff like bacon and sausages plus eggs etc, I could do us a nice fry up."

Ray looked thoughtful for a moment, "Nope, I fancy a pint and something with chips tonight. Fry up in the morning sounds good though!"

Grace rolled her eyes, "Honestly, Uncle Ray, how you don't weigh at least 20 stone is a miracle!" As she was saying this she was constructing a humungous open sandwich consisting of a couple of thick slices of ham and a wedge of cheddar atop a doorstop of bread spread thickly with butter.

Ray raised his eyebrows "Pot, kettle, black," he chuckled just as the sandwich reached Grace's mouth; she snorted with laughter, dislodging the cheese in the process.

"Must be genetic," she giggled, retrieving the cheese and settling it back into position before taking a large bite.

They spent the rest of the day in happy contemplation of the various findings Ray and Adam had made so far in respect of the family tree, before Grace excused herself to go and change into something with a bit more leg coverage for their trip to the pub. It was deliciously dark and cool in the house in contrast to the warmth of the summer day outside and as Grace headed upstairs she thought she caught the faint scent of lavender.

Replete after a hearty meal in the pub down the road and feeling the effects of the best part of a bottle of a quite decent red wine, Grace linked her arm through that of her uncle as they walked somewhat unsteadily back to the house. Not yet fully dark, the air was full of bothersome midges, but the scent of wildflowers from hedgerows and nearby fields was heady and in a rush of bonhomie Grace turned and hugged her uncle.

"It's good to be alive," she proclaimed, "and here with you."

Ray hugged her back, "I'm very glad you are here, my Gracie, and it's good to see you happy again, although how much of that is wine I wonder?"

Grace hiccupped and then giggled, "I'm a little out of practice these days I'm afraid. There was a time when a bottle of wine would have just been the start! Anyway, you had some of the wine AND four pints of ale, it'll be you with headache tomorrow, not me."

Ray nodded sagely, "Indeed, I shall probably suffer a little tomorrow, but life is for living, Gracie, and it's a headache I won't regret."

The first stars had begun to glitter in the deepening blue of the sky by the time they reached the front door; they heard the hoot of an owl and glimpsed a couple of bats sweeping to and fro in their quest for insects; it was a beautiful night, warm but not humid and the moon rose full and bright above them. Grace took a deep inhalation noting the loamy smell of the rich soil, the scent of the wisteria and sweet peas in the garden and overlaying all this the fresh clean, pollution free air. She had forgotten just how much better she felt in the country, although a city girl through and through having lived most of her life in and around Manchester, she had always found respite in the open air and regularly drove out to the nearby Peak District whenever she felt the city was suffocating her. Uncle Ray's apparent declaration that the house would ultimately pass to her was unexpected yet somehow felt right; comfortable, and gave her a different kind of future to look forward to, one of starry nights, clean air and an absence of traffic noise.

Upon reaching her room she opened the window to its widest extent and dragged the white wicker chair over; stripping off her clothes and wrapping herself in her cotton robe, she perched on the edge of the seat and gazed out of the window at the multitude of stars and at the large silver bright moon. She could be happy here, really happy, but there were still things she needed to do, places she wanted to visit and (her heart added) she wanted to find a man to share her life with. Sighing deeply she looked out at the stars, trying to spot constellations and failing dismally; the pin points of brightness dazzled her and seemed to send individual beams of light her way until all the beams converged into one blazing ray aimed directly at her. Transfixed, Grace could not tear her gaze away, then, as if from far away, she distinctly heard the words, "I will find you." Goosebumps prickled up her arms and she shivered, by nature she was a pragmatic girl, not given to flights of fancy, but she had definitely heard something. Rubbing her arms, she moved to the bed and, shedding her robe, climbed under the covers.

Tired and tipsy as she felt, it was sometime before sleep overcame Grace and her dreams were of warm nights and strong arms holding her tight.

Chapter 4 – And So They Meet

The sun was high in the sky before Grace opened her eyes the following morning; she'd slept well, eventually, and no dreams lingered on the peripheries of her mind. Her head was a little muzzy from the after effects of the wine but thankfully there was no headache; she was, however, ravenously hungry and the smell of cooking bacon was wafting tantalisingly up the stairs, spurring her into dressing rapidly and heading in search of sustenance.

Uncle Ray was seated at the table nursing a large mug of tea whilst Mrs Parkes (the wonderful Mrs Parkes) stood by the Aga busily frying bacon, sausages, mushrooms and eggs. She turned when Grace entered the room, "I thought the smell of food would rouse you from your slumbers, Miss Grace!" she grinned. "Plenty for all. Sit down and pour yourself some tea whilst I finish this off."

It was only as Grace headed for the table that she noticed the dark-haired young, late twenties she guessed, man seated across from Ray, cup of tea to hand. He stood to greet her, and Grace suddenly became aware that in her hurry to reach the kitchen she had donned her shortest shorts and a thin vest top, sans bra, and had left her curly hair to its own devices; she felt ridiculously exposed and embarrassed, although she couldn't say why precisely, and felt herself blushing profusely. *What must I look like?* she thought, as she took the proffered hand and shook it firmly while Uncle Ray introduced him as, "Adam, the researcher I've told you about. Adam, this is Grace, my beautiful niece." Grace shot him a glance, he didn't sound his usual bouncy self, obviously his headache premonition had materialised - looked a little green around the gills too.

Adam had been acutely aware of Grace from the moment she had entered the room, *I was right* he thought, *she does indeed have hazel eyes.* He watched entranced as the colour flooded her face when she realised he was there, *probably regretting wearing that outfit* he speculated wickedly, admiring the trim body barely covered by the top and shorts, whilst taking her small hand in his own large strong one.

"Grace, it's a pleasure to finally meet you," he said. "Ray has told me so much about you and he really hasn't done you justice." Her deep hazel eyes met his clear blue ones and for a moment they were locked in a gaze which seemed timeless. *I'm sure I know him*, thought Grace, lost in his eyes, *yet I know I've only just met him.*

"Hrmphh!" Ray interrupted whatever it was happening between the two of them. "She's my niece, man, I've known her since the day she was born and I'm not in the habit of describing how lovely she is, although she definitely is!"

Grace could not have blushed anymore if she tried, abruptly tearing her hand from Adam's and took a seat opposite him. "Uncle Ray!" she exclaimed, "you really know how to embarrass me!"

Ray grinned amiably, "Well I'm a man and I know when another chap finds a lady attractive, and he certainly thinks you are, my girl," he said, nodding in the direction of his younger friend, who by now was a similar shade of embarrassment as Grace.

Mrs Parkes spared any more blushes by plonking a plate heaped with food in front of her employer. "Get your teeth into that," she commanded, "and leave these two youngsters alone!". Similarly piled plates appeared in front of Grace and Adam and for ten minutes or so the only sounds to be heard were appreciative chewing ones.

The three of them finished their repast almost simultaneously and Adam looked at Grace's clean plate with admiration, "Crikey, you can pack it away, can't you?!" he said, without thinking. Both Grace and her Uncle cracked up in giggles and any residual tension disappeared.

"It seems to be a family trait," commented Mrs Parkes drily as she collected Ray's also empty plate.

Grace grinned widely, "It's your fabulous food, Mrs Parkes. I'll end up as fat as a bacon pig if you keep serving me food like that."

"I doubt it," snorted Mrs Parkes, "you've your uncle's genes and he's been eating my food for longer than I care to remember, yet he's still as skinny as a beanpole!"

Adam studied Grace as unobtrusively as he could, the high blush of earlier had been replaced by the normal healthy flush of a young woman, her skin was clear and very slightly olive toned and her lips were full - he imagined kissing them - the hazel eyes were wide, fringed with long black eyelashes (no trace of mascara) and surmounted by gently arched dark brows; her wavy dark hair curled in wispy tendrils around the high cheek-boned face and reached down to just past shoulder level. She was without doubt one of the most attractive women he had ever met yet she clearly didn't recognise that in herself, she appeared utterly devoid of artifice and Adam found that charming.

For her part Grace was also surreptitiously surveying Adam; he was tall, this much had registered when he'd risen to greet her; the dark hair was cut short in an almost military style showing off a well formed skull; his face was...chiselled...that was the only fitting description and almost overtly masculine but it was his eyes that commanded attention being a startling bright shade of blue highlighted by black eyelashes and set beneath strong, straight, dark brows. Her eyes drifted to his chest where curly dark hair could be seen in the open collar of the dark blue shirt he wore - she wondered how far down his obviously lean and toned body the hairs reached - before dragging her eyes back to his face to find he appeared to be studying her too; cheek of the man she thought before accepting she'd been guilty of the same thing. As their eyes met, each acknowledged the others attention with a barely perceptible nod, an acceptance as it were, that they liked what they saw.

Mrs Parkes and Uncle Ray had both been watching the silent interplay and inwardly congratulated themselves, they had suspected the couple would be attracted to each other and felt somehow personally responsible for bringing them together.

Ray cleared his throat to break the silence before announcing, "Adam, if we're to get to our meeting we need to think about leaving soon."

Adam tore his eyes away from Grace and nodded, "Just my cuppa to finish, Ray, and then I'm good to go."
 Turning back to Grace he asked, "What are your plans today then as I'm dragging your uncle away?"

She liked his voice, it was deep and rumbly, dark and warm. "I've arranged to go and visit an old friend who has just had a baby," she informed him, "we used to hang around together whenever I came here as a kid, but I haven't seen her for a while."

"You like babies?" Adam enquired, anxious to prolong the conversation but inwardly berating himself for asking such a question.

"Have to," she answered, "I'm training to be a midwife - would be the wrong career for me if I didn't! Not that I plan to have them myself any time soon...I still haven't found the right man yet." Grace mentally kicked herself - why in God's name had she felt the need to say that?
Adam however had registered only that if she hadn't found the right man, YET, she must be single and his heart gave a leap...it had been a long time since he'd met a girl that he thought he would like to be with for anything more than a one night stand. Something about Grace captivated him and had done from the moment he had spied her in tears the other day, he wanted desperately to spend time with her, to be the one to ignite the smile that caused tiny dimples at the sides of her mouth; to make her laugh; to be the one to hold her

41

when she cried...He shook himself, what was going on? He'd spent less than 40 minutes in this woman's company, had touched her only once when they shook hands, yet he was feeling things he couldn't ever remember experiencing before.

Ray drained his tea, "Right young man," he said, "time to go. Grace, we should be back around tea time...what about you?"

"About the same, I suppose," she responded, "although Jenny did say if it got too late I could stay over. If you don't see my car when you get back it's because I decided to stay. I would offer to text you but I doubt you have a mobile, do you?"

Ray laughed, "Err no, a phone in the house is enough for me."

Adam interjected with, "I have a mobile and here," he tore a page from a small notepad he had in his pocket and scrawled a number, "is my number. You could text me and I can let this luddite know if you're staying at your friends."

He held out the slip of paper to Grace and as she took it their fingers brushed, causing a shiver to run up her spine.

"Thanks, Adam," she said quickly to mask the confusion she felt, "I'll try to remember to actually put it on the phone!" *What on earth was happening*? she berated herself, *I'm 26 not 13, you'd think I'd never met an attractive man before!*

The two men left and after helping Mrs Parkes clear away the dishes Grace returned to her room. The old cheval mirror reflected just how brief the outfit she had worn to breakfast was and inwardly she cringed, 'there were ways to make a first impression,' she thought, but this wasn't one she would normally have chosen. Still, her wicked side consoled her, it had obviously worked, there had been more than a spark of appreciation and attraction in those stunning blue eyes. Grace giggled to herself, *he needn't think I'll make it easy for him*, she thought, *this time I want a man who really wants me for me, not for what I can give him or do for him, and who's to say this, whatever this is, will go anywhere anyway?*

Shrugging her shoulders, she took herself off for a shower, returning ten minutes later to dress in jeans and t-shirt for her trip. She left her hair to dry naturally and applied a touch of mascara and clear lip-gloss, it never took her long to get ready and applying tons of make-up had always been an anathema to her. Picking up her soft leather handbag she checked that Jenny's address was still on the notes section of her phone, it was, so device in hand, she headed back to the kitchen to quiz Mrs Parkes on the best route to her friend's house.

Not being in any hurry to depart, Grace spent a while chatting to Mrs Parkes, who, font of all local knowledge as she was, seemed to know everything that was going on with anyone within a 10 mile radius of Duntisbourne Abbots. She knew all about Jenny and her new baby despite the fact that Jenny had left the area several years ago, and did indeed know the best route between Duntisbourne and the address Grace had on her phone.

43

Finally, at around 10.30 Grace said her goodbyes to Mrs Parkes who handed her a spare key for the back door.

"Just in case you get back before your uncle," she said, "I shall leave around midday today," she added as an afterthought, "and I'll leave a cottage pie in the fridge for your supper which will just need reheating."

"Thanks, Mrs P," said Grace, hugging the woman before she took her leave. "You are an absolute gem!"

Seated in her little Mini, Grace studied the directions she had jotted down on the back of the piece of paper Adam had written his phone number on, it involved a route through the village she hadn't used before, but which seemed to lead out onto the road to Cirencester in a much more direct fashion. The engine made its usual protest upon being rudely awakened after a few days standing but none the less fired up obligingly, belching a cloud of smoke as it did so. Grace grimaced, she really should get the damn thing looked at, it was the thought of the potential expense which had so far deterred her - that plus a general dislike of mechanics who seemed, in her admittedly limited experience, to think that it was fine to discuss the workings of the internal combustion engine whilst staring fixedly at her breasts. The problem, whatever it was, did seem to be getting worse however and she resolved to ask her uncle if he could recommend anyone locally to take a look; preferably someone who wouldn't come onto her.

Route committed to memory and Adam's note dropped onto the passenger seat, she did a three- point turn and exited the drive, turning up the narrow road. Within what seemed a matter of minutes she was on the road leading directly towards Cirencester. The journey should have been straightforward, lasting no more than 20 minutes door to door but 10 minutes in and the aging Mini was protesting vigorously, spewing out black smoke before juddering to a halt adjacent a sign for a Bed and Breakfast establishment. Fortunately for Grace the road was quiet at that time of day and she had managed to steer the car onto the grassy verge so wasn't blocking any traffic.

"Bugger, bugger and buggeration!" she exclaimed, beating her hands on the steering wheel, "now what do I do?!" Rummaging through her bag she found and extracted her phone, who to call? Uncle Ray and Adam would be in Bath by now and Mrs Parkes didn't drive; she tried Jenny but her husband had the car so couldn't help - but she asked Grace if she had AA cover.

"Now why didn't I think of that?!" Grace laughed into the handset, "I'm such a prat, I do have cover!!" After apologising to Jenny and promising to visit another day once the car was fixed, Grace pressed the screen to dial the AA who promised to attend within the hour.

An hour and a half later Grace was awoken from a dozy day-dreamy state by the rat a tat-tat of knuckles on the car window; she jumped at the noise and managed to bang her elbow sharply on the car door. About to swear loudly at the pain in her funny bone, she somehow managed not to let the expletive out upon recognising the AA uniform on the middle-aged man who had knocked on the window. He stood back to allow her to get out of the car and then introduced himself as, "Andrew from the AA, what seems to be the problem?" It was on the tip of Grace's tongue to say, "If I knew that I probably wouldn't have called you lot," but she managed instead to explain what had happened to the car and that there seemed to have been a bit of a problem developing for a while. In a typically mechanic style fashion he drew in a sharp breath.

"Oooh, Miss, you'd have saved yourself a lot of bother if you'd got that looked at straight away."

Grace smiled blandly, letting him think she was just a helpless female - experience having told her it was often easiest that way!

Andrew lifted the bonnet and for several minutes fiddled and twiddled, all the while sucking in his cheeks and shaking his head. Finally, he declared that the car would need towing to a garage and did she have a regular one she used? Explaining she was a visitor and that her 'usual' garage (not that she in fact had one) was in Wilmslow, Grace suggested they took the Mini to whatever garage he recommended, which it turned out was not far from Duntisbourne Abbots. The car was hitched to the AA van and with Grace seated uneasily in the driver's seat (having never been towed before) they set off back up the road she had originally driven down, arriving at the garage 10 minutes later.

Andrew the AA man explained to the garage owner the problem he had identified, which went right over Grace's head, but sounded expensive, and went on his merry way leaving her to stroll the short distance back to the house.

Chapter 5 – Slipping Back

It was another glorious day and Grace thoroughly enjoyed herself as she ambled slowly back, it was disappointing not seeing Jenny but there'd be other days to do that, she hadn't after all set any kind of limit on how long she planned to stay, and she knew her uncle was in no hurry to see her go. She had to admit, if only to herself for the moment, that having finally met Adam she would like to get to know him better, the brief encounter over breakfast having whetted her appetite for more than Mrs Parkes food! This particular train of thought made her smile, he was gorgeous and imagining those eyes on hers whilst his hands did...

"STOP IT!" she said out loud, "You aren't sure he even likes you!"

An echo from somewhere seemed to say, "But he does, he's been searching for you."

Grace let herself into the house using the back-door key provided by Mrs Parkes, who had obviously left for the day, leaving behind her a blend of aromas ranging from bleach to fresh baked bread, cottage pie and furniture polish. Grace sniffed the air appreciatively and decided tea and a sandwich, using the fresh loaf she espied on the kitchen side, was first on her agenda. Several minutes later and she was munching on a cheese and chilli jam door stopper of a sandwich washed down by a mug of tea, whilst wondering what to do with her unexpectedly free afternoon. *First things first,* she thought, *I'll text Adam and let him and Uncle Ray know what's happened.* As she picked up her phone she remembered the bit of paper with his number was still in the Mini and she'd never gotten around to actually storing the number on the mobile.

"Dork!" she proclaimed, "Still, I only said I'd text if I was staying over." She realised she had merely wanted to make contact with Adam, any pretext would have done, which made her smile a little.

Impromptu lunch finished and the kitchen restored to the pristine state in which Mrs Parkes had left it, Grace decided that she'd have a proper nosey around the house which, according to her uncle's passing comment the other day, would one day be hers. Other than the large kitchen extension, the downstairs of the house consisted of a small library, a formal dining room which had long since become known as 'the den' and then at the front of the house and either side of the hallway, two equally matched in size reception rooms. Ray appeared to have taken one of these over as his office and the enormous old desk he'd installed was brimming over with sheaves of paper, books and charts all appearing to relate to his passion for tracing their family tree. Grace smiled, there seemed to be no order, in fact the desk top looked rather like the contents of a box had been upended on it, but she would bet her last penny that her uncle knew precisely where every article in that chaos was. The other reception room was rather an austere place, rarely used, the only TV was in the den as was the comfy leather sofa. It was sparsely furnished with an old-fashioned three-piece-suite and a couple of side tables. Grace wrinkled her nose, the potential was there to make a lovely living room; the mullioned windows let in a lot of natural light and the enormous original fireplace was still in place, although no fire appeared to have warmed the grate for a very long time. Grace imagined the room redecorated, a couple of large squashy sofas, a blazing fire and a large Christmas tree. In her mind's eye she pictured herself and a tall dark man with a couple of young children running around. The image was very clear and seemed so real.

Shaking herself out of the daydream, Grace ascended the stairs, aside from her bedroom there was Uncle Ray's room which she decided not to enter as it felt too much like snooping, a couple of bathrooms and two smaller bedrooms only one of which currently contained a bed, the other seeming to have become a general dumping ground for stuff her uncle obviously didn't need but couldn't bear to throw out. She grinned, Ray was a natural born hoarder and she guessed it was only Mrs Parkes fanatical tidiness that kept his collection restricted to one room.

One final door off the small landing led to a steep set of stairs up to the attics. As a child Grace had been forbidden from entering the attic rooms and the door from the landing had always been kept locked, she half suspected it still would be so was delighted to discover the door opened easily when she tried.

The stairway was dark and narrow and Grace couldn't locate a light switch, so she moved carefully up the steep steps holding onto the well-worn bannister rail as she did so. At the top of the stairs were two further doors; opening the one on the left revealed a room, empty save for a dilapidated old iron bedstead - once upon a time Grace guessed these attic rooms must have housed a couple of servants. A sudden draft of air, from what looked like a badly fitting window, blew past her and the door at the bottom of the stairs banged shut causing Grace to jump half out of her skin.

"Bloody hell!" she exclaimed, her heart beating overtime.

She closed the first door and opened the second cautiously, not wanting to create any more loud noises. *Now this looks more interesting*, she thought as she spied various pieces of old furniture and several tea chests, which on first inspection, contained items ranging from old curtains to photograph albums...another sign of Ray's inability to get rid of anything. Of most interest, however, was a large and seemingly very old wooden chest, quite plain apart from a heavy iron clasp and deeply incised marks on the lid which looked like a very ornate 'Y' entwined with a 'G'. Grace lifted the iron clasp from the matching hasp and opened the chest.

The scent of lavender was overpowering as the lid of the ancient oak chest lifted to reveal a yellowing linen covering. Grace wrinkled her nose at the pungent musty smell and sneezed violently - lavender, much as she appreciated the scent always had that effect on her - then carefully lifted the folded linen to discover what it was concealing.

"Wow!" The chest's contents appeared at first glance to be a selection of neatly folded garments, obviously old, very old but it wasn't immediately apparent if the clothes were male or female in design. Pushing the chest nearer to the attic's window, choking a little on the clouds of dust this created, Grace began to lift out the items one by one and drape them over the various pieces of decrepit furniture stored in the attic room.

Thus unfolded, the garments showed themselves to be dresses of what Grace thought Medieval design. "Although they can't be," she scolded herself, "even stored away in a big chest like this they'd not be in this condition, they must be copies."

Still, despite her doubts, the clothing did appear to be of the style she associated with female dress in the Medieval period. There were several of what she thought were linen under robes, cut very plain with a drawstring neckline; two over dresses, one in a deep blue the other a soft grey, each of them with elaborate braiding around the edge of the wide sleeves and around the scooped neckline; a couple of long cord like strips with metal tips at either end, belts Grace assumed, and finally a pair of leather slippers, somewhat cracked with time but still recognisable. At the very bottom of the chest and wrapped in another linen cloth was a heavy cloak of a deep red fabric, resembling velvet but rougher, the edges of which were richly decorated with embroidery.

Grace sat back and surveyed her treasure, *they really are in remarkable condition,* she thought to herself, absently fingering the heavy material of the cloak. *Good enough to try on, in fact.* Of course, once thought, the idea was not going to disappear and within minutes Grace had stripped down to her bra and knickers and was reaching for one of the linen shifts. *Hang on*, she said to herself, *women back then didn't have lingerie!* Grinning self-consciously at the sight she would have presented to anyone entering the room, she discarded her underwear and pulled the linen over her head, drawing in the neck cords so the garment didn't slip from her shoulders. The smell of lavender once again assailed her, but she was getting used to the perfume now.

Standing back, Grace examined the two over dresses, the blue one seemed to be more richly embellished than the grey, the bands at neck and sleeves were wider and worked in with the colourful embroidery were fine gold threads – definitely a dress worn to impress. Choosing the plainer dress, she struggled to get into the garment before realising that there was lacing at either side of the waist; once these were loosened the dress slid easily over her head. Re-tying the laces resulted in a garment which fit tightly from chest to waist before flaring out into quite a full skirt, the wide sleeves draped to knee level on the side nearest the body but ended precisely on Grace's wrist on the outer side. The whole ensemble could have been made for her, so well did it fit, and she felt very comfortable in it, although the lack of knickers was somewhat disturbing.

Choosing the most elaborate of the corded belts, blue and gold with gold coloured end tips, Grace wrapped it loosely twice around her waist before tying in a single knot to the front and allowing the ends to hang. The battered shoes completed her outfit, once she had removed a somewhat crumpled piece of very fine linen and what appeared to be a headband from inside the footwear. Reaching out she picked up the heavy cloak and draped it over her arm, as she did so the room appeared to waver, the walls seemed to dissolve and Grace sank to the floor, consciousness deserting her.

Chapter 6 – The Awakening

Through a haze of dizziness, Grace heard a woman's voice shouting, she couldn't quite make out the words, which in any case didn't seem to be English, and she drifted back into unconsciousness; only to be jolted out of her dead faint by a rough shake to the shoulder.

"Ysabella, Ysabella, what are you doing, girl? Get up! Get up!"

The strident voice roused Grace and she opened first one eye then the other, to be confronted by a ruddy female face mere inches from her own.

"Ysabella, how many times have you been told to wear your veil when outside?" The woman tutted loudly and grasped the crumpled linen square and headband lying next to Grace, which she vaguely remembered removing from the leather slippers before putting them on in the attic room.

ATTIC ROOM! Grace suddenly sat bolt upright, precipitating such a wave of dizziness and nausea that she keeled right back over. Through the uncomfortable feel of blood rushing to her head, Grace realised that instead of being in the stuffy attic she in fact appeared to be lying outside in a grassy meadow; the sun was warm on her face and she could hear the drone and buzz of many insects.

Her collapse back onto the ground had obviously unnerved her companion who was anxiously fanning Grace's face with the rumpled piece of linen, alternating between the phrases, "Ysabella, you wicked girl," and, "Ysabella, my sweet one."

Grace opened her eyes once more and sat, more cautiously this time, upright – resting her head upon her knees as the dizziness again threatened to overwhelm her. The woman placed her large careworn hand on the back of Grace's neck.

"You are burning up, my child!" then, a shade smugly. "Haven't you been told a thousand times never to go out in the sun without your veil?"

Although Grace could understand every word that had been said, she *knew* the language wasn't English; French she thought, but not like any French she had heard before, maybe more Spanish, perhaps a mixture of both, or neither! Her head was spinning and she still felt very sick - sick and clammy; she was aware of small rivulets of sweat trickling between her breasts and her hair was clinging damply to the back of her neck, fine tendrils curling onto her face. Where on God's good earth was she and who the hell was Ysabella?

Reluctantly raising her head towards the still chastising woman, Grace took in the kindly but irate face in front of her; dark beetled brows were drawn in a frown above a pair of brown eyes, heavy lines chased through the skin, leaving latticed wrinkles around mouth and forehead and deep crow's feet at the eyes. Not a gentle face but nevertheless full of care and compassion for Grace. One large hand was extended, she took it and was hauled unceremoniously to her feet, whereupon she discovered that she barely reached the woman's shoulder.

Tut-tutting, the woman, Favia, a name rose to the surface of Grace's mind, shook out the fine linen she had picked up from the ground earlier and, holding the fabric between her teeth, quickly and efficiently parted Grace's curly brown hair and tamed it into two thick plaits which she fastened off with ribbons from a capacious pocket in her gown. The linen was then placed on Grace's head and secured into place with the woven head band. Throughout these ministrations Grace never uttered a word, so confused did she feel.

Favia stood back and admired her handiwork, "Much better," she declared. "Now, young madam, it is time to get you home," a hand on her shoulder urged her to turn and Grace meekly complied, only to nearly collapse once more at the view which thus confronted her.

Some way in the distance, the warm sunshine illuminated the yellow stone walls of a fortified citadel atop a hill; a wide river, its water glinting in the bright light, wound its course to the rear of the knoll and in between Grace and this vision was an expanse of heat-dried meadow.

Bizarrely, a line from The Wizard of Oz sprang into Grace's head, "Toto, I don't think we're in Kansas anymore."

She blinked her eyes in amazement, she couldn't be sure and it wasn't exactly as she remembered, especially since there were no other buildings in view, BUT the walls on the hill looked like Carcassonne, a place she had visited briefly as a child on a tour of southern France with her parents. But how on earth could she possibly be in

France? Only moments before she'd been in the dusty attic of her uncle's house in the Cotswolds, it must be a dream.

Dream or not, the woman by her side looked, felt and sounded very real and was obviously rather irritated as she perceived Grace's inaction to be outright defiance. A further loud 'tut' issued from her companion as she spied the dark red cloak on the ground where Grace had been lying.

"Ysabella, why do you have your best winter mantle with you, child, 'tis the middle of summer!"

Grace, in her guise as Ysabella, had no answer to give and so merely flashed a rather wan and apologetic smile. She really didn't feel so good, if it was all a dream it was a very real one and she rather hoped she'd wake up soon.

Favia, if that was her name, picked up the discarded mantle and, with a firm hand on Grace's shoulder, indicated that they should begin walking towards the walled town on the hill.

The route took them around the base of the hillock, heading towards the river. It was hot and the long dress she wore felt like an encumbrance, wrapping around her legs as she attempted the lithe strides of her usual gait; she felt the puzzled gaze of her companion on her as she struggled to maintain a brisk pace and eventually worked out that smaller steps resulted in less entanglement.

Favia maintained a constant chatter as they walked along, none of it apparently requiring any response, being concerned as it was, with various tittle tattle relating to people Grace didn't know, although she quite obviously was expected to be intimately acquainted with the individuals in question. The names Agnes, Helena and Marguerida were mentioned several times, so Grace assumed they must be close connections to Favia, if not to her, or rather Ysabella, personally. By dint of occasional nods and muted exclamations at appropriate intervals, Grace managed to give the impression that she was listening intently, whereas she was actually trying to make sense of what was happening. She clung to the notion of a dream but the sweat trickling down her back, the heat of the sun and the slightly out of breath sensation caused by the brisk walk, all felt very, very real – more realistic than any dream she had ever experienced.

After some ten minutes walking, the pair began the ascent to the citadel up a clearly defined track, wide enough for a couple of horses to ascend side by side but perhaps not a cart, there must be another approach thought Grace. Within a matter of minutes, the two women reached a gate which until then Grace hadn't noticed, slightly hidden from sight as it was by a protuberance in the wall. The protuberance, a rounding in the wall, seemingly formed a part of a red tile topped tower.

Favia rapped loudly on the thick wooden gate whilst proclaiming loudly that, "Favia, former nurse to the Vescomtat, and Ysabella, lady-in-waiting to Agnes, wife of the Vescomtat, require entry forthwith."

Grace hid a giggle behind her hands, *pompous woman* she thought, rapidly followed by, *oh so I'm a lady-in-waiting then?* She recalled the tittle tattle she had paid scant attention to on the walk up the hill, Agnes had been mentioned several times but she was unable to recall the details. *That'll teach me,* she rued internally. From some hidden recess of her brain, an image surfaced of a gentle, slender woman, a girl really, with long fine dark hair and pale blue eyes; Agnes, the commentary in her head announced.

With some obvious reluctance the heavy gate swung open, allowing Favia and Grace to enter a courtyard bustling with activity; people of all ages were going about their everyday business, it was loud, colourful and, to Grace's modern senses, smelly. Assailed by such a sensory overload, and suffering from the combined effects of the heat and her unexpected arrival into what to all intents and purposes appeared to be Medieval France, Grace felt the dizziness of earlier return and she crumpled into an inelegant faint at the feet of the young soldier who had opened the gate.

"First time a maiden as pretty as this one has fallen at my feet," he quipped, bright blue eyes twinkling mischievously in a tanned face.

Favia cast a stern eye at the young man and demanded he carry Grace to their quarters across the courtyard. Nodding his assent, he bent and effortlessly lifted Grace into his arms, setting off in the direction indicated by Favia who bustled ahead.

"In here," she commanded, as they reached the living quarters. The soldier gently deposited his burden on the bed indicated; as he did so Grace's eyes opened, brown eyes met blue, inches apart. *I'm going to faint again* thought Grace, as she took in the handsome face so close to hers, *this must be heaven!*

A cherry-red blush suffused her delicate features and she promptly shut her eyes again, daring to re-open them a few seconds later to double check the young man's face. *I was right* she thought, *this is heaven and he's an angel,* and then, spotting the glint in the azure blue eyes, *hmmm, a fallen angel!* This notion further increased the flush to her face, and the soldier stifled a laugh at her discomfort, obviously used to this sort of reaction from members of the opposite sex. He really was very good looking, dark hair, left long and tied at the nape of his neck with a leather thong, a fine narrow patrician nose, high cheekbones and those blue, blue eyes surrounded by long black eyelashes and topped by well-drawn dark eyebrows. He reminded Grace of Adam, not so much in looks, he certainly wasn't Adam's double, more the feeling of outright masculinity that they both conveyed.

The man released his hold on Grace and stood, his lithe frame well-muscled yet lean. "I bid you farewell," he said to her and then, turning, he addressed Favia, "Your servant, Madame."

Even Favia was not immune to his charms and twittered in a most unlikely fashion, "My thanks, Guilhem."

"At your service," he responded.

"Away with you," she muttered, making shooing gestures with her hands, "we thank you for your service."

"My pleasure," was his reply, then, looking directly at Grace, "I hope to have such a pleasure again."
Lost for words, but feeling a distinct melting internal heat, to add to her external blushes, Grace merely nodded.

"Well!" exclaimed Favia once the young man was out of sight, "a forward young scoundrel, that one is."

Lost in daydreams of the departed Guilhem, Grace didn't hear Favia enquiring as to her well-being, until the question was repeated loudly right next to her. "I'm fine," said she, struggling to sit, "just rather warm."

Favia snorted, "Hardly surprising in that winter gown. I know the colour becomes you, young Ysabella, but as the daughter of a Bon Crestian aren't you supposed to be immune to such fancies? Come, let's remove your gown and you can splash your face with cooling water," she indicated a copper bowl and jug atop a chest, "whilst I fetch you one of your lighter gowns."

Grace struggled upright and off the low framed bed, which was a roughly made affair topped with a pallet stuffed with what felt, and sounded, rustling as it did, like hay. Looking around the stone walled room which was made more homely by colourful wall hangings depicting scenes of hunting, as well as more pastoral imagery, she spotted three other beds. *Looks like I share this space then,* she mused as Favia helped her out of the blue gown.

Several minutes later, feeling much cooler in a dress of a similar design to the grey, although with narrower sleeves, and fashioned in a lighter, finer fabric in a soft green colour and with a belt of red cordage, Grace was deemed fit to "resume her duties."

Duties. What duties? Oh heavens, how am I going to get through this? Grace felt panicky and scared, so far she had managed to get by in this strange old world she had woken in but there had been minimal interaction with anyone other than Favia and, a slight blush at the recollection, Guilhem. Having no idea what would be expected of her and even less idea how, or even IF, she could get back to her own time, Grace meekly followed Favia through a series of passageways, all the way chanting to herself, *it's only a dream, I'll wake up soon*, until they reached a stone staircase.

"Up you go, child," ordered the older woman, "Agnes awaits you, she's feeling rather out of sorts in this hot weather and requested you brush and dress her hair, she finds it soothing apparently." Grace relaxed a little, hair she could manage - a childhood love of Barbies had seen to that.

At the top of the narrow staircase Grace was confronted by a heavy wooden door guarded by a soldier a little older and definitely less handsome than Guilhem. Without a word he opened the door and bid her enter. The room within was quiet, with only a low murmur of female voices, the walls were curved and hung with richly embroidered tapestries. It was stifling, little air was circulating and the whole atmosphere was one of ennui.

61

"Ysabella," a low pitched and pleasant voice greeted her. "At last! I have need of your soothing hands."

Grace turned to the source of the voice and met the pale blue eyes of a very pretty and very pregnant young woman. A sheen of sweat was on her face and she looked tired and uncomfortable.

"Lady Agnes," the words left Grace's lips without conscious thought, "forgive me, I went out to the meadows to find some air and became unwell. Favia had to find me."

"As well she did," commented one of the other women, there were three excluding Grace and the Lady Agnes, "this infernal sun would have turned you as dark as a peasant otherwise."

The other women giggled and one commented, "But Ysabella is happy in the outdoors, mayhaps she is indeed a peasant!"

This roused more laughter from the group, abruptly ceased by the Lady Agnes who demanded, in a quiet yet firm tone, that they all leave as she required some peace and quiet.

The women made a great show of departing in a swirl of skirts and veils, embroidery abandoned where they had been sitting. One, the oldest looking of the three, cast daggers eyes in Grace's direction as she passed.

When, finally, the room was emptied of all save Grace, Lady Agnes let out a deep, deep sigh, "At last! They have fussed like hens around me all day and I have had no peace nor rest! Ysabella, please soothe me, your hands are so gentle and my head aches so."

She did indeed look very wan and tired, and Grace's heart went out to the young woman. Moving to stand behind the chair in which Lady Agnes sat, she gently removed the veil and carefully unpinned the plait wrapped on top of her head. The mind of Ysabella, her apparent alter ego in this very real-feeling dream, seemed to take over as Grace began what seemed to be a regular ritual, unplaiting the hair and gently combing the dark tresses through with an ivory comb. Her strong fingers then massaged the lady's skull, back of the neck and shoulders, the tension visibly lessening as she performed the task.

Suddenly the door swung open, revealing a handsome man whom Grace thought to be in his mid-20's, "Agnes my beloved, how goes it with you?" a deep baritone enquired.

Lady Agnes' eyes lit up. "My Lord, Raimond," she breathed. "All is well, the child kicks and wearies me, but Ysabella always finds a way to relax me."

Raimond bestowed a smile in Ysabella's direction, "Leave us, and return within the hour to ready My Lady for the evening meal."

Grace effected a curtsey and exited the room. Her head was spinning, who was she, where was she and WHEN was she?

After some false turns she managed to navigate her way back to the room which the young soldier had carried her to. The space was now occupied by the young women who had been with Lady Agnes earlier. They seemed to range in age from early teens to late twenties and were engaged in a deep discussion about a certain recently arrived young soldier by the name of Guilhem Bastier. Hearing the name 'Bastier' made Grace jump internally in recognition, it was the same name her uncle had mentioned whilst discussing their shared family tree!

"I hear he has the bluest of eyes and is well made," giggled one of the girls.

"And a handsome face and is tall," added another.

Grace listened for a few moments, apparently the appreciation of an attractive man was much the same in whatever era this was, as in the 21st Century, well maybe a little less crude, she noted.

Unable to resist any longer, as the discussion had moved onto how to best to ensnare the young man in question, Grace joined the fray. "He is indeed handsome and strong and very forward."

"What do you know?" the eldest looking woman sneered, "you pay no attention to the men in the great hall or the courtyard."

"I pay heed...I just choose not to gossip," retorted Grace. "As it happens, Guilhem picked me up and carried me back here when I fainted outside the gates earlier. He was very kind."

"Guilhem! First name terms already," snorted the same woman who had sneered previously, her narrow, sallow-skinned face creased in a waspish frown, "you'll be telling us all about him then?"

"No, but I might IF you all prepare yourselves for supper!" boomed a voice from the doorway.

The girls swung around to find Favia, hands on hips, surveying them and not looking too pleased. "Helena, as the eldest, you should know better than to indulge in such idle gossip." This sharp comment was addressed to the sallow-skinned woman, who had the grace at least to blush, whilst simultaneously flashing an 'I'll get even with you look' towards Grace.

As the young women splashed faces, re-plaited hair and adjusted veils, Favia proceeded to impart what knowledge she had of Guilhem Bastier.

"He is 24, the same age as our Vescomtat and comes from Narbona. His parents are dead, he is related to Raimond Rogier on his father's side and as yet has taken no wife. His mother was a Bon Crestian, so you share something in common with him, Ysabella."

"A heretic then," Helena derided, "not worth the trouble of pursuit." Although internally she winced, several months previously she had spoken to Lady Agnes about the possibility of marriage to one of Raimond Rogier's many relatives, Guilhem Bastier would have been amongst them, he had obviously rejected her approach without even meeting her. If this was the same man and as attractive as the other girls were indicating she may have to try again.

"Not that he'd look twice at you even if you caught him," snorted one of the women; a buxom girl with fair hair whom Grace's alter ego identified as Marguerida, "I daresay a man so favoured would prefer a more comely pursuer!"

"Marguerida," chided yet another voice, this time belonging to a serene looking dark-haired girl, "there is no need to be so cruel!"

"Quite so," Favia admonished. "Now girls, please finish getting ready and head for the great hall, I hear a troubadour has arrived. Ysabella, you are to return to the Lady Agnes and assist her."

Grace nodded and headed out of the door, as she did so she brushed past Helena who hissed in her ear, "Be careful, it's not good to be associated with the heretics."

Recoiling, Grace continued to the door, somewhat shaken at the venom displayed by the other woman. As she walked through the maze of corridors to The Bower (Lady Agnes' rooms) she tried to recall what the tour guide had said about the Bon Crestians (Cathars as they were called in her time) when she had visited Carcassonne as a child. All she could remember was that a Pope had declared Cathars as heretics and thus sanctioned their persecution and deaths. Of Cathars themselves, she could recall very little.

Chapter 7 – Duties And Desires

It didn't take her long to reach Lady Agnes and help her change into a loose-fitting robe of the clearest blue, *like Guilhem's eyes*, the thought rose unbidden in Grace's head. She carefully combed out the lustrous hair and made to braid it as usual.

"No, leave it loose, it pleases me thus," the deep voice of the Vescomtat said from the doorway. Both women jumped, neither had heard him enter, nor knew how long he had been there.

"Come, My Lady," he said, crossing the room and taking Agnes' arm, "let me escort you, my love."

The couple left the room, Grace trailing behind and soon all reached the great hall where noisy laughter and a loud buzz of conversation could be heard even before they entered. Grace assisted Agnes to her padded chair on the raised dais before heading to where Marguerida, the buxom lady-in-waiting, was frantically waving to catch her attention. Past the assembled lords and ladies to her designated area further down the rows of trestle tables and benches she marched, still trying to unravel the Cathar mystery in her head. So preoccupied was she that she didn't notice a gap in the rushes laid on the floor and tripped, falling headlong.

A strong hand was extended and she grasped it, grateful for the help in regaining her feet. "Well, well," said a sardonic voice, "it would seem, mistress Ysabella, that you make a habit of prostrating yourself at my feet!"

Blushing furiously, Grace raised her eyes to meet the dazzling blue of Guilhem Bastier's. Very aware that the rest of the ladies-in-waiting were witness to all this, Grace curtseyed prettily for their benefit whilst through clenched teeth she addressed him. "Sir, once more I thank you. It can only be your extraordinary handsomeness causing such weakness that I am unable to stand in your presence!"

Whirling around as elegantly as she could, Grace headed for her companions, but not before she noticed a speculative gleam in Guilhem's eyes and the nod of appreciation at her temerity. *Hah*! she thought, *I'm not one of the simpering ninnies who will hover around you begging for attention. You want me, you come after me!* Guilhem sat back at the bench he had vacated in such a hurry in order to assist Grace; he'd watched her from the minute she had entered the hall behind the Vescomtat and his wife, had been unable to take his eyes of her in fact. Something about her intrigued him, not for her the girlish coquetry he was so used to, and frankly bored of, but instead a mature and almost worldly demeanour. Seeing her tumble right in front of him had almost changed his mind, perhaps she was indeed just another maiden eager to attract his attention but her acidic response to his quip restored his former opinion. Here was a woman with fire and strength, one he could respect as well as desire. He looked down the length of the table to where Grace was now safely seated within the bevy of other young women; a slight flush still stained her cheeks and her hazel brown eyes were flashing dangerously, obviously in response to something one of the women had said to her. As his gaze lingered, taking in the smooth curve of cheek, the swell of her bosom under the tight-fitting bodice and her vivacious attitude, her head suddenly swivelled in his direction. Brown eyes met his blue, boldly and with almost a challenge in them. Guilhem dropped his gaze first, a slight smile on his lips, *truly a worthy conquest she would be,* he thought.

Grace had walked as steadily as she could down to where her comrades were seated. Her heart was pounding and her breathing heavy, she could still feel the strong fingers as they had enveloped her small hand and couldn't help but think to herself how wonderful it would be if that hand was stroking and caressing other areas of her body. The Ysabella part of her, for that's how it felt – as if she were two people, was appalled by such thoughts, but not so aghast that Grace's 21st century lusts were quashed in their entirety. It was a most disturbing sensation to feel two contrasting, yet in many ways so similar, personalities inhabiting one mind, one body; at times Grace felt more an observer, seeing things through Ysabella's eyes and behaving as the younger woman would; yet at others it was as if she, Grace, was the dominant character. *This is the weirdest dream I've ever had* she had thought to herself as she walked.

Composing herself as best she could, Grace joined the ladies-in-waiting and seated herself in the gap between Marguerida and the youngest of the girls, whom the Ysabella part of Grace was aware bore the name Peyronella.

"You did that on purpose," Marguerida giggled, "I really didn't think you had it in you!"

"Throwing yourself at him," sniffed Helena, "what an indescribably vulgar thing to do. Do you really think a man such as him would be interested in a trollop like you?!"

Grace felt her ire rising at Helena's snide remarks but chose not to rise to the bait. "In all honesty I wouldn't dream of throwing myself at any man, Helena, I merely tripped because there was a gap in the rushes and I wasn't looking where I was going. It was sheer misfortune that it happened right in front of Sènher Bastier."

"Don't you mean Vescomtat Bastier?" sneered Helena, "seems Favia missed out this piece of information, it appears that our handsome visitor is more than simply a distant relative of Raimond Rogier, he holds the fortress of Minerve for the Trencavels. All the more reason for someone like you to try and attract his attention!"

Still keeping her temper in check, although her anger seethed dangerously close to the surface, Grace replied as calmly as she could, and with knowledge that seemed to surface as she spoke. "I had no idea of his status and even if I had known, I would feel no need to, as you say, throw myself at him. My mother's family is one of the most ancient in Occitania and I hold my head high, the man I finally choose will befit my standing, not I his."

Eyes flashing she looked past her companions and back down the trestle tables, to find the gaze of Guilhem Bastier, Vescomtat of Minerve, fixed on her. She held his stare, challenging him; he was first to break the gaze, a smile seeming to lighten his face as he dropped his eyes.

Grace felt the heat rise in her face and averted her own eyes, concentrating on the food arranged in a haphazard fashion down the centre of the tables and being constantly replenished by an army of servants; suddenly she felt very hungry. There appeared to be a mixture of sweet and savoury foods, both hot and cold, and people were helping themselves to whatever they liked. She selected what looked like a bread roll, and using a wooden spoon, scooped a serving of a fish stew of some sort onto the wooden platter in front of her. For the next few minutes her attention was fully occupied with eating. Stew and bread consumed she ventured to try a small pastry which proved to be a sweet concoction of figs, raisins and possibly lemon zest, following this with other small morsels and finally a few small tart grapes.

Peyronella seemed amused at Grace's determined consumption and finally couldn't resist commenting. "Ysabella, how is it for one so small and slender you can eat so much?"

On her other side Marguerida snorted. "It simply isn't fair, is it? I only have to sniff the sweets and I get rounder whereas this one eats and eats and remains as delicate as a faery queen!"

Glad that the topic of conversation appeared to have moved away from her supposed intentions towards Guilhem, Grace shrugged her shoulders, "I have always been able to eat and eat; when I was a child mama said it was because I was never still and needed the food to keep my energy high. Perhaps one day I will just go pfffooof and explode into a fat old woman!" This caused gales of laughter amongst the assembled women, Helena

71

excepted, who seemed to find the idea of their slender colleague suddenly becoming fat hysterically funny.

Grace picked up the goblet in front of her and took a cautious sip of the contents; some sort of wine, fruity and not tasting too alcoholic, very pleasant in fact, so she drained it in one go, eliciting further giggles from the women. Conversation lapsed into a discussion of the design of a new gown for Agnes once the child was birthed and Grace breathed a sigh of relief, accepting a refill of her goblet from a passing servant. Dishes began to be cleared from the tables, although the wine kept flowing and an excited buzz began to permeate the hall – the troubadour had obviously eaten and drunk his full and was beginning to strum his gittern.

Grace procured another goblet of wine for herself from a passing servant and turned to where the troubadour had positioned himself, underneath the dais where Raimond Rogier and Agnes were seated. The musician was small, dark and wiry and possessed an impressively shaped goatee style beard. His keen eyes were surveying the assembled personnel seeking out someone to whom he would direct his first offering. He liked to start with something quite bawdy to warm up the listener before moving onto a selection of satirical pieces and finally to a soulful mix of songs telling of courtly love. His experience was that, much as the ladies liked it, if the love songs came first, the men, some in their cups with drink, would be snoring long before his performance ended. Spotting Guilhem his eyes lit up, familiar as he was with the seemingly irresistible attraction the young man appeared to stir within any females present. He had his 'victim'.

Strumming his gittern a little more loudly, he caught the eye of Raimond Rogier who clapped his hands for attention; as the hall settled somewhat the Vescomtat introduced the troubadour who went by the name of Peirol.

Peirol rose to his feet and executed a courtly bow in the direction of Lady Agnes, who graciously tipped her head in acknowledgment. The diminutive troubadour began to pick out a tune on his instrument and, looking directly at Guilhem, began a series of verses extolling the handsomeness of a certain individual, how all the women desired to make him their own but how, despite many, many temptations, "he did not yet wear the yoke". This last line raised a hearty guffaw from the male section of the audience. All the while Peirol allowed his wicked gaze to rest on Guilhem who, to his credit smiled and clapped along, maintaining eye contact with the artist; until that is he chanced a sideways glance at Grace who was giggling unashamedly at the character assassination being meted out. The troubadour, well versed as he obviously was with human nature, followed where Guilhem's eyes led and saw the delicately flushed Grace, tendrils of dark hair escaping from beneath her veil. He noted her slender figure, her unabashed laughter and understated beauty and concluded that perhaps the unattainable Guilhem had finally found a woman to desire above all others.

Nodding slightly in Grace's direction he continued his song with an exclamation that, "at last it seems the man in question has met one to whom he would pledge his heart!" and began to describe in some detail what he thought the main subject of his song should do if he had the chance to capture the object of his attention.

Grace hadn't really noticed the troubadour looking at her and thus, not associating herself as the topic of such lascivious language, continued to laugh and clap along. Others however HAD made the link and Guilhem was writhing internally and wishing he could wring the minstrel's neck. Agnes also having noted the brief interaction between the pair when the young woman had stumbled, looked on with some amusement at Guilhem's obvious discomfort and her lady-in-waiting's apparent lack of awareness. She filed the information away, Guilhem had so far refused to take a wife, perhaps Ysabella would be suitable? A mental note was made to confer with her husband.

Closer to Grace, one other had made the connection. Helena glowered, dark brows drawn together. She had intended to speak to Lady Agnes about the possibility of herself being proffered as Guilhem's bride; as the eldest of the ladies-in-waiting she felt it was her turn to be found a marriage partner, she had a small dowry, her family line was well thought of – in her head she was already Vescomtessa of Minerve and yet the upstart Ysabella, daughter of a Bon Crestian, was the one Guilhem desired! *Well, we shall see about that!* she snarled internally, fixing a daggers stare at Grace, *throw yourself at him will you? Well a man like that needs more than a pretty face, I will have him. You wait and see.*

Conscious of someone looking at her, Grace turned and met the venomous stare of Helena head on. *Now what have I done?* she thought before turning back to join in the laughter at the final line of Peirol's ditty, which seemed to infer that the object of Guilhem's desire, "was as clay in his hands to be moulded as he saw fit." She snorted with derision, *hmm...like to see him try that with me!* she thought contemptuously. Then she noticed Guilhem looking her way again and this time he appeared uncomfortable and decidedly out of sorts, the former arrogance diminished somewhat; she remembered the brief nod directed her way by the troubadour and suddenly the reason for Guilhem's discomfit became glaringly obvious to her! *Oh my good god! That was about me!* Colour flooded her face, why had she not realised earlier? Other members of the audience had spotted her reaction and some were openly pointing her out. She had to get out. NOW.

Trying to draw as little further attention to herself as possible, Grace made an excuse to her companions and swiftly exited the hall, not pausing to look back. Once out of the main hall she increased her pace through the corridors until she reached a door to the courtyard, the guard stationed there opened the portal and she stood gulping in great lungfuls of air, somewhat muggy it had to be said, but certainly fresher than that in the hall itself. Regaining a little composure, she rested her burning cheek on the stone wall, relishing its coolness against her skin. The modern Grace was unsure of the gravitas of being made the lewd participant in a troubadour's song, but she was sure it wasn't something a well brought up woman of this time would encourage.

The door she had just exited swung open again to reveal Guilhem. She made a vain attempt to merge into the stone work, but he spotted her nonetheless and headed straight towards her. Grace found her heart was pounding in a most uncharacteristic fashion and her cooled cheeks were once more flaming, what was the matter with her and what was it about this damn man that caused such a reaction?

Guilhem had reached her side now and was stammering some kind of apology. "I don't know why he singled you out for that," he seemed to be saying. "He knows me of old and I am often the butt of his jokes, but he had no right to say such things of you. I am sorry, Ysabella, for any insult caused."

Grace whirled around to face him, eyes flashing an anger which was soon dissipated at the truly apologetic look in his eyes; it wasn't his fault she tried to reason, she'd even laughed along with everyone else until the realisation that she was part of the song. She wanted to be angry, but she couldn't, not at him. Something was happening to her insides, they seemed to be full of butterflies and she felt her heart pounding once more – this time at his nearness, his sheer masculinity was overwhelming, she couldn't ever remember desiring anyone this much - it was almost a physical pain.

Their eyes locked and without either knowing who made the first move, they found themselves in a passionate embrace. Guilhem's strong arms enfolded her, one hand at the small of her back held her tightly against his torso, the other cupped the back of her head, dislodging her veil in the process. Grace reached with one hand to stroke his dark hair, now freed from the binding of earlier in the day, her other hand trapped between their bodies, held against his chest. She could feel his heart beating as wildly as hers and then they were kissing.

Guilhem broke away first, panting and fraught with tension his eyes searched Grace's and finding only a reflection of his own feelings he relaxed a little whilst remaining a firm hold on the trembling woman in his arms. "I'm sorry," he began to say until Grace rested a finger on his lips.

"Don't be," she said, "I didn't try to stop you, did I?"

She was acutely aware of the feel of Guilhem's arousal through the layers of both their clothing and equally aware of the throbbing of her own reciprocal reaction. For two pennies she would have let him lift her dress and take her there and then in the courtyard, not caring who may witness the union. God, how she wanted this man! How had this happened? *It's a dream* said the voice inside, *anything can happen in a dream.*

The mutual spell was broken by the sound of voices and the door being opened again. Guilhem came to his senses first, abruptly releasing his tight hold which almost caused Grace to collapse, "Don't fall," he hissed. "We cannot be caught thus, your reputation would be shattered!"

"I don't care about…" Grace began sotto voce before Guilhem's voice drowned her out.

"Madomaisèla Ysabella," he was saying, quite loudly. "I apologise if the fool Peirol upset you but please know his words were not meant for you, but for a serving girl who mopes after me. I remain as always your servant." Then low and under his breath he whispered, "I WILL have you. You will be mine." Then in a final flourish he bent from the waist in a low bow and offered the veil he had earlier dislodged, "Please, take this, you dropped it in your eagerness to escape."

Seeing the look in his eyes, Grace played along and executed a pretty curtsey. "No need to apologise, Sir, I was merely somewhat embarrassed by the language and the meaning of the song." She accepted the proffered piece of linen and added, "I bid you sleep well," eyes twinkling as she recognised the look on his face, which seemed to convey the idea that he probably wouldn't. *Serve you right. I likely won't rest much either mate!* she thought.

With one last look, Guilhem departed and Grace headed back to the doorway. Just as she was about to knock for admission, it opened to disclose a worried looking Marguerida.

"Ysabella, thank heavens. We were worried you left so quickly and didn't go to our chamber. Lady Agnes is asking for you to help her prepare for bed. We must hurry!"

Without waiting for any kind of response, the blonde woman grasped Grace by the arm and chivvied her along the corridors and up Lady Agnes' chamber. Grace, glad not to have to explain any further went along quietly, her head full of the delicious interlude she had just shared. *Dream or not* she thought, *I want him too!*

Chapter 8 – Danger In Waiting

After allowing enough time to elapse for his all too obvious arousal to diminish, Guilhem returned to the hall. Damn, what had that woman done to him? He had rarely experienced such a rush of passion as Ysabella had engendered in him, the feel of her in his arms, the way her body had moulded against his, the soft fullness of the lips he had crushed with his own, and the taste of her.

"God..." he groaned as the memory caused further tumescence in his groin, "I'm like a boy who never had a woman!"

Shifting uncomfortably on the bench, he picked up his goblet and drained what was left of the contents in one swallow before beckoning for one of the serving lasses who hovered attentively around the hall to refill it to the brim. Guilhem eyed the servants, wondering if any of them would be good for a tumble in the stables, or indeed anywhere, in order to slake his lust. *Bah!* he remonstrated with himself, *better drink to collapse then bed one of those!* In his mind's eye he could envisage Ysabella finding him rutting like an animal in heat with one of the serving girls to whom he had perhaps paid a penny for the dubious privilege. It surprised him somewhat to find that her opinion already mattered to him, they had shared one brief moment of intimacy and yet he cared what she thought. What had she done to him?

Face still flushed with desire, Grace chased after Marguerida who was chattering away about this and that, mostly inconsequential gossip, but she did laughingly refer to the troubador and his ditty about Guilhem. Grace found herself blushing once more and none too gently asked the girl not to mention it again. If Marguerida was surprised by the vehemence in Grace's request, she wisely chose not to respond. They had in any case by this stage reached Lady Agnes' chamber and the door was being opened for them.

Once inside the bedchamber the two girls hastened to their Lady who looked tired and wan.

"My Lady!" exclaimed Marguerida, "is something amiss? Are you unwell?"

Grace was covertly eying the heavily pregnant woman through a midwife's eyes. She was pale, possibly anaemic she thought, and had dark circles under her clear eyes but there were no signs of swelling nor indications that the woman was unwell. She thought it likely that rest and possibly the introduction of a little more red meat into the diet would be all that was required to restore Agnes' healthy appearance. She wasn't really listening to Marguerida and not paying close attention to Lady Agnes' responses but couldn't miss the look of surprise and shock which flitted across the lady-in-waiting's pretty, plump face in reaction to something she had heard.

Dragging her attention back to the room she heard Lady Agnes say, "Yes, since his uncle agreed to join the crusade in order to have his excommunication lifted, my husband has been trying to find a way to protect us all. It now seems the only way is to visit Arnaud Amaury at Montpellier and surrender to the Church."

"Who is Arnaud Amaury?" Grace asked.

"He is Pope Innocent's legate and so-called spiritual leader of this shameful crusade," was the response. "Although I doubt any of this mess is much to do with religion, more the northern lords and the church wishing to steal our lands and wealth."

"Are we in danger, My Lady?" enquired Marguerida in a tremulous voice.

"My husband says no," came the response, "but I have less faith than him, he sees goodness where there is none and I...yes I, I fear for us."

Grace blanched, the knowledge she barely remembered from her childhood visit came back to her, Carcassonne would fall but the heretics, the Bon Crestian, would not be slaughtered...not here at any rate, other towns would not fare so well.

Lady Agnes spotted Grace's white face and attempted to console her. "Ysabella, do not worry, console yourself, as it would seem you may have a suitor, my dear...one who would be more than able to protect you should the worst happen."

"Guilhem Bastier?!" laughed Marguerida delightedly. "He has spoken to your husband already? Ysabella - you certainly HAVE made an impression!"

Grace blushed furiously but remained silent whilst Lady Agnes shook her head at Marguerida, "No, he has said nothing...yet, but he will, even Raimond noticed the way he looked at our Ysabella - he has been trying to find a suitable match for Guilhem for some time, but all his suggestions are rebuffed. This time I think may be different." She winked conspiratorially at Marguerida. "What say you, Ysabella? Would you find a marriage to my husband's kinsman appealing?" she winked again.

Guilhem Bastier was a handsome man with land and he held Minerve for his cousin, many women would jump at the chance of such a marriage.

Grace tried diplomacy, her heart was racing and she was terrified of saying or doing the wrong thing. "My Lady, the gentleman in question has many fine attributes and I would not wish to go against the wishes of you or my Lord Trencavel but, romantic fool that I am, I would prefer that it be love not duty which sees me marry."

Lady Agnes smiled, "And who is to say that it won't be Ysabella, I have known Guilhem for many years and have never seen him look at any woman the way I saw him watching you tonight."

Grace bowed her head, "We shall see, My Lady, we shall see."

The two ladies-in-waiting helped their Lady to disrobe and Grace had her first chance to covertly examine the woman's swollen abdomen. She was further along in the pregnancy than she had first suspected, maybe nearly at term. As she observed, the white mound heaved convulsively as the child within adjusted position in its ever tighter confines.

Agnes sighed, "I do so hate it when the child does that...it makes me feel sick!"

"You carry a healthy, vigorous child, My Lady," Grace interjected, "better that than one that moves little or not at all."

"Agreed," said her mistress, "yet I shall be very glad when the time comes to birth this one!"

"Not long," soothed Marguerida, "surely only a few weeks more."

The Lady Agnes was by now safely ensconced in the large bed, the heavy drapes held back to allow air to circulate as the room was hot and stuffy, and drawing them shut as was the usual custom would have rendered sleep almost impossible.

"My Lord will not join me tonight," she announced, "he wishes an early start in the morning. Ysabella, would you mind sleeping in here tonight? I don't want to be alone." Seeing Grace's hesitation, she added, "Marguerida can fetch anything you may need from your room."

Grace acquiesced, what did it matter where she slept, this was all a weird dream and she was going to wake up eventually and find herself back in the rose patterned room in Duntisbourne Abbots.

Several hours later Grace did wake from a dream where Adam and Guilhem had seemed to merge into one person pursuing her up a rocky slope; sticky with sweat she pushed back the covers to cool herself. She was surprised to find she was apparently still out of her own time. Lying as still as possible so as not to disturb the woman next to her, she tried to recall as much as she could of the era but her knowledge was limited, all that came to mind was that the heretics, Cathars, Bon Crestians or whatever they actually called themselves in the here and now didn't ultimately fare well. She remembered stories of mass burnings of persecution, torture, false confessions and felt suddenly terrified. What if she was permanently trapped in this? Hadn't that nasty piece of work Helena intimated that her mother in this time was a Cathar? Would she, could she, be harmed because her mother here was a heretic? She wished she knew more - but she didn't, so, for as long as she was here, she would have to do the best she could to stay alive and stay safe.

Grace heard movement from the woman next to her, then quiet sobbing noises assailed her ears. Sitting up she asked quietly, "My Lady, are you alright? May I help in anyway?"

Sniffles ensued, then a muffled voice replied, "Forgive me, Ysabella, I did not mean to wake you. Nothing you can do except pray for our safety, but I must confess I am deeply worried for my lord. He is sure he can persuade his uncle and the priest that he is no heretic, but I know him, he won't allow any of his people to suffer for their beliefs and thus he will not, cannot, condone this damn crusade. I fear his meeting will not go well...and then what?" her voice trailed away.

Grace had no response, no real words of comfort; as far as she could remember, Agnes and her children were allowed to leave safely but her husband was not so lucky. She wished she had no foreshadowing of events, no knowledge at all of what was going to transpire; even more fervently she wished she would wake from this dream which was becoming more real by the minute.

The following morning, Grace woke hollow-eyed and despondent. Lady Agnes appeared to still be asleep so she carefully extricated herself from the bed, made use of the wooden bucket in a curtained alcove and pulled her gown on over her head before loosely plaiting her hair. Movement from the big bed alerted her to the fact that her mistress was stirring.

"Should I call for your morning meal to be brought here, My Lady?" she enquired, as Agnes hauled herself up the bed.

"Yes. Please. That would be nice, Ysabella. I barely slept, the child moved all night and I could not help but worry over my lord's safety - all of our safety."

Lady Agnes looked pretty much how Grace herself felt, minus of course the hugely pregnant belly. Dark shadows circled the pretty eyes and her face was pale and drawn with worry. *Should I tell her she'll be fine?* Grace thought, *but if I do, she'll want to know how I know, and she'll ask about her husband and everyone else and I won't have the answers. Oh God, how did I end up here, am I even here, or am I dreaming - reliving someone else's life?* Grace's brain went into overload, thoughts span around her head with such rapidity that it made her dizzy. However she looked at it and thought about it, the fact remained that everything which had happened since her awakening by Favia in the meadow outside Carcassonne felt very real, as real as her existence in the 21st century in fact; nothing she had so far experienced felt like any sort of dream she had ever had before. She had felt hunger, thirst, joy, anger, lust (oh heavens she had felt lust!), fear, empathy; the heat of the Midi had made her sweat and the troubador's song had made her laugh. Her dreams were not usually so vivid, nor so prolonged. As a pragmatic, down to earth individual, Grace was not given to wild imaginings BUT her presence in the Midi seemed more akin to time travel than anything else. However, that didn't explain the fact that she appeared to have entered this time period in the guise of a young female, younger than the 'real her' she thought, who was patently part of the fixtures and fittings of the place; had she somehow *stolen* Ysabella's consciousness AND body? A thought suddenly struck her, perhaps Ysabella was one of the ancestors Uncle Ray had discussed - maybe this was a genetic link to the past.

Shaking herself free of this train of thoughts, Grace allowed the part of her which knew exactly how to act in this time period to take over the routine task of assisting Lady Agnes with her morning ablutions, calling for a breakfast to be brought to the chamber and dressing her mistress. They were joined in due course by Helena and Peyronella who escorted Lady Agnes to a room called 'the solar', where her son was brought along to play with his mother and her ladies. Little Raimond was a delightful child of four with the dark hair of both his parents and serious grey eyes.

In the fuss and noise occasioned by the child, Grace took the opportunity to make her way to her quarters; once there she sat disconsolately on her bed. "What should I do?" she asked out loud.

"Do about what?" a voice replied.

Grace started, she'd thought herself alone in the room. Favia bustled over, she had been in the far corner of the chamber, out of her line of vision.

"Do about what, girl?" she asked again.

Grace thought rapidly. "It's nothing really, simply that Lady Agnes seems to think her husband is going to suggest a match between myself and Guilhem Bastier, I was, I AM surprised and don't know what to do."

"Why you will marry him of course, foolish girl! Why wouldn't you?!"

Grace smiled weakly but didn't reply. Favia however had the bit between her teeth and was chattering on about what a wonderful match it would be, what a handsome man he was, what beautiful children they would produce.

Eventually Grace snapped. "Oh do be quiet, Favia!" she admonished, "nothing is sorted, he hasn't asked me and as far as I know Vescomtat Trencavel hasn't said anything to him. I think he probably has more important things on his mind to be honest!"

Favia shut up mid-sentence and cast a withering glance in Grace's direction. "No need to be rude, young lady, and what pray will be occupying the Vescomtat if the marriage of his cousin is not important?"

"He's on his way to Montpellier," Grace replied, unsure as to whether the fact was common knowledge.

"Nothing untowards there, I saw him leave," sniffed Favia.

"There may be something 'untoward' coming our way soon if Raimond Rogier can't persuade Arnaud Amaury that the Trencavels don't sanction heresy! That's why he's gone. The Pope wants the Bon Crestians gone and the Northern Crusaders are all too happy to help if it means land and money for themselves; it would seem they don't care who gets in the way."

Favia seemed little disturbed by the information. "Raimond Rogier will convince whomever he needs to. He's always had a silver tongue but if it does come to fighting we shall be safe here in the ciutat, these walls have NEVER been breached."

She appeared so confident in her proclamation that Grace didn't have the heart to contradict her and instead changed the subject to that of Lady Agnes and the pregnancy. "When is Lady Agnes due to birth the baby?" she enquired. "When I helped her into her nightgown last night I thought she looked almost ready, yet she says she still has several weeks to go."

Favia pursed her lips. "You know, I thought that too. Mayhaps she has her dates muddled, we should make sure there is a midwife ready should the need arise sooner than planned. I'll send word today."

The unpleasant topic of heretics and war was pushed to one side, at least as far as Favia was concerned, Grace however had suddenly remembered something.

"What's the date today?" she asked.

"July 15th," came the response. "How could you forget, it is less than a week until your birthday, child!"

Grace ducked her head, "Perhaps I am too old for birthdays now."

Favia smiled, "17 is not too old, my child."

So, one thing at least was confirmed, Ysabella was, as Grace suspected, several years younger than her own 26, but she supposed people matured more quickly in this time.

This thought was supported when Favia added, "You are too old to still be unmarried though, the sooner Guilhem Bastier can make you his wife the better as far as I'm concerned. I promised your mother I would take care of you when she decided to take the 'Consolamentum', but I won't be around forever."

Grace winced, not quite 17 was considered too old to be unwed, she was so glad the passage of centuries had changed some things! The date Favia had provided had shocked her, although she hadn't given any outward sign of her disquiet; a memory of her visit as a child had surfaced. Carcassonne fell *(would fall)* on August 15th. A matter of weeks away yet no one here had any idea of the scale of the disaster soon to befall them, and she couldn't say anything- not, she reckoned that she would be believed if indeed she was to give voice to her prescient knowledge.

It was an unenviable position to be in, made worse by the fact that she had no idea what would happen to her if anything were to befall Ysabella. A thought suddenly struck which caused her legs to shake and would have required a less than graceful collapse onto the bed had she not already been seated: if, as she had begun to think, she was a many times removed descendent of Ysabella, it stood to reason that Ysabella would at some stage produce at least one child. The thought gave her consolation whilst at the same time making her wonder if she would still be in here, in this time, in this body when that momentous event occurred. It couldn't happen anytime soon she reasoned, the girl wasn't even betrothed - to Guilhem Bastier or anyone else - and the strictures of this time would surely frown on sex out of wedlock. No, Grace decided, the chances were, she would wake up back in her own time long before her ancestress produced the next branch on the family tree. Although, she pondered, she wouldn't mind sticking around long enough to see if indeed Guilhem Bastier did wed and bed the girl. He had an animal attraction she found overwhelming, her reaction to him had been as strong and instantaneous as it had to Adam.

"I'd like to find out anyway," she said out loud to the bemusement of Favia, who merely shook her head in bewilderment.

90

The remainder of the morning was spent assisting Favia in repairing some of the young Raimond's clothing, like all children in any time he had a habit of ripping, tearing or otherwise damaging his apparel. It was a boring, mundane task which left her mind free to wander, and wander it did as she tried in vain to remember as much of the history of Carcassonne and the wider Midi as she could; only to realise that her knowledge, such as it was, was almost entirely derived from two novels - one by Kate Mosse and the other from the pen of Elizabeth Chadwick. Grace remained convinced, however, that Lady Agnes and indeed all the inhabitants of the Ciutat were allowed to leave unharmed, although minus all their belongings, after the Crusaders took control. She was less sure of the fate of Vescomtat Raimond Rogier Trencavel, Carcassonne would fall but did the young Vescomtat survive? She simply could not remember.

Chapter 9 – Falling For Him

After several hours cooped inside with the garrulous Favia painstakingly inserting tiny stitches into small items of clothing, Grace was ready to scream. Never one to enjoy sitting still and even less enamoured of sewing, she was developing a pounding headache. Eventually she tossed a mended garment onto the pile beside Favia and announced she needed fresh air. Before the elder woman could say anything, Grace was across the room and out of the door. Moving swiftly, she let her alter ego navigate to a door, which proved to open out into the large courtyard in front of the castel.

Outside at last Grace took a deep inhalation, savouring the air without the overlay of wood smoke and human sweat. It was only slightly fresher than the confines of the castel if truth be known, it was around midday and the hot sun of the Midi was at its zenith beating down unmercifully; the scent of scorched earth and less pleasant odours of over ripe fruit, rotting vegetal matter and animal and human waste pervaded the atmosphere. Grace wrinkled her nose, she supposed that after a while one grew accustomed to the smell and didn't really notice it, but to someone from her time it was an almost physical assault on the olfactory gland. Still, she was outside without the damned needlework.

Two large elm trees offering welcome but limited shade dominated the courtyard but otherwise the area was quiet. Grace moved across to the large gated exit, guarded currently by a couple of the castel's soldiers who waved Grace on with barely a second glance; she presumed people leaving the area were considered less of a problem than those trying to gain access. She crossed the bridge over the grassy ditch which surrounded the castel on three sides; the huge curved and towered wall she recalled from her time wasn't there and she could see directly into the Ciutat itself. Hardly anyone was stirring in the town, the heat presumably having temporarily driven people inside, but dogs could be heard yipping and barking as they fought over scraps, and somewhere out of direct eyesight Grace could hear the cries of someone selling their wares, it sounded as if fruit of some description was the main offering. To her right and just above a sturdy wooden door, which she assumed it was the point of entry for herself and Favia yesterday, Grace spotted one of the towers, topped now with a roof of red tiles as opposed to the conical grey slated edifices she recalled from the future. A wooden ladder led up into the squat structure and Grace headed for that. Climbing a ladder in a long gown was not as easy as scrambling up in jeans or shorts would have been but eventually she reached the platform and could see out over the ramparts. The view, when she looked out of the front of the tower, was spectacular down to the river and an unprotected suburb consisting of a gaggle of wooden houses and beyond that to the fields and farmland. Upon turning around she could see out over the Ciutat and two other suburbs, which were walled and abutted the main ramparts of Carcassonne. Far away in the distance the snow-capped peaks of the Pyrenees and Sabarthe mountains shimmered in the heat haze. It was a beautiful, yet forbidding landscape, unchanged and unchanging, rich in history, myth and legend; Grace felt her breath catching as she surveyed the terrain, Carcassonne surely should be impregnable, yet she knew differently and her heart pounded with fear for both herself and Ysabella's friends and family.

"What in God's good name are you doing up there, woman?" a deep voice sounded, interrupting her reverie. Grace jumped and swung guiltily around to see who had issued the question. Guilhem Bastier stood at the base of the tower, hand on hips and, despite what she interpreted as a 'twinkle' in his eyes, looked none too pleased to find her in her lofty situ. She refrained from answering, turning instead to make her descent. If climbing up in her long dress had been tricky, getting back down was a thousand times worse and she cursed as the gown repeatedly caught around her legs.

"No wonder women now seem so useless," she muttered, "it's difficult to be anything else in outfits like this!"

She was about halfway down when a sudden small gust of wind whipped the offending garment around her ankles causing her to miss the next rung. Her hands slid painfully down the rough sides of the ladder as she slipped and fell backwards uttering a loud expletive. Guilhem caught her in his strong arms, unsure whether to laugh or remonstrate with her for her stupidity. In the end he initially contented himself with merely holding her, relishing the feel of her body against his.

Grace struggled, "Put me down!" she demanded, "at once!"

Guilhem laughed and reluctantly set her onto her feet, "Now you throw yourself at me," he quipped. "But you were foolish to climb up there, Ysabella, you could have been seriously hurt if I hadn't been here to catch you. What were you doing up there anyway?"

Grace felt the colour rise in her cheeks and went immediately into her default defensive mode. "I am perfectly capable of looking after myself! The worst that could have happened is I would have twisted my ankle or winded myself...I wasn't far off the ground!"

"But you could have been and if you'd fallen from the top you could have killed yourself!" Guilhem retorted angrily.

Grace bristled ready to counter with some clever comment and then the realisation hit that he was right and she could have badly injured herself. The fight went out of her and she replied a little more meekly than she intended, "You're right, I was just so bored mending little Raimond's clothes, I'm no good at sitting still and I needed fresh air - not that there is any - that's why I climbed up, to see if the air was any cooler up there."

"And was it?" Guilhem asked drily.

"No," she grinned. "But it's a wonderful view!"

Guilhem laughed, a full, throaty chuckle. "You are incorrigible, Ysabella, quite the most interesting woman I have met."

"And from what I've heard you've met a few." Grace lingered on the word met, making it abundantly obvious she was aware of his reputation as a womaniser.

It was Guilhem's turn to flush, "What if I was to say I intend to *meet* you one of these days, Ysabella?"

"I'd say you would need to ask very nicely before I would even consider it," she flashed back at him. Her pulse was racing, the nearness of him was intoxicating and he obviously felt the same way.

"I told you last night that I will have you; and so, my incorrigible Ysabella, you'd better get used to the idea. Oh, don't worry," he added as he saw her about to respond, "It will be after I have made you my wife."

"WHAT?!" Grace exclaimed, "Do I get no say in the matter? Will all this be arranged whether I like it or not?"

"And you do not like the idea of being my wife? Your words say one thing but your body is saying another, isn't it?"

Grace had no response to this as it was so obviously true, she yearned to kiss him again, to feel the hard leanness of his body pressed against her.

"That may very well be true," she said, gaining a large degree of satisfaction as she saw Guilhem's dark eyebrows raise in surprise at her audacity, "I can hardly deny the way I reacted last night, can I...BUT you barely know me and apart from the fact that I think you are very handsome, all I know of you is by reputation and not a particularly good one at that!" Guilhem tried to interrupt but Grace was having none of it. "I don't know what it's like where you come from, but to me it's necessary to get to know a prospective spouse BEFORE saying I do."

"You know I could go to the Vescomtat and he would sanction our marriage immediately, God knows he's tried to pair me off enough times in the past. He'd be ecstatic to see me settling down at long last."

"Lady Agnes said as much this morning, she thought we would be a good match and that she would speak to her husband," Grace responded before she could stop herself.

"Did she now? Interesting, I fear, sweet Ysabella, that you may indeed have no choice in the matter, Lady Agnes is difficult to sway once she has made her mind up." His face darkened, "Then there's the whole matter of this damn crusade, if my cousin cannot reconcile with the church we are all in danger, you more than most with your mother a Bon Crestian Perfecti. As my wife you would be under my protection, and I would protect you, to the death if need be."

Grace was surprised by the vehemence in his voice, could it be that he was actually genuinely enamoured with Ysabella and not just desiring her physically as his past history would demonstrate. Looking into his eyes it certainly seemed so and she felt herself melt internally - perhaps it would be a good match for the girl and after all, she - Grace, wouldn't be around forever (or at least she fervently hoped she wouldn't be - she had her own life to live in 2018).

"At least you could court me," she countered, "get to know me, perhaps you won't like me when you know me better."

"I intend to know you very well and as soon as I can," Guilhem smiled, taking one of her small hands in both his own, "but in the meantime, I will, as you say, pay court in so far as I can." He lifted her hand to his lips and brushed a kiss on the back of it before turning it palm upwards and kissing there too.

Grace's innards did somersaults and her loins tightened with pent up desire; it had been a long time, if ever, since she'd slept with a man who made her feel this way; Dave had been a pretty hopeless lover - once he came (and it didn't take long) he would fall asleep leaving her to finish on her own or lay in frustrated silence until she too dropped off.

"I will speak to Raimond Rogier upon his return," Guilhem announced, "If he has been successful in his endeavours then I shall woo you, my lady, BUT if not then I will marry you as soon as can be arranged. I want you under my protection should the worst come to the worst. And of course," he positively smirked at this, "I want you in my bed!"

Grace blushed but left her hand in Guilhem's. "I suppose that's the best I'm going to get in terms of a marriage proposal, isn't it?"

Suddenly she realised that she, or rather Ysabella, could be this man's wife in a matter of days because she knew, as he didn't, that Raimond Rogier Trencavel would fail in his attempt to persuade the papal legate of his devotion to the Catholic church and that Carcassonne would fall. She felt herself grow pale, much as she wanted to bed this man the thought that it would likely happen as a result of a war - crusade - she corrected herself, was not in any way an aphrodisiac. The fact that her alter ego could be so easily married off, with or without her consent, also irked her greatly; not that there was much she could do about that and if she, Grace, could ensure that Ysabella married a man in the prime of life then surely that was better than her ending up with some middle-aged lothario...wasn't it?

"Ysabella, what's wrong? You've gone really pale. Is the thought of sharing my bed so repulsive? I promise I won't hurt you, in fact I promise to take care of you for as long as God grants us time together."

He looked genuinely concerned and not a little upset at what he obviously perceived as her reluctance to share his bed and his life; it was patently clear to Grace that Guilhem Bastier did not generally offer marriage to any female he wished to take to his bed (and there had, by his own admission, been more than a few) and her heart warmed to him even further. Her ancestress, if indeed that's what she was, would be safe and possibly even happy with this man.

She smiled up at him. "I find the idea far from repulsive," she said. "In fact, if it wasn't for the morals of this time I would have you take me somewhere quiet right now." Guilhem looked a tad shocked by this statement, "but I would as soon not ruin my reputation for a quick fumble in a scruffy inn, thank you very much!" she continued. Guilhem was now laughing.

"Conversely, I would just as much wish to not marry someone simply in order to find out if we were compatible in the bed chamber."

Spluttering with barely concealed mirth, Guilhem responded, "Ysabella, with your fire and forthrightness together with my desire for you I really don't think compatibility in the bedchamber is going to be an issue." He bent down onto one knee and, still holding her hand in his, declared, "Ysabella de Valentes, please do me the honour of accepting me as your suitor, to woo you in accordance with your wishes until the day I may make you my wife. There, is that a better proposal, my sweet Ysabella?!"

Grace grinned widely, "Much better."

"Ysabella, Ysabella! Where are you, you lazy creature!" an unpleasant whiney voice interrupted the moment and Helena appeared in view. "Oh... I see, this is what you do is it, seduce the Vescomtat's relatives when you should be working?" she opined as soon as she saw Grace and her companion.

Guilhem rose to his feet and glowered down at the diminutive woman, "Mistress, I assure you I require no seducing, and in fact it is I pursuing this wonderful creature," he nodded at Ysabella, still holding onto her hand, "Truth be told, if my cousin permits I wish to wed her and as soon as may be arranged."

Helena's narrow pinched face took on a blotchy puce hue and her dark eyes swivelled from Guilhem's determined face to Ysabella's prettily flushed one. "I shouldn't be too sure of that happening, Sire, I'm sure your cousin has someone more suitable in mind for you than this daughter of a heretic," this last was uttered with a sneer of contempt.

"Madame," thundered Guilhem, "I would remind you that my own mother follows the path of the bon crestian and for your information my **cousin,**" he stressed the word, "will be only too happy that I finally wish to settle down, and I happen to know that his wife has suggested Ysabella to him as a suitable match for me." Not strictly true, at least at that moment in time, but only slightly stretching the truth, thought Grace as she watched the emotions play across Helena's face.

Helena sniffed, her already unattractive features made more so by the green-eyed monster of jealousy which was so clearly infecting her. Deciding against inciting Guilhem any further she directed her ire towards Grace,

"Favia is looking for you, you are to assist in selecting a midwife for Lady Agnes apparently, although what you would know about childbirth I don't know." She turned, flounced really, and without another word or backwards glance marched off.

Grace smiled internally, *much, much more than you may think,* she thought to herself but refrained from saying, instead commenting, "I don't know what I've done to that woman but she certainly doesn't like me!"

"I shouldn't lose any sleep over it," her companion said drily, "she looks like the sort of person who wouldn't get on with anyone unless there was something in it for her.

Be careful, Ysabella, I doubt there is much she could do to harm you, but it may be best to stay out of her way whenever possible."

"You really think she would act against me in some way?" Grace asked with some surprise, "but why?"

"Because she is a jealous, dried up woman whom no one wishes to take to their bed; she was suggested to me some time ago as being a suitable match, needless to say I turned her down, despite her dowry, which would have come in handy I have to say!"

"Jealous of me?" Grace interrupted.

"Yes because you are vibrant, young and beautiful, of course she's jealous and she's just nasty enough to find some way to hurt you. Particularly as it was she herself who apparently put herself forward to be my bride. I only found that out yesterday from Raimond, he was laughing about it and saying he needed to find me a good woman as soon as possible so that she couldn't try getting her claws into me again. Mind you, I gather she would have accepted any of my cousin's relatives if truth be told. However, the fact that I have chosen you will no doubt be twisted in her head to you having stolen me! Just be careful, Ysabella, I will look out for you as best I can but I won't truly feel you are safe until our vows are said."

"Guilhem," Grace said pensively, aware that it was the first time she had addressed him to his face by his name, "Do you not think you are trying to move things too quickly? I mean, we met for the first time yesterday and this is the longest conversation we have had. What basis is that for a marriage?"

"Some people don't have even this long," Guilhem retorted, "they meet for the first time on the day of their marriage. Ysabella, from the first moment I saw you I knew I had to have you, I can't explain any better than to say it's as if I was waiting for you. I am not a romantic man, Ysabella but you, you have made my heart come alive; it may be too soon to say I love you, but I know that I will." He paused and ran his free hand through his hair, "Am I making any sense?" he pleaded.

Her heart melted, if only she could meet a man like this in her own time, an image of Adam flashed into her head, perhaps she had but would she ever see him again? "You are making sense, I just never expected that I would be able to marry a man who chose me and wanted to love me. I suppose I thought I would be given, to someone wanting a brood mare; a man who would use me for his own ends without thought for me." Grace was aware she was saying the words but they didn't seem to come from her thought process. "Guilhem Bastier, if Raimond Rogier agrees I would be happy to become your wife."

Guilhem smiled broadly and raised her hand to his mouth, kissing first the back and then the palm before folding her hand into a fist and wrapping both his large but slender hands around it, "Keep this kiss with you until I make you mine," he said, executing a small bow.

Grace curtsied, "Gladly," she said. "Now I had better go and find Favia." Guilhem relinquished her hand and escorted her back into the castel, where she was immediately set upon by Peyronella and Marguerida, who had apparently come across Helena in a high dudgeon after her run in with the couple; although not repeating her words directly they certainly implied that the eldest of the ladies-in-waiting was not best pleased with Guilhem's interest in Ysabella.

"She all but accuses you of stealing him from her," snorted Marguerida, "honestly, the woman lives in a world of her own making. She was turned down by Senher Bastier, and others I may add, when the Vescomtat suggested her as potential bride. That fact appears to have escaped her however and she chooses to blame you!"

"Why was I not aware she was husband-seeking?" Grace asked.

"Perhaps because you didn't involve yourself in her silly schemes," Peyronella suggested. "She wittered away about her so-called suitors when you first arrived at the castel but you very wisely took little notice. If she spent more time being pleasant and less plotting her own rise up the social ladder she may have more success in interesting a suitor."

"She'll be less than pleased to hear that one of the older knights may be interested in her," laughed Marguerida, "Drogos de Merlon lost his second wife earlier this year and rumour has it that he asked the Vescomtat about Helena...her dowry is apparently the main attraction."

"Marguerida, how on earth do you know that?" Grace chided, "It's likely just gossip."

"Gossip it may be, but it comes straight from the horse's mouth...well from the wet nurse to de Merlon's youngest child anyway!" Marguerida retorted.

The pair of them then rounded on Grace, demanding she tell them about her 'tryst' with Guilhem.

"It wasn't a tryst," Grace exclaimed, "I went outside to get some air and he found me, there was nothing pre-arranged, I assure you."

"Methinks the lady does protest too much," scoffed Peyronella. "So, tell us...what did he say to you? Did he kiss you?" her eyes widened with enquiry.

"No he didn't kiss me!" Grace exclaimed, "Well at least not on the lips anyway," she added.

Marguerida giggled, "Ysabella, you are so wicked!"

"No...kissing him on the lips would have been wicked." Peyronella smirked. "I bet he asked you to marry him, didn't he? Do tell!"
"There's nothing to tell," Grace protested, but her face flushed at the lie and Marguerida, spotting this, grasped her by the hands and exclaimed,

"He did, didn't he? I can read your face like a book, Ysabella, you are incapable of lying I fear! Oh my...a wedding! When will it be, I wonder?"

Grace attempted to maintain a dignified silence as the young woman rattled on and on, finally and thankfully being halted by the sound of Favia bellowing down the corridor.

"I have to go," she said, wrenching her hands out of Marguerida's, "Favia is on the warpath." With this she turned and ran towards the sound of Favia's less than pleased sounding voice.

"I don't want to know," Favia stated firmly when Grace appeared. "Helena has already tried bending my ear and I told her the same. Nothing can be decided without the say so of Raimond Rogier, although between you and me it won't be a problem, so until then nothing has changed. Is that clear, child?"

Grace flushed. "How did you know?"

"I saw the foolish man on his knees in front of you and assumed he wasn't on them for the good of his health," came the dry response, "Now come, we need to visit Castellare to select a suitable midwife for Lady Agnes, the child seems to have dropped to me, so it may not be much longer."

Chapter 10 – Call To A Midwife

The pair walked back into the searing heat of outside and, with one of the younger soldiers as an escort, headed out of the Ciutat towards the suburb of Castellare, which lay to the south of the original Ciutat and boasted its own set of defensive walls abutting Carcassonne's. It was unbearably hot and within a very few minutes Grace felt the sweat pooling between her breasts and under her arms the thick plait of hair hanging heavily down her back didn't help. Favia fanned her face with a scrap of parchment succeeding only in wafting the warm air in Grace's direction until, in exasperation, she grasped the older woman's arm and demanded she stop.

"Hmmph!" Favia sounded, "I'm only trying to cool myself."

"Well all you're doing is moving hot air about," Grace said crossly. "Surely this little visit could have waited until later in the day."

"It could," Favia agreed amiably, "But I wanted you out of Senher Bastier's way for a while. I saw how he held your hand and it seems to me he is eager to hold quite a lot more of you!"

"Favia!" exclaimed Grace, feigning shock, "How can you say such a thing. He is a gentleman and I am perfectly capable of saying no to his advances. Not that he made any."

A loud snort of derision issued from Favia, "Ysabella, his reputation precedes him and I can guarantee he will have

107

suggested more than just a sharing a nice cup of wine somewhere!"

Grace had to grin, "Well he did but insisted it be AFTER we wed, IF that should ever happen that is."

"Well there's a relief anyway! He appears to have some morals at least. Now, this is the house." Favia stopped outside a small dwelling and rapped sharply on the poorly constructed wooden door. "Dama Balsace has the reputation as being the best midwife in the area and she assisted when the young Raimond made his appearance," she informed Grace in explanation.

The door opened a crack and a face as brown and wrinkled as a walnut peeked through. Upon seeing the two respectably dressed females the door opened wider and, in an accent Grace found almost impenetrable, welcomed them in. The dwelling was hot and airless but spotlessly clean, with bunches of herbs and an assortment of glass vessels containing who knows what potions, arranged neatly on shallow shelves attached to the walls.

Favia conducted what Grace assumed was an interview which ended with nods, smiles, the exchange of a small purse of silver coins and a promise that a message and escort would be despatched from the castel when her services were required. During these exchanges Grace wandered around the small space, sniffing the herbs - she identified lavender, which made her sneeze violently, as well as others she identified as rosemary and sage, some bundles eluded her completely and after cautiously opening one of the glass vials and nearly gagging at the scent she decided against further exploration. Whilst she was sure some of the potions and ointments on view could possibly offer some relief to certain symptoms, she was of no mind to expose the Lady Agnes to them if at all possible. Grace had, as a part of her studies, looked at the use of herbal remedies in pregnancy, and had nothing against the use of such things as raspberry leaf tea in the latter stages as anecdotal evidence suggested it could help with contractions; infusions of things like chamomile, valerian and St John's Wort did no harm, tasted pleasant (especially if honey was added) and did assist relaxation. Bottom line was, if it helped a woman through pregnancy and birth and did no harm to the mother or child, then Grace would happily employ it.

As they began the walk back to the castel, Grace quizzed Favia on the uses of some of the herbs she had identified in the old woman's house; it quickly became apparent that she had only vague notions of the efficacy of the lotions and potions in so far as they related to midwifery practices. She did however seem more informed on the use of love philtres and the like, the manufacture of which apparently Dama Balsace was also reknown, a fact which made Grace giggle.

"Really, Favia?" she asked. "You've actually made use of love potions and the like?"

Favia's dark complexion took on a rosier hue than it usually bore, "When I was young child, yes. There was a lad took my fancy back when I was maid to Raimond Rogier's mother and I bought a charm from her to aid my chances with him."

"Did it work?" snorted Grace.

"Well no, not really," was the response, "I caught him in the stables with one of the kitchen girls and they weren't grooming the horses I can tell you; mind you, she and I did share quarters and I did misplace the charm so I've often wondered if she stole it and used it instead of me to bewitch the lad!"

Grace was really laughing now, "Oh Favia, really! What happened to the two of them?"

A smug expression descended on Favia's usually stern countenance, "She died in childbirth some nine months later and he broke his neck falling from a horse shortly after - poetic justice I always thought!"

By now Grace was hanging onto Favia's arm and in gales of laughter, she couldn't decide if it was the thought of Favia being young and in lust or simply a kind of release of all the strangeness she had experienced over the last couple of days - either way it was infectious and Favia joined in with a deep chuckle.

In the shadows between two buildings Helena looked on at the laughing pair and scowled, "I bet they're laughing at me," her twisted mind thought, "since that girl came on the scene no one has given me a second glance, even Lady Agnes prefers her company to mine. I HATE her." Watching until they were out of sight and earshot, she slipped out of the shadows and headed for Dama Balsace's little house, from where she emerged some minutes later clutching a scrap of fabric which was wrapped around a small article consisting of knotted cord and twigs. Dama Balsace's words rang in her ears, although she had, like Grace, found it difficult to understand the woman; "Put this in the bed of the one you seek to undermine and ill luck will happen their way. Be careful to ensure it is not found, for if it is the misfortune will turn to you."

Back in the castel Helena quickly stitched a small drawstring bag into which she tipped some dried lavender, the charm followed before she gathered the top shut and secreted it in the straw mattress of Grace's bed via a small cut. Satisfied that her handiwork wouldn't be spotted, she made her way to the solar where Lady Agnes and her fellow ladies-in-waiting would be at this time of day, *now let's see how long you stay happy* she thought, glowering at Grace over her embroidery. Grace, naturally unaware of Helena's machinations, chose to adopt a 'let's be pleasant' approach and met Helena's glare with a beaming smile which only enraged the woman further - although in such company she wisely chose to remain silent, *They'd only take her side anyway*, she reasoned.

Grace shrugged her shoulders, she'd try to be nice but wouldn't push for best friend status, not, she thought that Helena appeared to have ANY friends, it was noticeable that the other ladies-in-waiting kept their distance whenever possible and Helena rarely talked to either of them. There was definitely something about the woman which discouraged any kind of intimacy - obviously part of the reason for her lack of success in the marriage stakes thought Grace somewhat spitefully.
As she prepared for bed after a subdued evening meal, Lady Agnes having decreed that during her husband's

absence she would eat with her retinue away from the main hall, Grace became aware of Helen's eyes on her again. She stripped down to her undershift and sat on the edge of her bed combing out her unruly hair. Peyronella offered to finish the task and Grace sat with her eyes closed, enjoying the feeling of the young girl's hands carefully untangling the knots before loosely plaiting the hair. Eyes opened once more she realised that Helena was STILL looking, albeit covertly, her way and she saw red.

"Helena, why are you watching me? This afternoon you were glaring at me and now apparently, I am the most fascinating thing in this room. Stop it, it's unnerving and very, very rude." Without waiting for a reply she flung back the covering on her bed and jumped in, causing the straw mattress to rustle loudly, releasing a sudden burst of lavender scent. Grace sneezed, where had the lavender smell come from? She hadn't noticed it earlier - it wasn't as if she didn't care for the fragrance and lavender was a very useful herb, but it always made her sneeze.

Across the room Helena began a response, "Why would I watch you, Ysabella, you are paranoid, child."

She sniffed and was about to continue when Marguerida interrupted, "Yes you have been, Helena," she accused the older woman, "and you aren't very good at hiding the fact, you're either watching Ysabella or talking about her to anyone who will listen to your incessant grips. Once and for all IT IS NOT YSABELLA'S FAULT THAT Vescomtat de Minerve has set his sights in her direction, he turned you down BEFORE she even arrived here. Now get off her back, you silly woman!"

Helena was dumbfounded, Marguerida was normally a pleasant, placid young woman but she appeared to be absolutely livid, twin blotches of vivid colour stained her cheeks and her eyes were flashing. Grace sat up ready to join in but before she or Peyronella could intervene Favia bustled into the room; taking in the situation with one swift glance she turned immediately to Helena, sensing she would be at the root of the problem.

"Helena, please go to Lady Agnes, she doesn't wish to be alone tonight." Dragging her dress back on, the woman left the room without another word.

"Now then," continued Favia, seemingly unperturbed, "I neither know nor care what just went on BUT I can guess, Helena is not an easy person to get on with and neither was her mother - each thinking they are more important than they actually are. My advice to you all would be to keep your distance, don't get involved in her schemes and don't allow her to upset you. Now sleep - ALL of you." Without waiting for an answer from anyone she left the room, moving swiftly to catch up with Helena before she reached Lady Agnes' chamber.

In a matter of moments she had caught up with Helena and asked her to detour to the kitchens for a jug of watered wine; "The one in the bedchamber is almost empty," she explained.
Upon reaching the bedchamber Favia knocked for admittance and once in the room began an apology to Lady Agnes, "My Lady, forgive me; you asked that

Ysabella attend you but instead it will be Helena." Agnes looked ready to protest so Favia hurriedly continued; "When I reached their chamber it was to find an argument of sorts in progress, Helena is wildly jealous of Ysabella and it would seem has said or done something to demonstrate the fact, Marguerida was vigorously defending Ysabella when I arrived and it seemed best to remove Helena from the situation altogether!"

Agnes nodded sagely, "I had noticed Helena's resentment, quick thinking Favia. We should get either Ysabelle or Helena safely married and away from each other as quickly as possible. Methinks it will be easier to find a match for Ysabella somehow!"

Favia nodded and picked up the almost full jug of watered wine, "I think so too, My Lady, particularly as it would appear your husband's kinsman has taken a fancy to the girl."

"Guilhem?" questioned Agnes, "Good, I shall see that matter settled as quickly as I may. What in heaven's name are you doing woman?!" she enquired as Favia began pouring the drink out of the open window into the ditch below.

"I had to find a way to get Helena out of the way so I could come and warn you, My Lady, so I sent her for a fresh jug on the pretext that this was almost empty," Favia countered, "she would have arrived here expecting you to have asked for her and you were waiting for Ysabella - had Helena discovered that fact it would have added even more to her dislike of Ysabella, I didn't want to risk that."

"You are a very wise woman, Favia," smiled Agnes, "and I thank you for your warning."

At that moment a knock on the door announced Helena's arrival, she entered the room looking a little flustered, the kitchen staff had been surprised at her request for a fresh jug of watered wine and only invoking Favia's name had brought about the reluctant production of a filled vessel.

"Helena," Agnes said warmly, "thank you for agreeing to keep me company tonight."

Helena flushed with appreciation, nodded graciously at Lady Agnes and set the full jug on a table next to the recently emptied one. "It is my pleasure, My Lady," she replied.

Favia made her goodbyes and left for her own bed, she had succeeded in averting a major confrontation within the ladies-in-waiting, at least temporarily; and had made Lady Agnes aware of the situation as well as the possible solution - added to that Helena now believed herself back in Lady Agnes' favour, not that she'd ever really been out of it, and so would be less likely to cause problems for a day or so at least...all in all a good night's work.

Chapter 11 – Night Time Wandering

Grace had a terrible night, every time she turned over or moved at all, the straw mattress emitted a waft of lavender which made her sneeze. Finally, in what she assumed was the early hours of the morning she gave up on any chance of restful sleep and, pulling a woollen cloak over her shift, she rammed her feet into soft leather shoes and headed outside. A sleepy guard let her out without question.

The sky was a deep indigo, with no sign yet of impending dawn, silver bright stars pricked the velvet dark and a crescent moon hung low in the sky; the air was relatively cool, at least in comparison to the heat of the day, and Grace relished the feeling of it on her skin. For a brief moment she considered climbing up into one of the lookout towers but remembering her potential fall of earlier in the day decided against it, instead she sat on one of the wooden bench-like seats under one of the courtyard's large trees. Leaning back until her head rested on the rough bark she gazed upwards and tracked the moon's slow progress across the sky, knowing eventually it would duck out of her sight and be hidden to her behind the defensive walls.

Grace took a deep breath in, enjoying the silence, a peace broken only by the occasional bark or yap of a dog and the distant sound of an infant demanding attention. She realised that with the exception of the short interlude earlier this was the first time she had been alone since she had arrived in this strange place and time - for a woman used to her own company the close confines of the living arrangements in the castel were difficult to come to terms with. She also longed for a shower and a good scrub with a scented shower gel, not to mention shampoo and conditioner. Lifting an arm she cautiously sniffed, "Phew, eau du sweat!" she exclaimed quietly, still, no one else seemed to notice and on the whole most people were, if not exactly fragrant, not too unpleasant either. Her fellow ladies-in-waiting washed every day using fresh water from large jugs carried in by servants; naturally all over clean wasn't possible but using wash cloths and what seemed to be some sort of soap they cleaned and freshened themselves, Grace vowed to be first to the jug in the morning.

She must have briefly dozed off, head lolling against the tree and was rudely awoken by a hammering on the gate leading out to the Ciutat. Guards who had evidently been sound asleep in their stations by the gate jumped a little groggily to establish who was trying to gain entry at such an ungodly hour. Grace could hear little of the conversation but one of the guards set off at a run, evidently to seek a higher ranked soldier, whilst the other opened the gate just wide enough to admit the dishevelled traveller who was mounted on a horse whose lathered sides indicated he had been pressed into great exertions. As the man flung himself from his mount, Grace recognised him as one of Raimond Rogier's most trusted soldiers, he had accompanied the Vescomtat on the trip to Montpellier. A sudden commotion from the castel signalled the arrival of several of the Vescomtat's senior advisors, Guilhem amongst them. They crowded around the obviously exhausted man, all talking at the same time...no one seemed to have noticed Grace so she drew the cloak tightly around herself to disguise the paucity of clothing and sat quietly in the shadows of the tree.

After a minute or so Guilhem's strong voice rang out over the melee, "Enough!" it commanded, "the poor man cannot be heard or understood if we're all talking at once! Now," he asked, "please tell us why you have arrived here at this time of night, and alone. where is the Vescomtat and the rest of the group?"

Fortified by a long swig of wine from a proffered skin, the exhausted man took a deep breath and quickly explained. "We failed," he said, "Armand Amaury refused to believe the Vescomtat, said he had had many a chance to repent and turn back to the one true church but still seemed bent on offering succour to Jews and heretics. The Count of Toulouse was unable to intercede, not that I think he wanted to, and so Vescomtat Trencavel has ridden onto Beziers to warn the people there and to round up the Jews of the town to bring them here to Carcassonna." Pausing for breath and another deep draft of wine he continued, "I was bade to make haste back here to let you know in order that preparations may commence." A deathly silence greeted his announcement and Grace realised that no one had actually seriously expected Vescomtat Trencavel to fail in his bid to sway the papal legate.

Guilhem took control, thanking the man and instructing one of the others to take him to the kitchens to see if any food was forthcoming; another was ordered to take the poor horse, who was standing legs splayed, head down and sides still heaving, off to the stables. "The rest of us," he declared, "to the hall, we need to make plans."

"Who put you in charge?" a bullish older man queried truculently.

"No one," Guilhem responded, "but would you have done anything I haven't just done?" The protestor shook his head, "Well then, we're in agreement," he continued, "now let's adjourn to the hall." The man opened his mouth to protest further but apparently thought better of it, instead he led the group back inside with no further protest.

Guilhem lagged behind and once he saw everyone else disappear into the castel he spun around and headed towards Grace.

She didn't bother trying to conceal herself, instead she rose to her feet and said, "How the hell did you know I was here?! None of the other men noticed me."

"I saw you the minute I came out," he responded, closing the gap between them, "I don't know quite what it is but I seem to sense when you are near."

By now he had reached her and gathered her into his arms, crushing her against his chest. Unlike their first encounter there was minimal clothing separating them and Grace was immediately aware of both his animal heat and obvious arousal. Working one hand under her cloak, Guilhem groaned as he felt her flesh, barely covered by the sheer linen of her shift. His hand bunched up the fabric until it was able to snake underneath and caress the flesh of her waist, flank and breast. Grace was giddy with desire, she welcomed the hand roving freely around her body, even the sharp pain as his eager fingers located an erect nipple and pinched a little too hard. She allowed her hands to slide under his loose shirt the better to explore his lean torso and he drew a sharp intake of breath, before claiming her mouth in a deep forceful kiss. His hand dropped to her buttocks cupping a cheek and pulling her hard against him - she could feel his hardness straining against the confines of the loose braies he had hastily dragged on and felt an answering wetness between her own legs.

"God I want you, woman," Guilhem sighed, "but not here, not like this. If the only good thing to come out of this damned war is you in my bed then at least I shall have something to fight for. We will be married as soon as Raimond returns. I will wait no longer." At this last, he drew his hand gently against her slippery entrance, toyed there for a moment, eyes intent on her face and then, releasing her entirely he raised the hand, scented with her, to his mouth - sensuously tasting her desire. It was the most erotic of things to watch and Grace moaned softly, catching her bottom lip in her teeth - she needed the release of climax more than she could ever remember.

"Go!" he commanded, "before I change my mind and take you up against this tree!"

Too overwhelmed with lust to protest, Grace leaned in for one last kiss and allowed him to adjust her shift and cloak, his hands lingering as he did so. She walked sinuously back into the castel leaving Guilhem frustrated but knowing he had done the right thing,

"My little hussy," he whispered, "what delights we shall share." Hoping none of the other man would notice the outward sign of his amorous encounter he followed a discreet distance behind and headed for the hall.

Back in her shared chamber Grace slid as quietly as she could under the covers of her bed, the scent of lavender irritated her nose but her other senses were so stimulated by the encounter with Guilhem that she could ignore the itchiness. As surreptitiously as she could she pulled up her shift and began to gently massage herself to fulfilment; it didn't take long, images of Guilhem and the memory of his hands roaming over her body filled her head, as the orgasm peaked she tried to hold in a moan of release but feared she may have failed when a sleepy voice from across the room enquired, "Are you alright Ysabella?"

"I'm fine," she managed to say, "just can't sleep."

"Oh dear," the disembodied voice replied.

"Don't worry, go back to sleep, Peyronella, I'll be fine," Grace responded, having recognised the voice. The only response was a deep sigh and the sound of a mattress rustling as the occupant turned over.

It wasn't long before Grace herself dropped off to sleep, her dreams peppered with erotic imagery of Guilhem taking her forcefully against the tree.

Chapter 12 – Warnings Of War

The next morning, feeling surprisingly refreshed, Grace made use of the freshly drawn water and a washcloth together with a sweet-scented soap provided by Marguerida to freshen herself as thoroughly as she could. She still longed for a shower but managed a creditable job nonetheless and felt much better for it.

The day followed a similar path to the others Grace had experienced since her unexpected and unplanned arrival into the 13th century - apart from what appeared to be an unusual amount of activity amongst the garrison which Lady Agnes commented upon. Grace said nothing to her companions of what she had overheard the previous evening, not wanting to admit her late-night wanderings nor to upset or alarm the women. Then at around midday a sudden commotion from the courtyard caused the ladies-in-waiting to head for a window.

"It's the Vescomtat," Helena announced for the benefit of her mistress, "He seems angry, he's ordering men about."

Lady Agnes blanched, her worst fears seemed about to be realised.

Moments later the sound of heavy footsteps could be heard and the door was flung open; Lady Agnes half rose to her feet as her husband, dishevelled, dirty and looking anguished barrelled across the room.

Holding her tightly he seemed close to tears. "I have failed, my love, the legate denied my entreaties and my uncle," he almost spat the word, "refused to assist. The man is only concerned with his own wellbeing, may he rot in hell, the two-faced idiot."

"What will we do, my sweet?" replied his wife, stroking his stubbled face, "surely we are safe here in Carcassona?"

"I hope so but there is no doubt the northerners want our land - Guilhem has already initiated the building of the hoardings around the walls and towers and we shall need to gather in as many of the crops as we can. God willing, we should be able to withstand a lengthy siege and perhaps negotiate terms. The Crusaders, pah, they do not deserve the name, are still some days away and have other rich pickings to plunder before they reach us. Beziers is informed, I stopped there to let them know and the Jews from the city are on their way here as I speak - I offered them sanctuary, Carcassona is more easily defended than Beziers." He ran a hand through his hair at this point; to Grace, he looked absurdly young to have such a burden of responsibility and she felt a surge of pity for the man she knew would not live to see his children grow up. Filling a goblet with cool wine from a jug on a small table she offered it to the Vescomtat who accepted it gratefully and downed the contents in one swallow. "Thank you, Ysabella?" Her name became a question as his voice rose slightly; Grace nodded.

"I would speak with you directly, Mistress Ysabella," Vescomtat Trencavel continued, "once I have rested a little and made some arrangements. Come back here before the evening meal to assist your lady and we shall speak then. Now, all of you please leave, I wish to talk to my wife."

The other ladies-in-waiting turned as one to look at Grace who shrugged her shoulders. She had a fair idea what he wished to talk to her about BUT if it was the marriage issue he wished to discuss then Guilhem had certainly wasted no time in approaching his cousin. Grace smiled internally, well he had said he couldn't wait.

As the four women headed to the door Raimond Rogier suddenly said, "Oh, Helena, if you could also please attend with Ysabella, there is a matter I wish to discuss with you too."

Marguerida and Peyronella were wide-eyed with curiosity by this point and couldn't wait until the four of them were out of earshot before they began questioning their colleagues.

"WHAT was that all about?!" exclaimed Marguerida.

"Marriage!" exclaimed Peyronella. "This threat of the Crusaders has prompted declarations for the two of you! Ysabella's must be Guilhem Bastier but as for you Helena I'm not sure."

Helena pursed her lips, in truth she had no idea either, it was unlikely to be one of her choices, mores the pity, and unless the charm purchased from the Dame had already wrought bad luck against Ysabella, it was definitely not Guilhem.

Marguerida cast a covert glance at Ysabella, she was pretty sure she knew who had asked for Helena but decided to say nothing, instead she said, "It could be something completely different, taking care of the Lady Agnes, for example, whilst Vescomtat Trencavel is organising the defence of Carcassona."

"True," Peyronella smiled, "but somehow I don't think so."

"Well we shall find out soon enough," Grace interjected, keen to change the subject. "Now do you think we should find Favia and see if there is anything we four can do to help prepare the Ciutat for siege?"

"Good idea," Marguerida and Peyronella said in unison. The four young women went in search of Favia and after a hasty lunch of cheese, figs and bread they found themselves engaged in winding strips of worn linen, torn from damaged sheets and the like, into bandage rolls.

"I do hope none of these will be needed," Marguerida said uneasily, as she surveyed the growing pile.

"Better to be prepared than not," was Helena's caustic response.

Grace remained silent, she couldn't remember if the people of Carcassonne saw much of a battle, in fact all she could really recall was that the citizens were eventually allowed to leave but all the same, it made sense to be ready. She wondered and worried about the sanitary side of things, from what she was seeing, little thought was being given to the sterility of the wrappings

- should she suggest something? Eventually she decided she should.

"Favia, my mother once told me to boil any clothes to be used as bandages, she said it helped prevent..." and here she struggled for a word, her alter ego came to the rescue and, "putrefaction," completed the sentence.

Favia looked doubtful but conceded that she too had heard this. "We could boil them, but they would come unwrapped," she declared.

"Not if we tie them of like this," Grace demonstrated by tearing the end of the bandage she was rolling in two, taking one end one way around the bundle and the other in the opposite direction she then tied the two ends tightly together to secure the whole thing. "See?"

They all nodded in agreement, but Helena protested, "It will take forever to go back over that lot," she jerked her head at the ever-growing pile, "not to mention drying them out."

Favia nodded, "A valid point, Helena. Ysabella, you may start knotting off the bandages and may boil as many as you manage to tie, the rest of us will continue to wrap."

It was a reasonable compromise and Grace set to work, it was harder work ripping and tying than it was simply winding, and although she managed to get through a fair number of the linen rolls it was by no means all. Finally Favia decreed an end to their work as it was approaching supper time. Grace gathered up the pile of knotted bandages she had accrued and went off to the kitchen in search of a large cauldron in which to sterilise them. Initially no one seemed too keen to provide what she required and only a timely intervention by Favia saved the day. Grace found a young girl who, for a sous was prepared to watch over the pot as it boiled.

"It MUST boil," stressed Grace, "a fast boil and for at least ten minutes." The girl, child really, seemed flummoxed by the notion of ten minutes and Grace realised that with no accurate timepiece guesswork would have to suffice. "Until the first servant begins to take food to the great hall," she said instead, estimating that was at least fifteen minutes away. "When that happens, have someone lift the pot for you and put it here," she indicated a spot which one of the cooks had said was suitable. "Cover the top with this," she passed the girl a large piece of worn but clean cloth. "I will return myself and see that the water is drained, until then you watch over it. Understand?" The dark-haired urchin nodded shyly and Grace smiled, this was the best she could do.

She realised she should already be back with Lady Agnes and straightening her hair, veil and clothing as best she could, hurried away, arriving just as Helena was departing, a look of thunder on her face.

"Whatever is wrong, Helena?" she enquired.

"I-have-been-sold," was the staccato response. "To an old man who has already seen off two wives. I deserve better than this, but it would seem I am the reward for the loyalty of Drogos de Merlon - or rather my dowry is!"

"Is there nothing you can do?" asked Grace, feeling genuinely quite sorry for the woman.

"It would appear not. The deal is done. We are to wed tomorrow, before the crusading army lays us siege," Helena retorted grimly, marching off with head held high.

Grace was a little stunned...tomorrow! She reached the door and the guard opened it for her without a word, although he gave her a wink and a broad smile.

Inside she saw Guilhem, his cousin and Lady Agnes, all of whom smiled. Guilhem crossed the room in a few strides and took her hand in his.

"My lady. My Ysabella. My Lord Trencavel has given his blessing, as I knew he would." He grinned at his cousin. "We will be wed tomorrow, assuming you would still have me?" He looked suddenly worried.

"Do I have a choice?" Grace asked, but she couldn't keep the smile from her eyes, nor indeed her lips. Guilhem pulled her towards him and kissed her thoroughly, to the delight of his cousin and his wife.
"No, you don't," he admonished her when the kiss was over. "I've told you on several occasions that you will be mine whether you like it or not."

Lady Agnes laughed, "Guilhem, don't scare the girl. Ysabella, come here, I have something for you."

Grace crossed to the chair where Agnes was seated and was handed a piece of exquisite lace. "There isn't much,"

Lady Agnes apologised, "but it will look fetching used instead of your linen." She indicated the fine linen veil on Grace's head. "And I thought maybe you could fasten it with this." From behind her back she retrieved a delicately wrought band of what seemed to be silver, patterned with leaves and flowers. It was beautiful and Grace said as much.

"I can't accept this, My Lady," she stated, "I am very grateful but it's too much, the lace is gift enough in itself."

"Nonsense," Agnes retorted, "we will be related once you have wed this reprobate, and in any case I don't wear this band at all."

Grace looked to Guilhem who nodded his head very slightly. "In that case, My Lady, I thank you most sincerely."

Agnes clapped her hands, "At least there is some cheer in these our darkest hours." She looked solemn. "The ceremonies will be held in the chapel here rather than St Nazaire and there will be no guests excepting ourselves. I would have wished for a better wedding day for the two of you," her eyes went misty as she recalled her own wedding several years before, "but at least you shall have the joy of each other before our troubles really begin."

Raimond Rogier Trencavel interceded, "Now let us all go to the hall and eat - it's important to maintain a degree of normalcy - at least for now". Agnes will see that all arrangements are made for tomorrow, won't you, my love?" Agnes nodded. "And I will make the announcements of the weddings but we must also prepare for siege...Guilhem, have your men gather after we have eaten. Messages have gone out to all my vassals instructing them to attend me tonight. We will plan our strategy."

The four of them made their way to the hall, somewhat subdued by the Vescomtat's final words, the reality of the dangerous situation they were soon to find themselves in was starting to hit home. This time Guilhem kept Grace firmly by his side, seating her next to him and much nearer the top of the hall than her accustomed position.

"As Raimond is to announce our betrothal and imminent wedding I want you here next to me," he insisted.

Grace acquiesced, what else could she do? Once seated she looked down to where the other ladies-in-waiting usually sat. Marguerida and Peyronella were there looking wide-eyed at Grace's apparent promotion.

Marguerida caught Grace's eye and mouthed, "I told you so!"

Grace grinned widely and shrugged her shoulders. Of Helena there was no sight. "I wonder where Helena is?" she asked her soon to be husband, "will she be seated next to her betrothed too?"

"I doubt it," Guilhem replied, "She was less than pleased at the news of her suitor. I think when she entered Lady Agnes' room and saw me there too she assumed I had belatedly accepted her as a suitable spouse. When she heard that it was actually Drogos de Merlon asking for her hand I honestly thought she was going to refuse! She still might I suppose but…"

Grace's face dropped, she hadn't realised that Guilhem was present when Helena was informed of her prospective groom, assuming instead that he had arrived just before she herself. It would be another reason for Helena to dislike her, no doubt she would right this minute be somewhere spreading malicious tattle.

"What is it, my Ysabella?" Guilhem had noticed the way her expression changed as he recited the events preceding her arrival.

"It's nothing really," she answered. "Only that lately Helena has chosen to blame me for all that befalls her, you yourself pointed out that I should take care around her and yet you witnessed what she will consider her humiliation. She'll have us both in her sights now."

"Pah, silly woman. She can do nothing after tomorrow when you will be in my protection. And in my bed!" he added lasciviously, winking at her as he slid a hand suggestively up her leg.

Grace giggled, she couldn't help it, his overstated leer was ham acting at its worse. He broke into a delighted smile, "I shall try and make you laugh at least once every day," he declared, "In fact it will be my new mission in life - making you happy." He took her left hand and raised it to his mouth, kissing each side as he done previously. His tone was light-hearted but his eyes revealed the truth in his words and Grace felt her heart contract.

Meanwhile, the subject matter of their conversation was sitting disconsolately on her bed; Guilhem had been correct, upon entering her mistress's room and espying him she had been momentarily convinced that he had agreed to wed her. To be told instead that she was expected to marry and bed a man old enough to be her father, one who had already seen off two previous wives (one younger than her) was a massive slap in the face. There was however little she could do, her parents were long since dead and she had been given over to the Trencavels care as a teenager. She was surprised she hadn't been married off long before in some small alliance. If she but knew it, Vescomtat Trencavel and his wife had been seeking a spouse for her for some time but her spikey disposition and less than pleasing appearance had proven obstacles too large to overcome; Drogos de Merlon had shown an interest in part because of her dowry but also because, unlike his first wife who had been remarkably pretty before near permanent pregnancy and childbirth had worn her down, Helena was unlikely to be the subject of any other man's interest. De Merlon was a petty jealous man who had never realised how lucky he had been to marry a beautiful vivacious girl, it had become almost a game for him to keep her pregnant, to assert his manliness despite the warnings of others. She bore him 7 children in as many years, 5 of whom survived but at the age of 25 and in her 8th pregnancy she fell ill, a 21st century midwife would have diagnosed a placental abruption and she may have survived after surgery and blood transfusions - 13th century medics could do nothing and she died a painful, protracted death, taking the unborn child with her. A doctor had cut the child from her womb at the last but it was malformed and de Merlon swore all to secrecy lest he be blamed for its misshaped head. The second wife had again died in childbirth - this time with her first baby - she had been a mere 15 years old, only a few years older than his eldest child.

Helena stared miserably at the floor - between the prospect of a marriage bed shared with an old man and the privations that would occur with the threatened siege, the next few weeks and months seemed nothing to be looked forward to. Suddenly she remembered the charm she had secreted in Grace's bed...she had forgotten the girl's reaction to lavender when she had disguised it in the scented sachet, should she remove it and try and hide it somewhere else before tomorrow's nuptials? She didn't expect that Grace would sleep on the narrow straw stuffed mattress after tonight. Glancing around she noticed Grace's personal storage chest, a heavy dark oak affair which she said had belonged to her mother; rooting around in the small slit she had previously made in the mattress she extracted the cotton bag and, opening the chest, pushed it right down to the bottom, underneath Grace's heavy winter mantle. There, she thought triumphantly, it was unlikely that the cloak would be needed for some months - a good hiding place.

Chapter 13 - Dual Betrothal

Back in the hall, Guilhem was searching out choice morsels of food for Grace, suggesting she try various things whilst all the while keeping a protective arm around her shoulder; eventually she snapped in mild irritation, "Guilhem, I am not a child! I am perfectly capable of choosing what I want to eat and I can even manage to put it on my platter!" She saw his face fall slightly and took his hand, "I love that you want to care for me but please, don't try and do everything for me - it will drive me insane!"

He looked a little shamefaced at her admonition and tried to explain, "I have never wished to care for anyone or anything other than myself. It feels so strange, so new and so wonderful to have someone that makes me feel this way - even after such a short time of knowing - I just want to spoil you, make you smile, make you laugh, make you happy."

She took his hand. "You have the rest of our lives to do that, Guilhem."

"As we don't know how long that will be, I want to start now!" was his answer. "Seriously, my Ysabella, the Crusaders could be here within days. I wish I could send you off to Minerve as soon as we are wed, keep you safe and away from here but if I do that I won't be with you." His voice broke a little..."and I want so much to hold you for as long as I can. We could perhaps send your things ahead though- anything you won't need for a while, they'll be safer away from Carcassona."

Grace thought for a moment, "We could pack things in my mother's oak chest, my winter clothes, the gifts from Lady Agnes and have one of your men take to Minerve. It will be one less thing to think about I suppose."

Her brain was whirring, she distinctly remembered reading or being told that when Carcassonne fell the inhabitants were allowed to leave carrying only what they stood up in but how could she suggest Guilhem include any of his belongings in the chest without telling him what she knew was going to happen? He'd think she was crazy if she were to confess that she knew the outcome of the siege to follow; worst still, others may hear and she may find herself accused of sorcery or such like. Grace's knowledge of the period was sketchy but she was sure that witchcraft was not considered a fitting occupation and foreknowledge, second sight or however it was termed was probably considered akin to witchcraft. No, on the whole it was probably best for now that she revealed as little as possible whilst trying to ensure the safety of as many people as she could with what little foreshadowing she possessed.

Guilhem nodded, "Perhaps if it's large enough I could include some of my belongings too."

He must have read my mind, Grace thought whilst saying, "It's a good size, maybe not long enough for a sword...but then again I suppose you may be needing that."

Guilhem grinned," I would prefer not to have to use it but you're right, that won't be going in the chest. I have a few items I won't need though so we will have your chest brought to our room before the wedding tomorrow."

"I'll bring all of me to the room...not just my chest," quipped Grace, causing him to snort into his goblet and spray the individual seated across from him in a fine mist of red wine.

"Forgive him," apologised Grace on behalf of Guilhem, "He's still learning how to drink from a cup."

The man laughed at Guilhem's discomfit and waved the apology away.

At that moment Raimond Rogier rose to his feet and briefly announced the betrothals, of Guilhem Bastier to Ysabella de Valentes and Drogos de Merlon to Helena Navarra. "The weddings will be tomorrow," he continued. "In light of the imminent arrival of Pope Innocent's crusading army. It is only proper that my cousin should have the comfort of a wife in this time as I find comfort in my own," he threw a dazzling smile at Lady Agnes. "Now, it is time for me to speak at length with my men, please, all of you accompany me to the council chamber."

All around the hall men were taking leave of their fellow diners and following Trencavel out of the room. Guilhem bent low over Grace brushing a light kiss against her cheek, "Until tomorrow, my sweet."

His departure left Grace seated with people who, whilst proffering their felicitations on her impending nuptials, otherwise left her to her own devices. Soon bored of sitting in silence, she excused herself and headed down the hall to her accustomed seat with the other ladies-in-waiting.

Peyronella and Marguerida greeted her with exuberance, clamouring to offer both their good wishes and, "We told you so's." Grace giggled, they were like a couple of excitable puppies - bright eyed and jostling for attention. She sat in the middle of the pair and enquired as to Helena's whereabouts.

"She stayed back in our chamber," Marguerida replied, "Doubtless disappointed that she didn't bag the handsome Senher Bastier but has to wed a fat old man!" She cackled with glee which made Peyronella laugh too.

"Really Marguerida, he's a nice enough man and he already has a brood of children so mayhaps he'll spare Helena the bedding."

"Doubt it. From what I hear he has a bit of a reputation, can't get enough of it. His first wife was constantly pregnant and that doesn't happen without bedding you know." Peyronella blushed puce at this.

"Marguerida!!"

Grace decided to intervene at this point to spare Peyronella's blushes.

"Girls, girls. The Vescomtat would not have agreed to the match if he thought Helena would be made truly unhappy by it. Marrying de Merlon is a good step for her, he has position and respect..."

"And a paunch!" interceded Marguerida.

Grace had to laugh, "and a paunch! But really, he seems pleasant enough and doesn't he have a house and land somewhere near Narbona? Helena could do much worse and he IS older than her, if you know what I mean."

Peyronella looked a tad confused but Marguerida got the point straight away.

"I suppose it could be worse for her, she'll become mistress of her own household whilst still quite young. THEN she'll be more of a catch!"

"All providing de Merlon doesn't kill her first with pregnancy like he did the first two." Peyronella added, having cottoned on. "But what about you, Ysabella? It's all very quick. By this time tomorrow you'll be a married woman about to get into bed with your new husband. How does THAT feel?"

"Wonderful! I hardly know him but I can't wait for him to take me to his bed. It just seems right." She was about to tell them about the night time encounter in the courtyard but thought better of it. Marguerida may understand but Peyronella would be shocked that she had allowed him to make so free with her body.

Her companions grinned, "Well he is a handsome man," they said almost in unison. "You definitely have the better deal," Marguerida added.

The conversation turned towards what she would wear. The two girls offered to dress her hair for her and were pleased to hear of the gift of the veil and circlet. Peyronella, who was a talented embroiderer, offered to stitch a fancy border around the neckline of Grace's blue dress but was dissuaded by the simple fact that she simply wouldn't have enough time. Then she jumped up having evidently remembered something and grabbed hold of Grace's hand.

"Come with me," she ordered, "I have an idea."

Grace and Marguerida were towed along in Peyronella's wake as she made her way swiftly back to their chamber, where they found Helena still sitting miserably on her bed. Despite her dislike of the woman, Grace moved to her side and hugged her, feeling her stiffen as she did so.

"I'm sure it will all work out," she offered. "Drogos de Merlon is an honorable man and apparently he asked for you, so that must be good, eh?"

Helena span around, eyes blazing. "He wanted my dowry!" she exclaimed "It's all very well for you; you get a virile and handsome man to take as husband. I get a fat old one...his belly is so large I doubt his cock is long enough to be useful."

Grace desperately wanted to laugh - she had every sympathy for Helena regarding her prospective bridegroom and had a sudden (and horrible) vision of a naked Helena on her hands and knees presenting her skinny rear to de Merlon. Shaking her head to rid herself of the thought Grace tried one more time, "Come now Helena, he is a man of property I gather, you will soon be mistress of your own household."

"And you, my dear Ysabella, will be mistress of the fortress of Minerve...again, you have the better deal so do not attempt to placate me! My only hope is that the fat old fart doesn't survive what is heading our way. Now get off me!" She shrugged Grace away and resumed her silent contemplations.

The two younger girls had remained silent but wide-eyed throughout these exchanges but now Peyronella took Grace by the hand and led her towards her portion of the room. "Sit," she ordered, pointing at her bed. She then began to rummage around in a chest not dissimilar to Grace's own but slightly smaller and made of a lighter coloured wood. Finally, she emerged holding a small flat package wrapped in a fine white fabric.

"I knew I still had it! This," she continued. "It will be perfect to edge your blue dress; it will brighten it, make it a bit special and won't take long for me to edge the neck and sleeves. What do you think?"

She unwrapped the parcel to reveal a piece of finely made tablet braid - it looked to have been created out of multi-coloured silk rather than the usual wool and was a vivid flowing ribbon of red, indigo and white, with a fine thread of gold...the pattern on its sinuous length reminding Grace of a river running over and around the rocks in its depths. White and gold edged the strip and the indigo formed the background whilst the deep red made four ripple-like waves along the length. It was beautiful and had obviously taken a great deal of work.

"It's gorgeous!" Marguerida said, echoing Grace's thoughts. "When on earth did you make that?"

Peyronella blushed at the praise and explained. "It was before I came here," she said, "mother helped me set up the tablets, that was the hardest part, the weaving is quite simple as long as you remember which way to turn the tablets."

Grace hugged the girl, "It is lovely but surely you will be saving this for your own use, won't you?"

"Ysabella, I have had this since I was 10 and as yet found no use for it - think of it as my wedding gift to you. Now where is the dress - I shall make a start right now!"

Nothing would dissuade her and so Grace gracefully acquiesced and sat watching as the nimble fingers placed the braid around the scoop neck of the dress and quickly tacked it into place. Within a matter of minutes or so, the braid was in place around both the neck and sleeves with a good length remaining.

"I'll sew it in place in the morning when the light is better," yawned Peyronella, "it won't take long."

Chapter 14 - Preparations

Grace suddenly remembered the cauldron of bandages in the kitchen and realised that if she didn't go back and deal with it now the contents would likely be tipped out onto a dirty floor. Sighing with annoyance, she left her room mates and headed towards the kitchens, arriving just in time to prevent a scruffy looking boy empty the whole lot onto the stone floor.

"Stop!" she commanded, almost causing the boy to fall into the depths of the large cauldron. "Those bandages need to be kept clean." Between them they tipped the water carefully away and Grace (after sluicing her hands in a bucket of fresh water) placed the sopping linen bandages on a wicker tray which she first covered with a piece of worn but clean linen from the earlier bandage rolling session; another piece went on top to protect the neat rolls.

The whole process took a little while and by the time Grace had hefted the tray back to the bedchamber where she planned to leave it so the bandages could dry out, she was exhausted, worn out by the extraordinary emotions of the day and by the previous night's excursion.

All four of the occupants of the room proceeded to disrobe and make preparations for bed. Helena was taciturn, silent and withdrawn but Peyronella and Marguerida made up for her silence by keeping up a running commentary on what tomorrow would bring. Eventually, and probably fortunately, just before Favia entered the room, they fell silent.

Favia looked around, the four young women were in bed; Peyronella and Marguerida looked giddy as children, Helena had the appearance of someone who has eaten a spoonful of salt when expecting sugar and Ysabella...well she resembled the cat who has drunk everyone's cream. She smiled internally, Ysabella's mother was an old and dear friend of hers and she had been instrumental in bringing the girl into the castel when her mother had expressed a wish to work towards taking the Consolamentum...the spiritual baptism of the Bon Crestian as they became Parfait. As far as she knew, Aelinor still hadn't taken the final step but lived with a group of other women in a house near Albi where they helped others, often the old or infirm who had no families to care for them. Aelinor may herself have rejected what she termed 'fleshly pleasures' but Favia knew she was well aware that her vivacious and attractive daughter was not ready to do so - hence the decision not to force Ysabella into the strictures of the Bon Crestian house but rather to find her employment with the Trencavels.

"Good night, girls" she said softly, "tomorrow will be a busy day - sleep well." She extinguished all but one of the candles in the chamber and left, closing the door softly behind her.

Marguerida attempted to make conversation but it quickly became apparent that tiredness had overcome her companions, so with a sigh she turned on her side and was quickly asleep. Helena and Grace however weren't sleeping, rather each was imagining what the morrow would bring; one had a warm glow in the pit of her stomach, the other an ice block. Grace was imagining

Guilhem's strong but sensitive hands moulding her flesh, stroking and rousing her whereas Helena was trying not to think of the calloused furry hands of her intended on ANY part of her. A greater contrast between the mindset of the two women would be harder to imagine.

Chapter 15 – Refuge

Grace awakened before any of the others the following morning and after dressing very quietly and tying back her wavy curls into as neat a plait as she could manage she crept quietly out of the room, determined to have a little time to herself before the others awoke.

She headed into the courtyard and was greeted by the sights and sounds of what seemed like an army of workmen building what appeared to be covered wooden walkways around the towers and walls. She gazed open-mouthed at the bustle and decided maybe a quieter spot for contemplation would be found within the castel. Passing back through the door she had just exited she asked the guard stationed there if he knew what was going on.

"They're the defensive hoardings, miss," the young guard said shyly, "makes it more difficult for attackers to get to the base of the towers because we can see them approach."

Grace thanked him and headed towards the hall to see if any breakfast was forthcoming.

The hall was crowded, noticeably more so than usual and Grace didn't recognise many faces - there seemed to be an influx of newcomers, a mixture of men, women and children - entire family groups by the looks of it and all were surrounded by bags and crudely tied parcels. It looked for all the world like a refugee camp, a resemblance, she soon discovered, which was not far from the truth - for the newly arrived were the Jewish population of Beziers...Raimond Rogier had offered them sanctuary and they seemed to have taken him up on the offer en masse.

From amidst the mass of people Favia emerged barking orders, behind her was one of the Vescomtat's administrators, a rather weedy ineffectual looking man who had been attempting to restore some sort of order and allocate food and temporary lodgings to the massed assemblage but had been failing miserably to make his voice heard. Favia however had no such problem, climbing onto one of the narrow benches she bellowed "QUIET!" The incessant racket in the hall immediately subsided into a quieter rumble of dissatisfied voices...still clamouring for attention.

"I said QUIET!" Favia reiterated. "You are here under the grace and protection of Vescomtat Trencavel. His representative, this good man here," she indicated the administrator with a wave of her hand, "is trying to sort out food and lodgings for you BUT..." she glared sternly around her, "he can do nothing if you are all talking at once and pushing and shoving your way to see him. Now IF you want our help, may I suggest that the head of each household form an orderly line HERE." She pointed to a trestle table where the administrator had now seated himself. "Whilst the rest of you find somewhere to sit and rest. IF you can't or won't do this then I suggest you collect your belongings and seek refuge elsewhere."

Grace watched in admiration, "Favia would make an excellent hospital matron," she thought to herself as the assemblage proceeded to organise themselves in the way suggested. Her thoughts were interrupted by the feel of someone tugging her hand, looking down she spied a tiny black haired, sloe-eyed girl with a tear-stained and grubby face. She bent to the child's level and gently asked what was wrong.

"I can't find my mama," sobbed the girl, "and I don't want to die. My brother says we're all going to get killed."

"We all die eventually my dove but this isn't your time," Grace reassured the child. "Come," she stood and held out her arms in invitation, "let me lift you up. If you are taller you may be able to see your mother." The little girl sprang into Grace's arms and she settled her on her hip. "What does your mother look like?" she asked but before the child could answer the question she obviously spied her missing parent because she suddenly shouted "MAMA!". A small worried looking woman of the same colouring as the girl turned and pushed her way through the crowd towards the pair.

"How many times? How many times!?" the woman enquired. "I have lost count how many times you have been told to stay with your brother, to keep hold of his hand and still you wander off. Esther, you will be the death of me!" The girl hugged Grace briefly and she set her down on the floor.

"I'm glad you found each other," she said addressing the reunited mother and daughter. "It's hard to lose a parent, even if only temporarily in this case." Smiling she watched as they re-joined a small group, the mother berating the child and the girl attempting to explain how she had become separated, each talking over the other.

Across the hall, Guilhem had watched the brief exchange and his heart swelled with what he assumed was love; Ysabella hadn't hesitated to sweep the dirty child into her arms and comfort her, many other ladies in the castel would have ignored the girl. *Actually*, he thought wryly, *most would not even BE in the hall at this hour, let alone unaccompanied and in the midst of such a throng of strangers.* He sighed, not long and she would officially be his but in the meantime he had to supervise the hasty harvest and storage of crops and vegetables from both within Carcassonne's two walled suburbs and the unprotected St Vincents nearer the river, as well as sending out parties to collect whatever could be gathered in the outlying areas. The plan was to denude the area of any food stuff which could assist the Crusaders; whatever could not be harvested and brought within the Ciutat walls was to be destroyed by fire. It was going to be a long, hard day but with a precious reward at the end of it.

Grace remained unaware of Guilhem's perusal and headed towards Favia who was surprised to see her in the hall so early and on her wedding day.

"I have to eat, Favia," she laughed, "even if I am getting married later!"

Favia gave a rather lascivious wink and said, "Yes, I suppose you'll need your strength, my girl!"

Snorting with laughter, Grace allowed Favia to lead her out of the chaos of the hall and into a smaller and richly decorated antechamber, where food was laid out for the household; it having been decided that as the influx of refugees from Beziers would be best dealt with in the hall, the usual residents should at least be able to breakfast in relative peace in this smaller room.

Much refreshed after demolishing a couple of warm bread-like rolls spread liberally with a sweet butter and a mug of what seemed to be milk with a good dollop of honey added (whilst internally bemoaning the fact that tea hadn't yet reached this time), Grace headed off towards Lady Agnes' chamber, unsure what, if anything else she was expected to do today - her wedding day.

Upon arrival at Lady Agnes' room Grace was startled to hear raised voices even through the heavy door.

"It isn't fair that I am expected to marry that odious man!" one of the voices, which Grace instantly recognised as belonging to Helena, shouted.

A second and calmer voice interjected, only to be drowned out again by Helena's hysterical tone; "Ysabella gets Bastier, I get HIM! Why? What have I ever done but serve you! I deserve better than this!"

Grace hesitated, not wanting to go in and be drawn into the argument. She heard Lady Agnes say, "It isn't a case of deserving anything, Helena. Guilhem ASKED for Ysabella, de Merlon ASKED for you and circumstances being what they are at the moment My Lord deemed it sensible to see the pair of you safely married. If of course you really can't go through with the marriage then I will speak to my husband; BUT I warn you Helena that there IS no one else waiting in line to wed you - in all seriousness it is he or life as an unmarried woman with no family. I beg of you to reconsider your position, we want only the best for you I swear."

"I have no real choice, do I?" the lady-in-waiting shrieked. At that moment the door flew open and Helena stormed out, colour high on her sallow cheeks.

"You!" she hissed. "One day you won't be so young, pretty and lucky!"

Flinching against the verbal onslaught Grace slipped passed the furious woman and into the bed chamber where a distraught Lady Agnes was sitting, still wearing her linen night shift. The angry exchanges had obviously taken their toll on the heavily pregnant young woman, her face was marred by twin red blotches on her cheekbones and her eyes were filled with angry tears. Grace felt a surge of sympathy for her mistress and crossing the room in a few strides she put her arms around her and hugged her tightly. Although a little surprised at the contact Agnes hugged back, it was unusual for any of her ladies to touch her, other than in the normal course of their duties and it felt good to have the strong young arms holding her tight.

Finally, with a deep breath, Agnes drew back. "Thank you, Ysabella, I needed that, I hate confrontations. I wish I knew what to do for the best for Helena, as it stands de Merlon is THE only man who has agreed to take her as wife, several have expressed interest in Peyronella and Marguerida but both I think need a little time to mature - plus with you leaving me," she smiled at this, "I need the pair of them to look after me a while longer. Helena is nearly 25, old for a first-time bride - we thought she would be pleased."

"Nothing ever really pleases Helena," Grace said wryly, "and if the truth be known what is causing her the most unhappiness is the fact that she wanted Guilhem, thought she was in some way entitled to him as she is the eldest of us."

Agnes laughed hollowly, "I guessed as much from the way she has been glaring at you. Actually Raimond did mention her to his cousin but that idea had been proposed and declined once before and Guilhem has eyes only for you, Ysabella. Now, help me dress - I have things to do if you and your betrothed are to wed this afternoon!"

Once Lady Agnes was dressed and escorted to the solar, where she immediately began ordering various servants to commence a myriad of tasks, Grace excused herself and headed back to her shared room with the intention of packing the oak chest. When she reached there, however, it was to discover that the heavy wooden box had already been moved, together with most of her belongings, apparently to a room which had been allocated to herself and Guilhem. There was no sign of Peyronella or Marguerida either and her blue dress was nowhere to be seen.

"Bugger!" she exclaimed, there being no one else to hear. "Now what am I supposed to do?" After a couple of seconds thought she decided her best bet was probably to find Favia, she seemed to know everything that was going on at any given moment - in fact, it was probably she who had organised the moving of her belongings. Somewhat irritated by the lack of information coming her way, Grace set off in pursuit of Favia, eventually finding her in the kitchens where she was haranguing an unfortunate servant.

"There you are!" Grace exclaimed. "Would you happen to know where my things are?!"

Favia ceased her admonishing of the servant lad and turned towards Grace, "Indeed I do but you are not allowed into that room until after you are wed, my girl."
"Not allowed! Well how am I supposed to get myself ready if I don't have anything to wear, eh?"

Favia simply laughed, "Ysabella, for once just trust that someone else will sort things out for you - you don't always have to know everything. Now come, sit here, take a drink of wine," she waved a hand and magically a cup filled with a spiced wine appeared, "and WAIT until I have finished, then I'll take you to Peyronella and Marguerida."

Grace opened her mouth to remonstrate but catching sight of Favia's face decided silent obedience was perhaps the safest option. She sipped the wine, it was delicious and once swallowed created a warm glow in the pit of her stomach. As she sat quietly drinking, her thoughts turned to the evening to come, the entire life she was currently experiencing still had all the elements of a dream to her, nothing truly seemed real except the feelings, both physical and emotional, engendered whenever she and Guilhem shared the same space. In the few brief days she had been in the castel he had woven his way into the fabric of her thoughts so completely that it was as if he was the reason she had somehow ended up 800 years out of her own time. Dreamily she envisaged his hands loosening the tie of her shift and pushing the garment from her shoulders until it puddled around her feet, her hand unconsciously toyed with the neckline of her dress and a soft smile formed on her full lips. From across the room Favia grinned inwardly.

"There'll be no problem for her new husband tonight I reckon!" said a voice next to her, echoing exactly Favia's own thoughts.

"Away with you!" she scolded the elderly woman, "You're here in case Lady Agnes births early, not to speculate on my charge's wedding night! Not that I don't agree with you mind!" she added, turning towards the midwife who had been instructed to move into the castel pending the arrival of the new baby.

The old crone grinned toothlessly, "She's certainly getting a handsome lad out of it anyways," she cackled, "not like the other one who came to see me just after you two visited. I hear she's to wed that fat old bugger de Merlon - is he still as rampant as he used to be or has age and belly slowed him down?!"

"Helena came to see you?" Favia asked. "What was she after, a love philtre mayhaps? Well it worked then but didn't get her who she wanted!"

"No, 'twas an ill luck charm the weasel-faced one was after, I sold her one of my best."

"Did she say who she wished ill to?" Favia questioned speculatively, a thought forming in her head.

"They never do, and I never ask," was the reply.

Favia strode back to Grace carrying a jug full of the spiced wine and three additional cups, "Come," she commanded, "time for you to let Peyronella and Marguerida entertain you for a while!"

"Can't I do something?" pleaded Grace, hurrying after the older woman. "I'm bored of sitting around, there must be plenty of things I can help with, what with the Crusaders and all."

"Not on your wedding day!" Favia admonished, "time enough for that tomorrow."

Chapter 16 – Hens

Grace realised somewhat belatedly that they were heading towards Lady Agnes' bed chamber. Once they arrived it was to find her fellow ladies-in-waiting AND Lady Agnes, plus a large wooden bathtub filled with rose scented water. Helena's skinny frame was wrapped in a linen towel and her dark hair hung limply down her narrow back...she had obviously had first dip in the tub.

Smiling graciously she said, "Your turn."

A giggling Peyronella began to unlace Grace's dress whilst Marguerida loosened the hair so hastily plaited that morning. In a matter of moments a rather bashful Grace was naked in the middle of the large room. The contrast between the two brides to be was marked; the one skinny and angular, narrow of hip and flat of chest, the other slender too, yet curvaceous, high, full, firm breasts tipped with dark nipples, leading down to a slim waist and gently sloping belly. Rounded hips, pert buttocks and slender shapely legs with a tangle of curly hair at their juncture completed the picture of femininity.

Lady Agnes looked on amused as Peyronella exclaimed, "I've never seen you naked before, you're beautiful and no hint of all the food you eat...where do you put it?!"

Grace grinned and blushed, "Thank you, I think!"

She was led to the bath and lowered herself in. The water was warm, not hot and it felt delightful to be submerged, from the chest down at least, not quite the shower she had been wishing for but a reasonable alternative.

She sighed deeply, "Whoever had this idea, thank you!"

Whilst Marguerida turned her attentions to Helena, gently combing out the fine hair with an ivory comb and rubbing a fragrant oil into her skin, Peyronella picked up wooden bowl from the side of the tub and, urging Grace's head forward, poured water over her before massaging a sweet-smelling lotion into her hair creating a small amount of lather. She dipped the bowl into the water and rinsed Grace's hair several times before declaring herself satisfied and allowing her to sit back and enjoy the soak.

A knock on the door heralded the arrival of a kitchen servant carrying a tray bearing small delicacies; little pies and pasties containing spiced meats, grapes, cheeses, bread, dates and dried fruits. Grace attempted to cover her breasts with her hands but the servant wasn't allowed over the doorstep, rather Favia took the tray from him and set it on one of the room's small tables.

"Mmmm, food!" exclaimed Grace, "I'm starving!".

They all laughed at her but insisted she soak a little longer, Favia handed her another full cup of the spiced wine she had so enjoyed earlier and she reclined in the tub feeling extremely decadent. In her world she had few close girl friends, certainly none with whom she would have felt comfortable to be naked in a bath in front of, and she was enjoying the sense of bonhomie and female camaraderie, even Helena, flushed from both the bath and the cup of wine she had downed seemed to be enjoying herself. This was, Grace suddenly thought, a 13th century version of a hen night!

Once she had finished her wine, Peyronella bade her stand and used a rough wash cloth to scrub her head to toe before helping her out of the bath and wrapping a linen towel around her. Grace made a bee line for the food and helped herself to several of the tasty mouthfuls and a further cup of wine.

The wine was liberating the tongues of the young women and soon the topic turned to what would (or wouldn't) happen in the marital bed chambers that evening. Well into her third large cup, Helena announced that she would simply close her eyes and let him get on with it.

"Surely it couldn't take much time, a man of his age wouldn't last long". Lady Agnes laughed.

"You may find you enjoy it Helena, he is, after all, an experienced man!"

"I doubt it," Helena retorted, "and I plan to keep my eyes shut so I don't have to see him. Ysabella will at least have something attractive to look at."

"My mother said all cocks are ugly!" Margueirda announced solemnly, "but I don't suppose you have to look much given where they are supposed to put it."

Grace whooped with laughter, Lady Agnes and Favia joined in whilst Peyronella looked bewildered and Helena blushed furiously. Struggling to keep a straight face, Favia waggled a finger at Marguerida and attempted to admonish her but the laughter of the others was infectious and she had to give into it.

Several minutes passed before the laughter subsided and calm was restored, Grace wiped tears from her eyes and succumbed to the very pleasant ministrations of both the younger women. Peyronella teased out the tangles in her curly wet hair whilst Marguerida massaged a sweet, slightly spicy smelling oil into her arms and hands.

Chapter 17 – Stag

Meanwhile one of the prospective bridegrooms, far from luxuriating in a scented bath, was up to his eyes in a myriad of freshly gathered food stuffs, bits of straw clung to his dark hair and his clothing was covered with a layer of fine dust. He'd spent the entire morning and the best part of the early afternoon supervising, as teams of men travelled through the fields and farms surrounding Carcassonne, entreating the occupants to hurriedly harvest whatever they could and make haste with it back to the Ciutat. He'd already ensured that any stocks within the walled suburbs and from St Vincents had been transported within the Ciutat walls and the area set aside to store the produce was so full that he doubted anything else could be crammed in. Now he was tired, hot and hungry so with a last instruction to the men working with him he headed back to the castel, he was, he suddenly realised a matter of hours away from becoming a married man. He looked down at his dusty clothes and sniffed cautiously at the sweat stains under his arms.

"God save me, I stink like a peasant! The poor girl won't want to get near me," he cursed as he hurried towards the chamber he knew Lady Agnes had arranged for himself and Ysabella.

Passing a servant on his way to the bedchamber he requested fresh water to wash in, a pitcher of wine and bread and cheese. The room itself when he arrived there was small and dominated by a huge bed with deep red drapes and matching coverlet. Guilhem grinned to himself imagining Ysabella stretched out naked upon it. The thought of a naked Ysabella was enough for him to feel a rising in his loose fitting braies; in deference to the scorching heat he had scorned the hose he would normally have donned atop the undergarment; a long linen shirt and sleeveless doublet complete his casual ensemble. He laughed at the state he was in, looking and smelling like a peasant fresh from the fields yet planning to bed a beautiful woman within a couple of hours.

A knock on the door heralded the arrival of servants with the food and water, he thanked the youngsters who had carried the heavy items and as soon as they were gone stripped naked. He was still semi-erect in anticipation of the night to come and he grinned ruefully, he'd never been a man to get a cockstand at the mere thought of a woman, at least not until he had met Ysabella, she intoxicated him, filled his waking thoughts and haunted his dreams. He'd known her a matter of days but felt as if she was the one he had been waiting for, it now seemed providence that he had turned down all the previously proposed marriage partners.

The cooler air of the chamber felt delicious on his sweat-soaked skin; the cold water provided to wash in was even better and he culminated his ablutions by dipping his entire head into the deep bowl - not exactly a hair wash he thought but better than nothing. Finding no towel to hand he spied Grace's wooden chest in the corner and opened it wondering if, along with the other items he had instructed added to the contents before it was carried to the chamber, that someone may have added such a thing.

Lifting the lid of the chest he was assailed by a strong smell of lavender, which surprised him as he seemed to recall Ysabella telling him the scent made her sneeze. Shrugging his shoulders, he rootled around the contents, failing to find a towel but locating the source of the lavender smell. Guilhem extracted the bag from the bottom of the chest and as he did so felt a hard lump in the middle of the poorly constructed thing. He was intrigued enough to cut the threads closing the neck of the bag and reach inside. The small article of bent twigs and knotted cords repelled him, he knew exactly what it was, an ill wish, but not why it would be in amongst Grace's possessions, especially hidden within something that she wouldn't use, a lavender bag. In a sudden flash of realisation he knew who would have put it there. Helena.

Snorting with annoyance he dressed hurriedly in the clean clothes which were, as instructed, in the chest and with his hair still dripping swiped up the ill wish and headed out of the bedchamber and down the corridor to where he knew the room for Helena and her groom had been readied. The door was open and he slipped inside, placing the ill wish under one of the pillows - it wouldn't remain hidden for long but then again he didn't want it to be. He smiled grimly to himself, Helena would have the shock of her life when she found her attempt at wishing Ysabella bad luck had misfired.

Task accomplished, he returned to his own room where he demolished the platter of bread and cheese and quaffed the jug of wine in the way only a fit and healthy young man who had taken part in hard physical labour could do. Finally, replete, he lay on the bed and within seconds was asleep.

Chapter 18 – A Tale Of Two Brides

In Lady Agnes' chamber the two brides to be were sitting wrapped in their linen towels whilst Marguerida and Peyronella, under the instruction of their mistress (and with minor intervention from Favia) were perfuming their skin with a heady, musky scent. Grace wrinkled her nose, she wasn't a huge fan of strong perfumes and this was very powerful.

"A small dab behind the ears, between the breasts and maybe a little behind each knee," suggested Lady Agnes.

"Perhaps also a tiny bit on the inner thighs?" enjoined Favia. "It is designed to drive the man wild with lust after all," she grinned wickedly.

"Yes, but I'm sure neither of the grooms needs a scent marker to show where they need to head!" laughed Agnes, "and this stuff is very expensive." She pointed to the exquisite and tiny glass vial which held the perfume. "Raimond's father brought it back from the Holy Land."

Much to Grace's relieve none of the perfume was applied between her legs and attention turned to dressing the pair of them. Shifts of a very fine linen came first, hers had a trim of the braid Peyronella had given her and she smiled gratefully at the younger girl. The neckline was drawn by the ribbon threaded through it so that it sat at mid chest level and her blue dress, now embellished with the braid was dropped over her head and the sides laced so that the garment fitted snuggly and enhanced her curves.

Helena's dress was of a deep red that Grace couldn't recall seeing her wear before. This supposition was confirmed when Marguerida commented on the gown and Helena explained that she had made it a few years ago in preparation for just such an occasion.

"Although," she added, "I'm not sure marrying Drogos de Merlon constitutes the type of occasion I had in mind." The sentence was concluded with a hiccup. Helena was a good way to being rather drunk, a fact which Grace decided was probably a good thing, given her aversion to de Merlon, a state of near inebriation may carry the woman through the ceremony and onto the evening. She just hoped Helena wouldn't turn out to be one of those aggressive drunks; although it would possibly be amusing to watch, she guessed a fair degree of the woman's vitriol would be released and as much of that appeared to be directed in her direction, she'd as soon it didn't happen.

Grace's apparel was completed by a red corded belt with gold coloured metal end pieces, which was passed twice around her waist before being knotted and the ends left to hang down, and a pair of embroidered slippers - another gift from Lady Agnes.

"My feet are too swollen to wear them," the woman explained, "and they're too pretty not to see some use."

The final item was the fine lace veil and silver circlet to hold it in place, but first Grace's curly hair was tamed into glossy waves by Peyronella. At last the pair of brides to be were ready and were instructed to stand side by side for a final inspection.

The wine and camaraderie had brought an attractive flush to Helena's normally sallow face and the deep red of her gown complemented her colouring in a way her usually more sober clothes couldn't - although, as Lady Agnes thought to herself, Grace was by far the prettier of the two, Helena could hold her own. De Merlon would be gratified.

"Beautiful!" exclaimed Favia. "Both of you look lovely. Now, sit the pair of you, finish the wine and the food whilst the rest of us make ready."

Forced to sit together whilst the other women dressed, the two attempted, or rather Grace did, a desultory conversation. Finding her overtures rebuffed as Helena drank her way determinedly down the remaining jug of spiced wine, Grace lapsed into silence and wondered yet again if she was dreaming all that was occurring or whether by some strange twist of fate she **was** actually in Carcassonne in 1209, about to be wed and suffer the privations of siege. It was all too much to take in and thinking about the whys and wherefores of her situation was headache inducing, better to just let whatever was happening run its course she decided. She'd just lapsed into a bath and wine induced snooze when a hand on her shoulder made her jump awake.

"Come on, sleepy head," laughed Peyronella. "It's time!"

"Time? Time for what?" asked Grace mazily.

"Your wedding," smiled Lady Agnes. "Come girls."
The women left the room, Favia leading, followed by the two brides then Lady Agnes with Peyronella one side of

her and Marguerida the other. Helena hiccupped gently as the party wended its way to the castel's small chapel and on occasion appeared to falter in her steps; the surfeit of spiced wine had obviously done its work and she was if not completely drunk at least partially anaesthetised. Sounds of activity from the outside met their ears and it was obvious that the hall was still under the occupation of the displaced Jews of Beziers and, by the sounds of it they had been joined by other refugees.

Grace felt unreasonably nervous, her palms were sweaty and her heart was racing; by the time they reached the outer door of the chapel she was a bag of nerves. Vescomtat Raimond Rogier was waiting for them, he bowed deeply and ushered all but Helena and Grace inside.

"You both look beautiful," he said quietly, positioning himself in the middle of them and drawing their arms through his. Neither girl said anything in response and then, as if at a signal from inside, the door opened. The chapel was small and dark, one of the oldest parts of the castel, candles illuminated the space and Grace could see a small group of people looking towards them. Bishop Berenger stood at the chapel's small altar, he looked uncomfortable and was sweating slightly, his jowly face was redder than usual and his little black eyes flicked betwixt the incoming brides and their intended spouses. In the far corner of the room the troubadour Peirol began to strum a gentle tune as the Vescomtat walked the two girls slowly towards the front of the chapel past the small assembly of well-wishers.

Guilhem locked eyes with Grace and she felt some of the nervous tension release, only to be replaced by a tension of an altogether more enjoyable and anticipatory sort. She smiled shyly and he returned in kind, his eyes never leaving her face as she walked towards him. Helena staggered slightly but the Vescomtat's strong arm supported her and no one seemed to notice, her groom was resplendent in a tunic of a rich ruby red, at least they had their choice of colours in sync, thought Grace as she noticed him stood next to Guilhem. The contrast between the two men was marked and Grace couldn't help but feel sorry for Helena. De Merlon was short and barrel chested with thinning brown hair liberally peppered with grey; his dark eyes were set in a round face which sported a straggly beard and a pair of impressive bushy eyebrows. Grace guessed he was somewhere in his mid to late forties against Helena's mid-twenties. Guilhem in contrast was tall, slim and muscular. Dressed simply in hose of dark blue with a long-sleeved tunic of fine linen and a sleeveless surcoat of a light blue edged with some kind of fur, he looked the very epitome of young virile masculinity.

Arriving at the altar, Raimond Rogier released the two girls to their future husbands and stepped to the side to stand with his wife. Guilhem reached for Grace's hand and held it tightly as they turned to face the Bishop. Helena and de Merlon barely acknowledged each other although he licked his lips in what, to some of the more wordly of the congregation looked to be a lascivious manner.

The Bishop began to recite the marriage vows, the process was lengthy and Grace felt her attention wander, only Guilhem's tight grip on her hand tethered her to her surroundings. Eventually she realised she was being called on to play her part and she dutifully repeated the words of the Bishop and thus it was done, she was married. Grace felt Guilhem's arms encircle her and his lips meet hers, her arms rose of their own volition and settled around his neck. The whole situation felt dreamlike and unreal to her; whether as a result of the afternoon's imbibing or merely because her entire sojurn in this time seemed improbable, she couldn't quite decide. Guilhem's kiss however felt very real and she concentrated on the sensations evoked. Finally drawing apart they were escorted to the room (where several hours earlier Grace had eaten breakfast) for the wedding feast. De Merlon and his bride were already seated and Helena had a goblet in her hand which she was calling to be refilled.

Glancing around Grace caught Helena's eyes. The women was flushed with drink and her eyes were slightly unfocused but she noticed Grace and raised her goblet ironically. Not quite sure how to react, Grace contented herself by nodding slightly.

Guilhem drew her towards a high-backed chair next to Lady Agnes and, having seen her comfortably ensconced, seated himself next to her. Servants laid multiple dishes before them; roasted meats of every variety, delicately spiced fish dishes and elaborate sweetmeats made of dates, spices egg yolks and breadcrumbs shaped into fantastical animals. The wine flowed constantly but Grace tasted little and drank less, so conscious was she of the man to her left. His hand was stroking her leg through her dress as he conversed nonchalantly with one of the other men; gradually the hand worked its way up until it reached the juncture of her thighs whereupon two long fingers began a slow circular motion. Grace moaned and her new husband turned solicitously towards her.

"What is it my sweet, do you feel unwell?" As he said this he increased the pressure of his hand, causing her to part her legs unconsciously thus allowing the roaming fingers easier access. Grace felt desire pulse through her, she was sure that if he continued his assault she would likely climax. In her mind's eye she pictured Meg Ryan in the famous scene from **When Harry Met Sally** and was entirely sure that the 13th century wedding guests would not appreciate her shouting out, "yes, yes, yes!"

With considerable difficulty she focussed on responding to the question whilst surreptitiously grasping Guilhem's wandering hand and firmly pinching the skin on the back of it.

"I am a little overwhelmed, my husband," she said, "and perhaps a little tired."

The man Guilhem had been talking to throughout snorted, "Well, mistress, if I know Senher Bastier you will be even more tired come morning!"
Grace blushed prettily and gasped slightly as Guilhem made one last assault on her causing a rush of moistness between her legs. He did however remove his hand whilst whispering (none too quietly) in her ear, "you will be doing more than gasping later, my Ysabella!"

Grace merely smiled and raised her glass to her new husband. "I rather think you may be gasping a little too," she parried before turning to address Lady Agnes, who had been watching the exchanges with some humour.

"Well done, Ysabella," she laughed, "start as you mean to go on!". The two women laughed and shared a platter of sweet pastries.

Peirol the troubadour put down his goblet and picked up his gittern. Obviously there was to be a little entertainment in addition to the feasting and the assembled crowd quieted somewhat as the musician thoughtfully strummed the stringed instrument, whilst glancing covertly at Guilhem and his bride. With a sudden flash of a smile he began to sing what appeared to be a continuation of the song he had created a few nights previously, as salacious as the original but this time clearly identifying Ysabella as the object of Guilhem's attentions. The guests roared with laughter at the newly married couple's discomfiture and Guilhem responded by grabbing Grace's hand and dragging her out of the room whilst simultaneously announcing his intention of carrying out some of Peirol's suggestions.

Chapter 19 – Wedding Nights

The pair ran hand in hand along the corridors in fits of giggles until they reached the door of their bedchamber. Guilhem flung it open and they collapsed in a heap on the floor, incapable of speech. With a certain presence of mind Guilhem managed to close and bolt the door, keen to prevent any guests who may have decided to follow them, from entering in a bid to perform any kind of bedding ceremony.

Finally their laughter began to subside and Grace became very aware that they were alone in a room which contained a large bed. She suddenly felt unaccountably nervous and licked her lips which for some reason felt dry, as did her mouth. Guilhem watched her, entranced. Her face was flushed, the veil she wore was adrift, as the circlet holding it in place had slipped in their precipitous flight, and tendrils of her dark hair curled onto her cheeks. He rose to his feet and extended a hand to her.

"Come, wife," he said, hauling Grace to her feet. "I have plans for you but first, sit and let us share a glass of wine."

Grace blushed furiously, angry at herself for feeling like a nervous virgin, *which of course I am* she thought, *in this body anyway*. That thought increased the butterfly sensations she had been experiencing since Guilhem's hand had incited such desires at the wedding banquet. Watching the emotions chasing across her face, Guilhem could resist no longer and pulled her tight to him, holding her buttocks in his hands he pressed her against him and kissed her thoroughly.

"There," he announced breathlessly, "let that be the start...on account! Now sit here, my love, and we will share this wine and talk until you are at ease with me."

He led Grace to the bed and she perched on the end as he poured them each a goblet of the wine which had thoughtfully been left. Sitting himself at her side, he rested his hand on the coverlet between the two of them.

"Hold my hand as we drink," he said quietly.

Grace, place her small hand in his and they took a few companionable sips of wine in silence. After a few moments it was she who punctuated the quiet by commenting.

"It's only a few days since we met yet here we are married - it seems so strange to me."

"I have noticed you in previous visits, Ysabella, but you were much younger and not so..." he paused, "well, not so curvy," he finally finished.

"I don't remember you," Grace (as Ysabella's memories kicked in) responded, "but I was never that interested in men and you were probably occupied by older and more curvacious girls!"

Guilhem grinned at her. "Well you have filled out nicely now," he laughed, "and appear to have developed an interest in the opposite sex, if our kisses so far have been anything to go on!"

Grace pulled her hand from his and punched him in the stomach spilling a little of her wine on him in the process.

Guillhem dabbed ineffectually at the wine soaking through his hose, "I'll need to get out of these, before I carry you to bed for the second time!"

"What do you mean, when did you carry me to bed for the first time?!" Grace demanded as Guilhem set down his wine, stood and began to untie the laces fastening his hose. Then, blushing she remembered her arrival at the Ciutat, "Oh," she smiled, "I forgot about that."

"And this time I won't be leaving you there alone," he said, kicking the discarded legwear across the room and standing hands on hips in his knee length linen braies, shirt and surcoat.

Grace began to giggle as he cut an incongruous sight, hairy legs beneath the braies looking wildy out of place in contrast with the linen shirt and finely made surcoat.

"What are you laughing at, impudent woman?" Guilhem demanded, a hint of laughter apparent in his voice.

"You," she replied, "you look so silly standing there like that - as if you can't decide whether to get dressed or undressed!"

"Oh, I very definitely intend to get undressed!" he grinned, "but there's no rush." He took a single step towards the bed and pushed Grace back onto the coverlet, before taking both her hands in one of his and drawing her arms above her head - she lay helplessly pinned beneath him, and he kissed her thoroughly, his lips demanding ever more. Finally, he drew back and commented mildly, "Well that stopped the giggles anyway."

Grace was far too breathless to respond and Guilhem, with his free hand, began to tickle her, mercilessly seeking out her sensitive spots with his long fingers until she was once again helpless with laughter.

Amidst her laughter, Grace begged him to stop and, by this time laughing almost as much as she, he eventually relented, rolling off her to half sit, half lay, next to her. Both were flushed and had tears of laughter running down their faces.

"Now that's better," Guilhem said. "My father always said the best way to get a pretty girl into bed was to make her laugh or marry her, and I've done both. Now, wife, if you could possibly contain yourself I should like you to come and stand. Just here..." He sat up and indicated a spot just in front of him.

Feeling nervous again, although the shared laughter had brought a closeness, a warmth to proceedings, Grace did as instructed.

His arms went around her pulling her close to him, his head rested between her breasts, his hands were firm on her buttocks. "I have wanted you since the day I picked you up in the courtyard, yet now I have you here I'm scared, scared I'll hurt you, scared you won't enjoy it, scared you won't want me, that I won't give you pleasure." His voice was muffled, "I want so much to make this good for you, but I don't know how."

Grace was unaccountably moved, she could remember little of her first time, it had hurt a bit and didn't last long was about all she could recall - that and feeling distinctly let down - "was that what all the fuss is about?" she remembered thinking. Yet here was this man, one whom by his own confession had had many lovers, worried that he would be unable to please his new wife as he took her virginity.

She pulled away slightly and said, "Guilhem, whatever you do will please me, this I swear." Breaking free from his grasp, she loosened the fastenings at the side of her gown until she was able to pull the wide neck down, letting the dress land in a puddle of blue on the floor.

Stepping out of the gown, she stood in front of him in the almost transparent shift...he gasped and felt himself harden. She was beautiful, the high breasts pressed against the sheer fabric and the dark hair between her legs was clearly visible. Standing, he moved towards her, her eyes left his face only briefly to note the obvious sign of his arousal. Guilhem's hands moved of their own volition to remove the silver circlet and lace veil, both of which he dropped unheedingly onto the floor, before tangling his hands into the glossy waves of hair and drawing her head towards his for a passionate kiss.

Withdrawing slightly, he discarded his surcoat and pulled the shirt over his head, leaving himself, out of some kind of false modesty, clad only in the braies. His hands reached out to the ties at the neckline of Grace's shift, they shook slightly as he untied the garment and pushed it off her shoulders, down past her breasts - the nipples hardening as the air met them, and onto the floor until she stood naked before him. He felt his eyes fill with tears of emotion, she was, to him, perfect as she stood nervous, yet proud in front of him, her eyes not leaving his. Suddenly overcome he fell to his knees in front of her, his head against her thighs, smelling her womanly scent, he was on the very edge of simply taking her, no foreplay, no preparation - so desperately did he wish to feel himself sheathed inside her - but, he reminded himself, he wanted her to enjoy the experience, not to feel like a tavern wench he'd bought for a few coins after an evening's carousing. Taking a deep breath, he rose once again to his feet and kissed Grace gently on the mouth.

Not saying a word, he allowed his hands to rest on her head, almost in benediction and then slowly, teasingly, gently he began to stroke down each side of her face, cupping it carefully before letting his hands slide down her neck shoulders, arms and back again and again - on and on in an almost hypnotic rhythm. Grace shut her eyes, her breath coming in small gasps, his touch was incredibly erotic and she lost herself in the sensations, feeling very much as if she was not only experiencing the moment but also watching it - as if from outside. Ysabella, if not totally reasserting control seemed more present than usual and it almost felt to Grace as if she were two women; the one, herself, experienced in matters of sex and the other, Ysabella, a virgin experiencing the delights of her body for the very first time.

175

Guilhem's hands ceased their relentless stroking of her arms and neck and back and instead moved to cup her breasts, his thumbs gently circling the nipples until they hardened; unable to resist he bent and suckled one brown nub, his tongue flicking around and around it, his thumb mirroring the action on her other breast. Grace moaned and felt a surge of wetness between her thighs; she wanted to feel him inside her very badly but the other part of her, Ysabella, still seemed wary, it didn't matter though, the intense desire Guilhem was creating was enough - for now.

Sensing how aroused she was Guilhem pushed her back onto the bed; her legs parted and he had to use every ounce of his self-control to prevent himself from dropping his braies and plunging into her. His desire was so urgent, so strong that he felt an almost physical pain as the primal urge to shoot his seed into her struggled with the need to make the moment last - to bring her to completion before he let himself go. Pulling her fully up onto the bed he bit his lip and began once more the teasing appreciation of her body. This time he started at her feet and slowly stroked and tickled his way via instep, calf and thigh until he reached the swell of hips. He maintained the stroking, nibbling and kissing for some time, assiduously avoiding the dark curly hair between her legs until, arching her back and moaning incoherently she begged him to touch her there.

He needed no further encouragement, his fingers parted her gently, she was as wet and slippery as waterweed; mentally he told himself, NO, not yet. Instead, finding the small nub of flesh already engorged, he began to rub and circle it steadily and rhythmically. Grace could feel the orgasm building and building, her insides tightened, her entire body seeming to exist of nerve endings - she was acutely aware of the feel of his fingers on her, in her; of his hair, escaped from his tie, brushing her thighs and belly, of the sound of her strangled moans and his rapid breathing, time ceased to exist, there was nothing but NOW. Then, as his lips and tongue joined his eager fingers, she imploded - all the pent-up sexual tension was released in a paroxysm of joy leaving her boneless, mindless.

Guilhem could wait no longer. With one hand he fumbled at the drawstring of his braies and raising himself pushed them down and off. Grace opened her eyes to the sight of him kneeling between her spread legs, a look of such intense emotion on his face that it made her smile inwardly. The blue eyes met hers as he lowered himself and pushed into the tender sensitised flesh. She felt a single sharp pain as her hips involuntarily lifted up to meet him, then her legs instinctively rose to clasp him tighter, pulling him deeper, welcoming him. Guilhem groaned knowing he wouldn't last long, he plunged into her, once, twice and then again and again, his hands underneath her clenching her buttocks and she met him at every thrust, urging him on. His eyes opened as climax overtook him and he found himself lost in Grace's gaze; an animalistic growl escaped him as he shuddered to a heart pounding finish and he fought an overwhelming urge to fall on her and bite the soft skin of her throat. Grace locked eyes with Guilhem and it seemed only the two of them existed, that somehow they were inextricably linked for all time, she found herself shouting (or at least she thought she had), "Mine. You are mine."

With coherent thought finally returning, Guilhem withdrew and drew a trembling Grace against his side. The pair of them were breathing heavily and to her astonishment Grace felt tears running down her face. Guilhem noticed and clutched her more tightly to him.

"My love!" he whispered tenderly, "What is wrong? Did I hurt you? I didn't mean to...I just couldn't wait any longer - at least not without exploding anyway!" he added.

Grace giggled through the tears at that. "No, you didn't hurt me, well maybe a little for a brief moment. I don't know why I'm crying, it's as if every emotion I have ever had just happened again all in one go." She sighed at her inability to find the words which could convey the complex mix of feelings, "I just never knew, never thought it could be like that," she concluded.

Guilhem stroked her back thoughtfully, "To be honest, my love, neither did I. I have no idea how many women I have bedded over the years - too many probably but never, ever have I wanted so much to please someone." He paused, "In fact I only ever thought of my own pleasure and took it where and when I wanted. This caring how the woman feels is brand new to me!"

"And do you like it then?" sniffled Grace, sounding a little worried.

"I could come to like it very, very much," he replied, "Especially if you react like that every time!"

"Like what exactly?" she blushed once more.

178

"So...so...errr...enthusiastically!" he countered, grinning, "I've bedded a few virgins in the past but none as willing as you, my love."

Grace snorted, "Well I sincerely hope I am the LAST virgin you take to your bed!" she retorted.

"The only woman I will ever need from this day forth," he assured her, clasping her tightly.

Grace sighed and snuggled against him, her head resting on the sweat-damp hair of his muscular chest, "I'm so glad to hear that."

Enveloped in a postcoital haze the two of them soon drifted into sleep, Grace's head still pillowed on Guilhem's chest. Twice they woke during the night, candles burned down and the room inky dark, and made love gently, slowly, before dropping back into slumber.

Chapter 20 – The Other Bride

The celebrations had continued long after the giggling departure of Guilhem and his bride. The guests seemingly intent on roistering through the night, all of them very aware that the Crusading army of Arnaud Amaury was close and that there may be few other chances for revelry. The exception to this being Raimond Rogier and his wife, who had retired to their chamber not long after Grace and Guilhem had left.

Helena had continued to drink, as had her new husband - his florid face becoming ever redder and his actions lewder as the evening progressed. Helena barely exchanged a word with him, nor indeed with anyone else, in fact she seemed inured to the noise and laughter around her, preferring instead to concentrate on the contents of her goblet.

Her seemingly peaceful reverie was interrupted when her husband grasped her firmly by the upper arm and loudly announced his intention to take his new wife to bed, "whilst he was still capable of a cockstand." Helena recoiled at both his crude words and the vice like grip on her arm, prompting jeers and comments from the assemblage as to the likelihood of de Merlon being able to service his latest wife.

Helena was mortified as he pulled her from her seat and towards the door through the laughing crowd of drunken revellers - having missed out on the opportunity of a bedding ceremony with Guillhem, they were not about to be short changed again and swept the couple down the corridor towards their chamber chanting lewd songs as they did so. Upon reaching the room the pair were unceremoniously shoved inside and rough hands began to attempt to disrobe them...Helena screamed at the affront but de Merlon laughed uproariously and allowed the crowd to strip him to his braies before ordering them out of the room, "so he could attend to business."

The room emptied relatively quickly, leaving a very drunk and very frightened Helena in the middle of the space clutching her gown (which had suffered a large tear to the neckline during the melee) tightly to her.

"Come now," de Merlon said, gruffly but not unkindly. "They meant no harm really and the dress can be repaired." He approached her and tried to help her remove the damaged gown but she backed away from him, his paunch was all too visible in his semi undressed state - as was his erection. "Take it off, girl!" he commanded, obviously irritated by her action, "You will do your duty by me." As Helena still showed no sign of compliance he tugged at the neckline of the dress enlarging the rip still further and revealing her breasts, covered only by the flimsy fabric of her shift. This glimpse of her body appeared to inflame the man and he tore at her garments until, despite her screams and attempts to fight back (which resulted in nail scores down one side of his face and a reciprocal split lip for her) she was naked.

Trembling with a combination of fury, fear and excess alcohol, Helena attempted to conceal her small high breasts with her left hand and forearm whilst her right hand covered her pubic area. De Merlon paced around her, poking her in the buttock, thigh and stomach, "I've seen more meat on a bone gnawed by one of my hounds, and bigger breasts on a pigeon," he said derisively, "Still, you're still youngish and a pregnancy or two will fatten you up."

Without warning he pushed her to her knees in front of him and discarding his undergarment, forced her head against his erect penis, "Open your mouth!" he demanded, and when - whimpering - she did so he forced himself in her making her gag and nearly vomit. After a few thrusts he withdrew, pulled her to her feet and then pushed her face down over the edge of the bed; forcing her legs open with his knees he roughly spread her and tried to push inside but she was, not unsurprisingly, dry. Cursing he spit on his fingers and rubbed briskly before plunging his fore and index fingers into her. Helena screamed and writhed trying to escape but he held her firmly, pushing her head into the covers. Grunting with the effort he positioned himself and took her in one fierce thrust, ramming into her right to the hilt leaving her momentarily stunned by the abrupt pain. She tried to get away but finding herself held fast with no means of escape she resorted to turning her face into bed cover and biting down hard to stifle the sobs which she couldn't seem to stop.

De Merlon thrust mindlessly in and out of his new bride, evidently caring not a whit that her only response was sobs and the occasional plea for him to stop. With one hand he began to slap her arse in time with his thrusts, hard stinging, painful smacks which left rosy handprints in the pale skin. Seeing the red marks appeared to encourage him further - as did Helena's increased attempts to escape his attentions. Maddened with lust he increased his pace, using his not inconsiderable weight to thrust harder as he began to smack her buttocks with both hands. Helena was nearly insensible with the pain and the shame of the violation by the time de Merlon reached his peak and jerking, shuddering, spilled himself inside her before collapsing on her back.

He farted loudly and with wine-sodden breath slobbered in her ear, "That wasn't so bad, was it?" he asked breathily. "Once I've rested we shall have another go. I last longer when I'm sober," he added jovially before biting her shoulder viciously.

He hauled himself off her and made use of the slop bucket before pulling back the covers and climbing in the bed. He was asleep and snoring loudly before Helena managed to stand. His semen trickled down her leg and she picked up the nearest cloth, which happened to be her shift, to wipe herself with. It hurt but she scrubbed viciously; the make do cloth came away blood-smeared and she threw it down in disgust. She was nauseous and dizzy, and her backside was on fire. On trembling legs she managed to get as far as the shelf, holding the bowl and jug of water which had presumably been left for washing purposes. Taking the jug she took a swig directly from it, wincing at the sting in her split lip, and swilled her mouth out - spitting into the bowl until her mouth felt cleared of the taste of him.

Looking around the chamber she realised that there was nowhere other than the bed to sit and so, grimacing at the thought of having to be so close to de Merlon, she reluctantly joined him, laying as close to the edge as she dared in order to avoid the possibility of touching him. Tears of pain and anger slid down her face and she bit down on the pillow to prevent herself from crying out; as she did so one hand slipped underneath the soft cushion and her fingers found the sharp edges of the wooden ill luck Guilhem had secreted there earlier in the day. Removing it from the hiding place, Helena recognised it as the same one she herself had purchased from the old woman and the words of warning echoed in her mind, "Be careful to ensure it is not found, for if it is, the misfortune will turn to you." She flung the small object across the room and made her way hurriedly to the bucket in which de Merlon had relieved himself, she needed to be sick and the smell of his urine made it worse. She vomited until her stomach was empty, leaving her weak and clutching her midsection in pain.

After rinsing her mouth again, she finally had to return to the bed where de Merlon had continued to snore, completely unaware of proceedings. Huddled in a tight ball of misery she eventually drifted into a fitful sleep, only to be woken what seemed mere minutes later by her husband pulling her onto her back to claim his conjugal rights again.

"Come here, wife," he demanded.

She made no attempt to resist but did not cooperate either - just lay there, face to one side until he finished and then she rolled back onto her side, arms locked around her knees, tears in her eyes.

"Bah!" snorted de Merlon. "It's like fucking a statue!"
His meaty hand crashed into her side and she gasped with pain but didn't move. Let him do what he wanted, it didn't matter, this was her life now - Ysabella had won.

Chapter 21 – The Happy Couple

Blissfully unaware of Helena's plight, Grace awoke in the soft light of the early morning as it filtered through the wooden shutter on the room's only window. She stretched and yawned, momentarily wondering where she was. Realisation came flooding back as the toes of her right foot collided with the solid calf of the man still soundly asleep at the side of her. Raising herself up onto her elbow she studied the peaceful face, softened by slumber, resisting the urge to push a lock of dark hair from his cheek. He was a handsome man by the standards of any century; in sleep the face lost its angular masculinity to the softer look of childhood, the ridiculously long eyelashes casting half-moon shadows on his cheeks. If she closed her eyes she could picture what a beautiful little boy he must have been, almost girlishly pretty perhaps, which, she thought to herself, could explain his overt masculinity in adulthood - a point to prove.

As if sensing her scrutiny Guilhem stirred, muttered something incomprehensible and turned onto his side, lapsing immediately back into his deep sleep. Grace smiled to herself and eased out from under the covers to look for the covered bucket she had worked out sufficed as a toilet in most of the castel's bedchambers. The only guarderobes with latrines appeared to be in the rooms which looked down over the hill to the river (the waste merely dropping to the ground to be, eventually, washed away by the rains) and this room wasn't one of them. The bucket was behind a heavy curtain in the corner of the room so at least there was some privacy but it was still, to a 21st century girl, an uncomfortable experience to squat over the pail (sitting on it was almost impossible) and relieve oneself, especially since the only means of wiping was usually a cloth which one dampened in the bowl of water provided. On this occasion Grace only needed to pee but she winced as the urine stung the tender flesh between her legs; legs which ached from the exertions of the previous night and which struggled to maintain the awkward squatting position.

Standing once more she took an inventory of her, or strictly speaking Ysabella's body, her legs ached as did her neck for some reason. There were several fingerprint-sized bruises on her sides from Guilhems strong hands, a bite mark on one breast and what seemed to be a purplish love bite on the other. She also had a deep inner ache, as if her internal organs had been re-arranged and her inner thighs were streaked with blood and other bodily fluids. She grimaced and emerged from behind the curtain with the provided cloth which she dampened in cool water from a jug on a shelf before gingerly cleaning herself.

As she finished she became aware of Guilhem's eyes on her and turned to face him. He was propped up against the pillows with a lascivious look on his face, a face which now bore little resemblance to the sweet child she had been imagining only minutes before, the transition to aroused adulthood underlined by the obvious rise of the covers.

"Come here, wife," he commanded in an unknowing echo of de Merlon's words to Helena the previous night. "I plan to ravish you once more." His face split into a wide grin.

Grace sauntered across the small room, hips swaying in an obviously provocative way. "Really?" she enquired, "I'm surprised you have anything left to offer in the ravishing department - what was it? Three times last night?"

"Only three times? I must be getting old," countered Guilhem. "Now come here!" As he spoke the last words he erupted from under the covers, jumped from the bed and landed next to Grace in one fluid movement. She squealed involuntarily as his arms and lips claimed her then was lost again in the power of his lovemaking.

Chapter 22 – The Day After The Night Before

Several hours later Grace awoke to find herself alone in the large bed. Sunlight streaming through the single window via the now opened shutter, indicated it was rather late in the morning to still be abed, but as no one had yet knocked on the door Grace assumed she was being allowed to rest after the wedding night. Smiling to herself as she recalled said wedding night, and the dawn hours, she stretched languorously. The boundaries between herself and Ysabella were blurring; it was almost as if she were looking at the world through the younger girl's eyes, her senses, her thoughts and feelings were as hers, yet somehow shared, Grace could still recall her own memories and experiences but they were melded with Ysabella's. It was a rather disquieting discovery, but if it was a dream it would have to run its course and if it wasn't - well that was too complicated to even imagine so Grace decided to push that particular thought to the back of her mind.

She was interrupted from her reveries by a sharp knock on the door, which then opened a mere crack.

"Ysabella, you lay abed! I've brought you some food, are you dressed?"

Grace sat up in the bed and pulled the covers up, capturing them under her arms. "No, I'm not dressed but I am hungry!"

The door opened revealing Favia, wearing a knowing smile and carrying a tray on which rested a couple of sweet rolls with a lump of a soft goat's cheese, some very ripe figs and a jug of wine.

"Well, judging from the lateness of the hour, your bridegroom's happy demeanour when I saw him earlier AND the way you look this morning, do I take it that last night was a pleasant experience?" Favia's eyes twinkled as she took in the purple shade of the mark on Ysabella's breast which was just visible above the bed sheets.

Grace felt the colour rise in her face but smiled sweetly back at the older woman. "It was more than I could have imagined. I only hope Helena is as satisfied this morning as I am."

Favia's face darkened at the mention of Helena. "I fear she fared less well than yourself, Ysabella. She seemed in some discomfort when I saw her earlier and she has what seems to be a cut lip, whilst de Merlon has a fine set of scratches on his face. He has bragged amongst the men that he managed, as he put it, to get his way with her, more than once and that he is sure she will add to his brood of children within the year if he keeps at it. Helena visibly shrank when she overheard that. Odious man!"

Grace, despite the way Helena had behaved towards her alter ego Ysabella, felt more than a twinge of sympathy for the woman. To be almost forcibly married to a man more than twice your age with whom you have spent little, if any, time prior to the nuptials and then to be used as merely a vessel to carry yet more children was a fate that she herself was glad to have avoided. She wondered how often a woman in this age would be pleased with, even love, the man who chose her or, as seemed to happen, was chosen for her?

Shaking her head, she simply said, "Poor Helena, I doubt she would accept my sympathy if I offered it, so perhaps it would be better to say little when I see her next."

"That may indeed be wise," Favia responded, "although one look at your face and she will know how things were better for you. You look like the kitchen cat when she has been allowed a dish of cream!"

Grace blushed again and began devouring the tray of food whist Favia busied herself by picking up the discarded clothes, folding the dress and fine linen shift and adding them to the contents of the large chest, whilst simultaneously removing a plain work a day gown and more coarsely woven undergarment.

"Hurry up, my girl," she commanded, "there's still lots of work to do to make the city ready should the Pope's Crusaders decide to pay us a visit."

Through a mouthful of food Grace asked, "Where is Guilhem? Have you seen him? What is he doing?"

"I haven't seen him since first thing this morning when the Vescomtat asked him to round up some men and begin bringing in as many of the people from the suburbs as would come, he feels it will be safer for them to be within the walls of the Ciutat when the Crusaders arrive." Grace blanched, she had forgotten about the peril facing Carcassonne and wished she could remember the key dates of the sequence of events to come but she had been young and relatively uninterested when she had visited as a girl in 2001. Stuffing the last of the food into her mouth and taking a large gulp of the watered wine to assist with the swallowing thereof, she threw back the covers, affording Favia a full view of the various small bites and bruises adorning her body, and headed for the curtained off area. A quick splash of water on her face and use of the bucket rendered her ready to dress and Favia, without commenting on the love marks, helped her into the dress, braided her hair and fixed a linen veil to her head with a strip of tablet woven braid. Grace protested at the necessity of the veil but, as she was now a married woman, Favia insisted she wear it and would brook no argument.

The pair of them, at Favia's insistence, sorted through the wooden coffer which Guilhem had apparently arranged to be transported to Minerve. Deciding what to leave in and what to remove for ongoing usage was problematical as neither of them had any idea what Guilhem planned, nor could they know what may happen with respect to the Crusading army. Eventually it was decided that only the very bare minimum of goods and chattels remain in Carcassonne, the remainder to be sealed away and taken to the fortress of Minerve. As they were rooting around and repacking the chest Grace came across the bag filled with lavender, she sneezed at the scent as she always did but, assuming it was something of Ysabella's she returned to the coffer without comment. After all, it made her sneeze but it wasn't an unpleasant aroma.

Chapter 23 – Tempers Rise

Throughout that hot day the inhabitants of the three suburbs and wider surrounding areas swarmed into the Ciutat which did its very best to accommodate all and sundry, but which quickly became uncomfortably full; families set up makeshift campsites wherever they could, seeking shaded areas, attempting to hide from the fierce Midi sun whilst Guilhem and his men continued to shepherd new arrivals through the main gates.

As the surrounding countryside was emptied of inhabitants, soldiers began to set light to whatever crops hadn't been collected in and brought into the Ciutat; Vescomtat Trencavel wanted to leave little by way of provisions for the invading army, hoping that the 40 day tenures of the foot soldiers would elapse and that the men would start to disperse whilst Carcassonne's citizens remained safe and well fed within the Ciutat walls.

In the castel, Grace and the other ladies-in-waiting, including a surly and obviously in pain Helena, attempted to assist in creating order within the various refugee groups. Women with young families were allowed to remain in the relative cool of the Great Hall, everyone else was moved to the courtyard where awnings, made of the tents the Ciutat's own soldiers would ordinarily use whilst on campaign, were hastily erected in order to offer some shade from the fierce sun. The able-bodied men and boys were set to work in constructing the wooden hoardings which sat atop the ramparts, projecting out past the outer wall so that attackers could be spotted before damage was done to the walls themselves. It was barely organised chaos - noisy, dirty and hot. The ladies-in-waiting, at Favia's request, were set to arranging the distribution of water which was being brought from the river Aude to supplement the Ciutat's wells and being stored in the biggest empty barrels that could be found. Most containers had been filled with the crops brought in but whatever was empty was utilised as a water store.

A sudden recollection came to Grace as she was using an enormous ladle to transfer some water to a cooking pot being held out by one of the displaced women; Carcassonne ultimately didn't fall due to the invading army, rather sickness caused by the overcrowding and lack of sanitation and clean water forced the Vescomtat to consider terms in order to protect his people.

"Oi! Watch what you're doing." A coarse voice interrupted her train of thoughts.

Smiling apologetically, for she had inadvertently tipped a quantity of water over the women in front of her, Grace handed the ladle to Peyronella who stood beside her and without a word set of in search of Guilhem. Finding him some minutes later engaged in ordering a group of men in the construction of one of the hoardings, she caught his eye and with a last barked instruction he hurried to her side.

"Is something wrong?" he enquired, looking worried.

"No. Well yes. I don't know!" was her muddled response. He drew her towards the shade offered by one of the large elm trees and kissed her gently. "What is it, my Ysabella? Something is troubling you, I can tell."

193

Grace took a deep breath, how much could she, should she say without seeming to be offering up some kind of premonition? "I was just portioning out water," she said, "when it occurred to me that the invaders could easily block our approach to the river and that with so many people in the Ciutat the wells could run dry. It is very hot, people need water, what happens if we run out?"

Guilhem looked concerned, "You're right. We have enough food stuffs to last out a long siege but what good is that if there is no water. The wells should be sufficient, even if we can't get to the river, but I think I will suggest that each well is assigned a guard to ensure that no one takes more than they need. I doubt that will be popular, I am already hearing that the local Ciutat dwellers are grumbling about the influx of refugees and they are used to simply helping themselves from the nearest well, limiting that will be another irritation."

"They'll be more irritated if they end up with NO water!" Grace retorted.

Guilhem laughed, "You're right. Now come here and kiss your husband then get back to your duties. I shall see you later, my love."

Grace stood on tiptoes to kiss him and was swept into a fierce embrace and passionate kiss, much to the delight of the nearby men who whistled and offered up ribald comments. She blushed as she was set down and sent on her way with an appreciative slap to the bottom.

"Bloody man!" she muttered under her breath but with a wide smile on her face.

The long, hot day dragged on, tempers becoming fractious with minor scuffles breaking out between the various groups of people encamped within the courtyard of the castel. Grace was sitting nursing her head between her hands, pressing fingers into her temples, in an attempt to relieve a mild but incessant headache, when she heard yet another argument break out. Rising to her feet she strode over to where two teenage boys were obviously about to come to blows over a disputed area for their respective families to set up a base.

Inserting herself between the youths, despite them both being considerably taller and broader than her diminutive stature, Grace shouted, "Stop it. Just stop it. We are about to be besieged and you are arguing over where to sleep! For the love of God, if the invaders so choose, NONE of us will have a place to rest unless it be our graves."

The boys were stunned but one, braver or more belligerent than the other, retorted, "I am from St Vincent and a true Christian, he and his family," he indicated the other boy, "are dirty Jews from Beziers. Who should have more right to select a place?"

Virtually incandescent with anger, Grace replied, "All here are under the protection of Vescomtat Trencavel, be they from St Vincents, the Ciutat, Beziers or indeed anywhere else. Whether they be Jew, Christian or Bon Crestian, ALL have EQUAL rights. Now sort this out or I will be forced to find my husband or one of his men and they will decide the matter for you!"

Head high, face flushed and trembling internally, she turned on her heels and came face to face with Helena, who had witnessed the entire scene and wore a sneer on a face marred by the split lip; "So, marriage has made you even more forthright, has it? Such a shame that if the Crusaders get here they will find out your parentage. I hear they don't take kindly to heretics, I wonder what your fate will be? It can't be any worse than mine stuck with a rutting old pig for a husband instead of a handsome Vescomtat. Perhaps justice will be done in the end, eh?"

Grace was stunned. Her instinct was to fight back, but she was saved the necessity of responding by the fierce voice of Raimond Rogier who was striding towards them. He had observed and overheard the whole scene from the reprimanding of the youths through to Helena's unwarranted attack on his cousin's new wife.

"Madòna de Merlon," he thundered, addressing with her married name. "Unless you wish to find yourself sleeping out here WITH your husband, which I venture will please him even less than being called a 'rutting pig', I suggest you think again about your words. Ysabella is not your enemy, but the Crusaders are, and they are on the way here. I doubt they will listen or take kindly to an obviously bitter woman trying to implicate others in heresy, even should they breach our walls! You are relieved of service to my wife forthwith. Now get out of my sight!"

Helena blanched, made to retaliate then thought again and spun on her heels, but not before giving Grace a look of pure venom which chilled to the bone despite the oppressive heat.

Raimond Rogier took Grace by the arm and led her back to the castel, "Well spoken to those boys," he said conversationally, "and please do not worry about Helena, she is nothing but a jealous woman and one I have been wanting away from my wife for some time. Pah! Her husband is welcome to her. Now, Ysabella, cousin, would you please be so kind as to attend to your mistress?"

Grace nodded silently, whilst inwardly still shaking; she hated confrontation of any sort, a part of her was pleased she would have no have further contact with Helena but she couldn't help feeling somewhat sorry for the woman. Real or perceived, Helena obviously felt she had been dealt a bad hand in life and her response to this was to attempt to make everyone else unhappy in whatever way she could. A shiver ran down her spine, this latest assault to Helena's wellbeing would doubtless be blamed on her.

Grace made her way to Lady Agnes, expecting at any moment to run into Helena, but luck was with her and she managed to reach the solar with no further incident. Upon arrival, her mistress immediately noticed something was amiss and gently questioned her. Fighting back tears, Grace explained as succinctly as possible what had happened, leaving out Helena's threat, merely saying that she had been unsupportive, and not mentioning the Vescomtat's dictate that she would no longer be required to serve as lady-in-waiting - it wasn't her place to pass on his orders, she thought to herself. Lady Agnes was aghast and immediately sent one of the waiting servants to fetch wine and refreshments for the obviously upset woman; knowing nothing of Helena's words she assumed her lady-in-waiting was troubled by the confrontation with the boys. This notion was soon disabused when her husband arrived.

Appalled yet not unsurprised by what he had to say, she turned to Grace. "Ysabella, why did you not tell me what she had said?"

Grace shrugged her shoulders and replied, "I didn't want to upset you, My Lady. Helena's words were hurtful but there's little chance she will be able to act on them. As for not mentioning that your husband dismissed her from your service, I felt it not my place to say."

"I would have sooner heard the full story from you but I appreciate you trying to spare me Helena's vindictiveness. I suppose her nature has always been apparent, but you certainly bring out the worst in her! I shall arrange for some small gift to be sent, perhaps something for her new household. In any case at some point soon she would have left my service to take up her place in her husband's house, that was the arrangement we reached when he accepted her as his bride." Lady Agnes looked worried as she concluded, "I hope we haven't made a bad choice for her, My Lord."

"He was the only choice," responded her husband, "no one was falling over themselves to wed her and de Merlon has status, a home and an income. She will adapt, provided we make it through the next few weeks."

The latter, added almost as an afterthought, caused Lady Agnes to blanch and Grace to catch her breath. Sensing the disquiet he had just incurred, Vescomtat Trencavel attempted to lighten the mood by enquiring if any of the wine and food brought up at his wife's behest could be diverted his way.

Chapter 24 – Love Is In The Air

By the end of that long, hot and wearying day Grace and Guilhem were too exhausted to repeat the previous night's lovemaking, instead falling asleep, her head pillowed on his chest, almost immediately they got into bed.

Awaking in the pre-dawn light as it filtered through the partially closed shutters, Guilhem raised himself onto his elbow and looked at his wife as she slept. Her lips were slightly parted and her cheeks bore the flush of sleep, whilst the dark hair curled in soft tendrils around her face and across the pillow; a feeling of love so intense rose within him causing him to catch his breath, he wanted to ravish her, wake her from her slumber, yet at the same time to hold her tenderly in his arms and listen to her gentle breathing.

Unshed tears filled his eyes and he said very quietly, "Ysabella, my love, my life, I promise I will protect you with the last breath of my body and when we leave this life, wherever and whatever shall become of us I vow to always find you. We are one now, my love."

Grace began to stir; some of Guilhem's words had penetrated the fog of sleep but they dissipated as she came to full awareness, opening her eyes to find him gazing at her.

"Good morning, my love," she smiled. "How long have you been staring at me?"

"Oh, a little while," he responded, "you are so beautiful and precious to me. I never thought I would find anyone to love, always assumed I would marry for duty, and then you fell at my feet, repeatedly. I think God was trying to make me notice you."   He finished on a smile and gathered her into his arms, "Now" he grinned, "I intend to make up for last night!"

It was some time before either of them was capable of coherent speech but at last, still breathless, resting with her head on his shoulder, Grace asked, "What were you saying as I awoke? It must have been important, you looked so serious."

Guilhem shrugged a little self-consciously, "Just how much I love you and that I will always, always look after you, my Ysabella."

Grace sighed contentedly, she may not be when or where she was supposed be but she was very much with the person she should be.

Their peaceful interlude was interrupted by a loud hammering on the door. Exclaiming in exasperation, Guilhem jumped from the bed and headed, still naked, towards the commotion. Grace admired his lean physique as he reached the door and opened it just wide enough for the person without to be heard more clearly.

"Well, what is it, man? Speak out or leave me in peace with my wife!"

The voice outside the door spoke tremulously, obviously a young page nervous to disturb a more senior personage. "My Lord, word has just been received that the Crusaders have reached Beziers and that Servian surrendered without a fight. Vescomtat Trencavel wishes you to meet him at once."

Guilhem thanked the messenger and sent him on his way, promising to attend the Vescomtat as soon as he was dressed. Returning to the bed he saw Grace, wide-eyed and white faced.

"It is beginning isn't it?" she said quietly.

"I am very much afraid it is, my love," her husband solemnly replied. "I must go to my cousin, I shall send word to you as soon as I am able but, in the meantime, please pack anything of value in the chest," he nodded to her oaken chest in the corner of the room, "and I will arrange for one of my men to take it directly to Minerve. I would send you too but I doubt you would go, would you?" he chanced to ask.

"NO! I would not go!" she replied, "My place is here with you and Lady Agnes!"

Guilhem shrugged his shoulders, he had expected as much. Quickly pulling on his clothes and running a hand through his hair he said, "Get dressed, my beloved, there will be much to do today. Regardless of what happens at Beziers, the Crusaders are close now - we need to be ready."

Grace was already dragging a shift over her head and reaching for her gown, she wished fervently that she could remember how events unfolded, what would happen at Beziers and how long it would be before disaster overtook Carcassonne and its inhabitants but she couldn't, and, in any case, she reasoned to herself, what good would it do, she wouldn't be able to change anything - would she? Once that thought took hold it preyed on her; could she say anything, give any warnings, suggest Raymond Rogier leave Carcassonne with his pregnant wife and son? One of the few things she remembered is that the Vescomtat most definitely would not survive the coming troubles, if he were to leave now could the sequence of events be changed? What if something she did or said actually made matters worse, perhaps everyone in Carcassonne would perish and she would have changed history. The possibilities made her head spin and she had to hurriedly sit back on the edge of the bed for fear of falling.

Guilhem, looking up from pulling on his boots, noticed how pale she had become and rushed to her side, "Ysabella, my heart, I WILL look after you, that I promise." He kissed her gently.

She smiled wanly and returned the kiss. "I know you will, but who will look after you? We are both the children of *Bon Crestians,* the very "heretics' this damned Crusade was established to destroy, if this fact is made known…" she broke off at this point, recalling Helena's threat of the previous day.

Guilhem hugged her tightly, "*We* are not Bon Crestians, my love, we were married under the laws of the Catholic church, a fact to which Bishop Berenger will attest. I think not that the Pope would see fit to persecute members of his own church."

It was on the tip of Grace's tongue to say that she wouldn't be surprised by anything anyone did in the name of religion, but she bit the words back and instead merely nodded and, getting to her feet, finished dressing.

With one last embrace and passionate kiss Guilhem departed, leaving her to plait her hair and fasten the veil in place, an item of clothing she could well do without she thought to herself, before leaving the sanctuary of their chamber to face whatever the day would bring. It was only as she walked disconsolately towards Lady Agnes' room that she realised today was Ysabella's - her - 18th birthday; what a day to celebrate your 18th, she thought as she remembered the fuss her parents had made on hers.

A subdued Lady Agnes greeted Grace; she was still in a night robe and with her hair loose upon her shoulders looked absurdly young to be the wife of a Vescomtat and about to give birth to a second child.

She appeared pale and worried. "My husband tells me that the Crusading army has reached Beziers. That's so close! What are we to do, Ysabella?"

Grace wondered if suggesting that Lady Agnes gather together her most precious possessions and have them removed to safety would cause too many questions to be directed her way? Guilhem had not thought it strange so she thought not, if she chose the words carefully, and at the very least the heavily pregnant women would find the task of selecting items a distraction.

"My Lady, I know little of armies and less of Crusaders but would it be possible to ensure that, should the worst happen, your most precious belongings are perhaps removed to safety now? Perhaps a small chest could be taken to your parent's home in Montpellier until you may reclaim them? Our husbands seem confident we will be safe here so God willing this will be unnecessary, but even so Guilhem is having most of our things transported to Minerve today..." She let her words tail away.

Agnes turned even paler, if that were possible, but squared her shoulders resolutely. "At least that would give me something to do. Raimond is determined that I stay here and not involve myself with the preparations in the rest of the Ciutat - 'for the sake of the child' he says! Pah - if Carcassona falls it won't matter if this child is born boy or girl, healthy or not for there will be nothing to inherit anyway."

A sudden movement of the child within her elicited a gasp from the woman and Grace moved rapidly to her side. "What is it, My Lady? Is your travail beginning? Should I call for Favia and Dama Balsace?"

"No, no." Lady Agnes waved the concerns away, "It was simply the child deciding to remind me of his presence by aiming a kick to my ribs. I will be glad when he does decide to arrive though, young Raimond was never as restless as this one is!" She stroked her straining abdomen lovingly and a ripple was clearly visible as the child responded to his mother's caress, Grace stared - she would never lose the fascination, the wonder of seeing a pregnant belly move with the motion of its unseen occupant.

"May I?' she asked, her hand poised above the white robed mound. Lady Agnes nodded and Grace rested her hand on the now quietened belly, pushing slightly evoked a kick and both she and the child's mother smiled in unison.

"A strong one," said a voice from the door where, unbeknownst to them, Favia had just entered the room.

"Indeed he is," replied Lady Agnes. "And one I would see safely birthed sooner rather than later."

As she busied herself helping her mistress dress, Grace wondered what the infant mortality rate was back in this period of history. She assumed that amongst the general population it was probably quite high, many babies not seeing their first birthday; even once that milestone was reached there would likely be no guarantee of reaching adulthood, surely though it was safer for the wealthy? Perhaps not given what she had learned about de Merlon's two previous wives - although it would seem all his first wife's offspring had survived so far, their mother hadn't been so lucky in her final pregnancy and the second wife hadn't lived through her first labour. She frowned, dangerous times not only for the men involved in war but for their womenfolk too. Both Favia and Lady Agnes spotted the frown and queried its reason.

Thinking quickly Grace said, "I was wondering if you should accompany your belongings to Montpellier, My Lady. We don't know what is going to happen here and at least your child would be born away from the immediate threat of conflict and you would be safe."

Favia nodded in agreement.

Agnes sighed, "It is a pleasant notion, Ysabella, but my place is here with my husband and his people and to be honest I do not think I could suffer the privations of a journey in this state. No, our child will be born here."

Grace dipped her head, she had expected no less and it would be even more unsafe should the child be delivered during the lengthy journey. In any case she realised with Ysabella's memories, the easiest route to Montpellier would doubtless take the traveller near Beziers, not the safest of places to send a heavily pregnant woman. A small group on horseback bearing her belongings could afford to travel cross country staying out of sight and could also act as a scouting party.

"In that case, My Lady, if you wish to begin packing your precious items perhaps I should find Guilhem and ask if men could be spared to take them to your parents. He could perhaps use the opportunity to have his men survey the countryside between here and Montpellier."

"Ysabella, I do believe you are becoming a military strategist," smiled Lady Agnes, "but yes, go and see what Guilhem can arrange, it will only be a small chest and perhaps some items suitable to carry in panniers, so a couple of men would suffice and would attract less attention. Favia and the other girls will help me."

"Indeed," agreed Favia, "Peyronella and Marguerida will be along shortly, they were assisting with the distribution of supplies to the refugees within the castel."

The mention of food made Grace realise she hadn't yet broken her fast and she left in search of both her husband and sustenance.

Chapter 25 – Military Strategist

Grace found Guilhem sometime later as he supervised the building of the protective wooden hoardings along the tops of the ramparts. He was in full agreement with her idea of Lady Agnes sending on some of her possessions and grinned in admiration when she pointed out that the mission could also be used as a scouting trip.

"You never cease to amaze me, my Ysabella! Tell Lady Agnes I shall have two men at her disposal within the hour and encourage her to complete her packing as quickly as she can; it's at least two days' hard ride to Montpellier and that would be on the direct paths, if they go into the hills to avoid detection it will be longer still, it would be best if they were underway before noon." He hugged her tightly and bade her return to her mistress to help with the packing, "I will send your oak chest with the men, it is only a short detour to Minerve, they can take a cart to transport that and leave it there whilst they progress to Montpellier. Make sure you have everything you need and then lock the chest."

Grace nodded in acquiescence and hurried back to her mistress's room where she found a flurry of activity underway as her fellow ladies-in-waiting were helping Lady Agnes select the possessions to be packed and transported to Montpellier. To Grace it looked as if the intention was to send just about everything Agnes owned, certainly far more than could be carried by two men on horseback. She had to step in.

"My Lady," she said quietly, "I know this is difficult but my husband can only spare two men, they will not be able to carry this much. The smaller chest and things which could fit into the panniers of two saddles are all they will be able to manage. Guilhem wishes they stay away from the main tracks and head up into the hills avoiding Beziers so the going will be hard. He is sending a cart as far as Minerve, if you desire perhaps some articles could be sent there until it is safe to send them on."

Peyronella and Marguerida looked shocked at the apparent temerity of their colleague, but Lady Agnes did not seem unduly perturbed, replying, "I know, I know. You are quite right, Ysabella, but it is so very difficult! I think perhaps less clothing, just my jewellery. May I leave it to you and the other girls? I am tired and my back hurts, I will rest for a while."

The younger girls, with Grace's guidance, quickly managed to reduce the piles of goods to a portable level, and Grace sent a serving boy to seek Guilhem and fetch the panniers so that they may judge what more, or less, could be fitted in; Lady Agnes having decided not to make use of the cart and send more of her belongings to Minerve for safe keeping. "After all," she had said, "this may all come to nothing and all will be well." Grace had merely smiled and agreed, no need to tell the woman that within a couple of weeks she would be forced to leave Carcassonne empty handed, never to return.

Just after noon the two horses were saddled, and a rather elderly looking donkey hitched to the small cart Guilhem had procured. Lady Agnes' goods, in both the panniers and small dark wooden casket, joined Grace's rather larger oak chest in the back of the cart, and a quantity of straw was piled on top to camouflage the items. It had been decided that one of Guilhem's retinue, an elderly man, would drive the cart whilst the riders went on ahead. An old man and a ramshackle straw-laden cart would attract less attention than one being driven by an armed soldier with an escort. The riders were to overnight in Minerve before heading to Montpellier at first light the following day, using tracks known only to the locals they would stay well away from Beziers and the crusading army, with any luck they would return to Carcassonne three days hence.

As Guilhem watched them leave he wished fervently that he were able to travel with them, taking Ysabella away to temporary safety at least. Guilhem Bastier was no fool and he knew that the Crusading army, whilst nominally intending to wipe out what they regarded as heresy, were in reality seeking nothing less than the destruction of the Occitan way of life. It was abundantly clear to him that the members of the Crusader's army, many impoverished noblemen from the north, wished to occupy the grand castles and fine houses of the Midi, whilst driving out the people who had built them and subverting the rich culture which was so very different from the northern lands.

"I swear," he muttered sotto voce, "that if we survive whatever is to come, I will take my Ysabella and leave this place." He wiped his face with the back of his hand, sweat poured off him, it was as hot as Hades and he hoped that the northern invaders, who would have no experience of such conditions, were suffering; although, if the rumours he had heard were true, more than one of his liege lord's neighbours had joined the Crusade in an effort to save their lands and they at least would be used to the heat. Guilhem shuddered, brought up to believe in the concept of *paratge* the very idea of betraying one's ancient lands and culture for continued wealth and privilege was utterly abhorrent to him, he would as soon lose an arm as turn against his lord and their people, any of the people.

Work continued during the rest of that day on the fortification of Carcassonne and by the time the evening meal was served, most of the wooden hoardings to the rear of the castel were completed and a good stretch on the Ciutat walls were well under construction. Guilhem returned to the chamber allocated to himself and his wife to wash and found Grace lying on the bed, face turned into the pillow.

"Ysabella, what's wrong?" He rushed to her side.

She turned her tear-stained face towards him and said quietly, "I'm scared."

He hugged her tightly to him, wishing he could keep her safe but knowing that it may not be possible. "I will always look after you," he promised, "if you are lost I will find you; if you cry I will dry your tears and when you laugh I will laugh with you. Ysabella, we cannot hope to control what may happen, but you must know I will always love you."

She sniffed, "I wish we were away from here, we are only just wed and yet I fear we may not see the anniversary of our joining. You know I was unsure about our marriage, I feared it all happened too quickly, yet now I wish you had found me sooner and made me yours."

Guilhem simply held her more tightly, there was little he could really do to reassure her, he simply did not, could not, know what would befall them. Suddenly he remembered something.

"There's one anniversary we can celebrate," he said, "Favia tells me today is your birthday. I have no gift for you, other than my love but tonight we will drink wine, listen to Peirol and try to forget, for a little while at least."

Chapter 26 – Imminent Delivery

The feast day of Mary Magdalene dawned hot and sunny. Grace awoke alone in the bed and stretched out, a muzzy headache and dry mouth indicated that she had imbibed far too much wine last night. Guilhem had been determined that she have some enjoyment on her birthday and there had indeed been a deal of merry making. She smiled wryly to herself, remembering how Peirol had woven an entire evening of songs around herself and Guilhem ranging from lewd to lovestruck. Everyone was aware that the evening may be the last chance for revelry and Peirol himself planned to leave the Ciutat that very day to return to his home in the foothills of the Pyrenees, safe he hoped from the Crusading army. Everyone would miss his easy charm and lightness of spirit, but Grace could not blame him for wishing to remove himself to safety and she had wished him well as she left the Great Hall, now devoid of its refugees who had been found places to settle outside the castel.

Reluctantly leaving the peace and comfort of the bed, she dressed and made her way out to see what was required of her that day. Firstly, she made her way to the Lady Agnes whom she discovered in bed, propped up by several pillows, enjoying cuddles with her son Raimond whilst feeding him morsels of food from a platter containing the usual mixture of fruits, soft creamy cheese, honey and bread. Peyronella and Marguerida were in attendance and both laughed at Grace's somewhat wan appearance.

"Too much wine last night, Ysabella?" quipped Marguerida with a large grin on her face.

"You could say that," Grace responded. "Guilhem was determined I enjoy the evening and kept refilling my cup!"

Lady Agnes smiled, "Come and share in our repast, Ysabella, a little food is all you need and perhaps some of this pomegranate wine."

Grace's stomach recoiled slightly at the mention of the wine, but she dutifully took a sip from the proffered cup and found it to be more like a fruit juice than the alcoholic beverage she had consumed to excess last night, so she took a larger mouthful and some of the bread and cheese. Several minutes passed in a companionable silence, broken only by the incessant chatter of the young Raimond, who wanted to know why he wasn't allowed a sword and to be able to fight with his father, "when the webels came." His mother patiently explained that he was still too small and that his father would worry too much if he were to fight which would mean he couldn't give his best. Raimond appeared to, albeit reluctantly, accept this reasoning and turned his attention to a very ripe peach which spurted juice all over him the moment he bit into it. The look of puzzlement on his face as the sticky liquid dribbled down his chin and onto his smock reduced the two younger ladies-in-waiting to helpless giggles. The laughter was contagious and soon all them were giggling en masse. Suddenly Lady Agnes caught her breath and clutched her stomach, Grace immediately stopped laughing and rushed to her mistress's side.

"What is it, My Lady, are you in pain?"

"It's eased now," the woman replied, "for a moment I thought it was the child coming but I think it is just a warning. I remember having such pains for a week or two before this one made an appearance," she ruffled Raimond's hair.

Grace rested her hands over the distended abdomen, all seemed calm, no further tightening was apparent and she breathed a sigh of relief. Still, it was likely a sign that delivery was close and she hoped the child would arrive swiftly and without complications well before the date she knew all would have to leave the castel and Carcassonne. She was glad the old woman, Dame Balsace was already in the Ciutat, for although she had been present at many births never had she had to cope alone; doubtless Dame Balsace would employ methods a 21st century midwife wouldn't BUT she was at least experienced.

At that moment Favia arrived with the aforementioned midwife and all but Grace were shooed out of the room whilst the old crone 'examined' the pregnant woman.

"Not yet, but soon," were about the only words Grace could decipher in the torrent of language emitting from the almost toothless mouth. Favia nodded her agreement and swiftly translated the heavy dialect.

"The dame says at most a couple of weeks, My Lady, she says the child is still not in position but he should turn soon."

216

Grace sensed a slight hint of concern emanating from the old lady, it was unusual for a nearly to term baby not to be in the head down position by now and a breech delivery was tricky enough in a modern hospital with all the attendant medical personnel; in a medieval bed chamber it could prove fatal to both mother and child. She chewed her lip thoughtfully remembering the ECV class she had attended where the process for turning a baby in uteri had been explained and demonstrated on a model; the lecturer had said that without an epidural or at least gas and air the pain to the mother could be considerable but she imagined considerably less so than trying to deliver a breech child with no pain relief. If it came to it she could suggest the procedure.

Examination over, the younger girls were allowed to return whereupon they set about assisting Lady Agnes out of bed and into a loose-fitting dress. Grace could see little for her to do and sensing her impatience to be busy, Favia suggested she accompany her to check food stores and fair distribution of water amongst the residents and refugees within the wall. Lady Agnes nodded acquiescence and Grace departed with Favia and the wizened midwife.

Once out of the room, Dame Balsace focussed black eyes on Grace and began chattering away in her unintelligible dialect. Shrugging her shoulders in non-understanding Grace turned to Favia who obligingly translated.

"She asks why you looked concerned when she told our Lady the child hadn't turned."

Thinking quickly, Grace replied, "I was remembering when one of my mother's serving women was trying to deliver, mother said the child was upside down and bade me help her turn the baby by pressing on the woman's stomach. It caused the woman a great deal of pain but the child was delivered sound and the woman recovered."

Dame Balsace nodded, apparently able to understand and directed a volley of sentences to Favia before hobbling off to the small chamber which had been found for her.

Favia looked dumbstruck and turned to Grace. "Well!" she huffed, "In all my days I have never heard that one insist someone else be present when she delivers a child. However, she says she sees a knowing in you which may be useful and demands you be there when Lady Agnes goes into her labour."

Grace merely nodded, she was glad she wouldn't have to ask or make an excuse to be present.

Chapter 27 – Honour And Obey

The courtyard of the castel was a seething mass of people under makeshift tents and awnings, the air redolent with wood-smoke from numerous small fires and the unmistakable odour of too many unwashed bodies in too small a space in murderously hot weather. Tempers among the displaced were obviously frayed and as she wandered amongst the masses, trying hard not to breathe through her nose, Grace overheard many a disgruntled person mutter that they would be better off in their own homes.

Eventually, growing sick of the dissent, she broke her silence and said to the group of refugees nearest her, "Beziers is at the moment surrounded by the Crusaders, if you truly think you would be better off there than here then I am sure Vescomtat Trencavel would be pleased to see you on your way. We need no disunity within these walls."

Without waiting for a response, she marched away to the guarded gateway of the castel and across the bridge into the Ciutat leaving behind a momentarily silenced band of individuals. One of the guards recognising her as his leader's new wife let her through but the moment she was past he sent one of the numerous young boys, who were milling around intent on talking to the soldiers, on an errand to locate Guilhem.

Once into the main body of the Ciutat the smells and overcrowding were, if anything, even worse than within the walls of the castel. People were crammed into every available space and the usual population seemed to have at least doubled. Enterprising individuals had set up makeshift stalls and were doing a roaring trade selling ripe peaches, nectarines and apricots and the discarded stones of the fruit littered the ground attracting wasps and flies. Grace wrinkled her nose in distaste, making a note to herself to tell Guilhem and see if he could find a way to issue a dictat to the effect that the inhabitants of the Ciutat needed to try and maintain a level of cleanliness to prevent the start and spread of disease.

It was unusual for a woman, especially one so young, attractive and of an obviously high social standing to be walking alone and Grace was garnering a lot of attention, not that she realised it, absorbed as she was with the strangeness of her environs. She was almost at the Porta Narbona, the eastern gateway, before she became aware of the stir her presence was creating. A group of young men were following her and making ribald comments, which were causing onlookers to laugh openly. They appeared to be addressing the fact that she was a woman alone and asking why her husband would let her wander without a chaperone. Seething with the indignity of being singled out for such castigation, Grace spun on her heels and turned to respond in vituperative kind, only to be roughly grabbed by the left arm. Her attention switched to the perpetrator and with her right hand balled into a fist she let leash a punch into the abdomen of her supposed attacker who "oofed" in response as the air was momentarily expelled.

"For the love of God woman," hissed Guilhem. "What was that for?"

Belatedly realising that her "attacker" was in actuality her husband, Grace muttered back, "Why are you following me? Am I not able to take a walk and see for myself what is happening out here? Do you expect me to stay caged within the castel like some sort of prisoner?"

Guilhem looked livid and tightening his grip on her arm he began to pull her back from the gate. "Yes, *wife,* I do expect you to stay within the walls of the castel, or at the very least tell me if you must go a wandering so I can arrange for one of my men to accompany you. There are too many strangers within the Ciutat now, it is dangerous!"

Spluttering with indignation, Grace began to retaliate. "I can look after myself, you know!" She shouted to the amusement of the onlookers. "Did I not just punch you?"

"Yes, you did," her husband responded grimly, "and had it been one of those young men you had hit, one or more of the others would have stepped into his place and then what could you have done? Will you not realise, woman, that these are dangerous times? I'd sooner not lose you to a fracas out here."

Grace took a breath to respond but bit back her words, he was right, these WERE dangerous times. 21st century Manchester undoubtedly had its unsafe aspects but compared to the 13th century, life was long and relatively trouble free for most people. When she had set off on her walk she genuinely hadn't thought that to leave the castel unaccompanied would be considered both rebellious and dangerous and she was suitably chagrined that Guilhem had felt it necessary to come after her himself.

Finally, as she was practically being frogmarched along at a speed that almost caused her to lose her footing, she shouted, "Guilhem. Husband. Stop! I cannot keep this pace!"

He stopped and spun her towards him, "If I could have locked you away in that chest of your mother's and sent you off to Minerve, I would."

"I'd have likely suffocated," retorted Grace, eyes still flashing angrily, but she was moved by the look of despair on his face and said no more.

"I'll likely throttle you, if you go off again like this," was the response but he too was calming down. "Ysabella, you are my life and I can't think of anything happening to you. I've never felt this way before and so I don't know how to act. I want to wrap you in soft blankets and keep you safe, yet at the same time I want to throw you to the ground and use your body as I might have once done a tavern whore. I want to dress you in fine silk and jewels but want to rip the clothes from you every time I see you. I want to hold you tenderly at the same time as I want to leave my marks on your breasts and bruises on your arms where I hold you down." His voice broke.

Grace was moved beyond words and so did the only thing she could, she took his face in her hands and on tiptoe reached to kiss him. Her heart was beating quickly and she was close to tears as initially he held back, then with an exhalation he gathered her into his chest and returned the kiss. When they broke apart each was breathless, flushed and aroused but the mutual anger of earlier had passed.

"I'm sorry," Grace said quietly, "I really didn't think, I just wanted to see how things stood outside the castel."

Guilhem sighed. "My love, my life. I only want to look after you and I am sorry if I hurt your arm."

"You didn't. Well not much. Before I forget though, I saw lots of rubbish being thrown onto the streets, it is attracting flies and is rotting - it's only going to get worse as time passes." She thought quickly, not sure if the link between filth and certain diseases had been made at this time and continued, "Mother is considered something of a healer and she taught me that cleanliness is a good way to keep the bloody flux at bay. Could you perhaps send word around that people should dispose of waste more carefully?"

Guilhem thought for a moment and then shook his head. "I am sure your mother has a point, Ysabella, but at the moment I don't think the populace is of a mind to listen. You probably heard mutterings that some folk think they should leave and go home, if we place more strictures on them many may leave, and we have no way of knowing at the moment what is happening beyond these walls. We have scouts out there, but none have yet returned. So, for now, we leave them be to wallow in their own filth and pray that the bloody flux does not add to our problems."

Grace thought about arguing but decided she wouldn't win, she could however minimise the risk of exposure to any of the people Ysabella loved and cared for. That was the best she could do under the circumstances.

Harmony restored, Guilhem escorted her back to the castel whilst he headed out to round up any remaining refugees and bring them back to the Ciutat. The whole area was in a kind of suspended animation, normal life held in abeyance pending news from Beziers.

Chapter 28 – Massacre

A loud hammering on the door of their chamber awoke Grace and Guilhem seemingly minutes after they had fallen asleep in each other's arms. Guilhem stumbled to the door and opened it just a fraction.

"What is it?" he asked grumpily.

Whatever the response had been, and Grace didn't hear, lost on the edge of sleep as she was, it was enough to send Guilhem scrambling to put his clothes on.

Grace sat up, "What's happening, why are you getting dressed, where are you going?"

Hopping on one leg as he tried to pull on his hose, Guilhem stated gruffly, "Beziers has fallen, one of our scouts has just returned with the news." He swallowed hard, "He says no one was spared. No one. What barbarism is this in the name of our Lord?"

Grace could see his blue eyes were brimming with unshed tears and he was clenching and unclenching his jaw spasmodically. She jumped from the bed and sped into his arms. He held her tightly and she felt his breathing calm and his heart rate slow, pulling back slightly she looked into his eyes and said simply,

"This is not Beziers. We will survive, I promise."

Guilhem sighed. "I wish I could believe that, my love, and I wish even more I had sent you to safety. Now I must go to Raimond and see if I can find out any more information. Try to get some sleep, my Ysabella."

"No. I should go to Lady Agnes, she will have been awoken also and will need some company. I will stay with her until you come for me. Help me dress and I will go with you."

Some five minutes later the pair of them traversed the dim corridors until they reached the Trencavel's rooms, Guilhem planted a kiss on Grace's head and she turned to the bed chamber whilst he headed to the council chamber next to the Great Hall.

"I love you," they said in unison.

Grace found Lady Agnes, as she had fully expected, sitting up in bed wide awake and holding onto her belly, the woman was pale and looked frightened.

"Oh, Ysabella, I am so glad you are here, Raimond left in such a hurry he never thought to send for anyone. I am so afraid, have you heard anything?"

Grace was unsure how much Raimond Rogier had told his heavily pregnant wife, but she guessed he probably wouldn't have imparted the news of a complete massacre of the inhabitants of Beziers, so she merely said that she had heard the city had been taken.

So frightened and upset was the older woman that she insisted Grace share the bed with her. Thus the pair spent a restless and largely sleepless night waiting for news from their respective husbands.

The sun was high in the sky and the two women had been joined by the younger ladies-in-waiting, Favia and young Raimond before their husbands returned, hollow-eyed and grim of face. Grace flew to Guilhem and he held her tightly, Raimond Rogier stepped slowly to where his wife was seated and bent low over her hand, neither man said a word, until the Vescomtat turned to Peyronella and Marguerida and asked them to take the young Raimond to the kitchens to see if there were any treats to be had. The little boy flung himself against his father's legs, hugging them in obvious pleasure at such a suggestion and then grabbed the girl's hands to drag them away. They were not as eager to leave as the child but had very little choice in the matter.

Once the door had closed behind, Guilhem took a seat, pulling Grace onto his lap; the Vescomtat preferred to stand and began to pace nervously along the length of the room.

"What news, my husband?" Lady Agnes finally asked.

Voice shaking, Vescomtat Raimond Rogier Trencavel relayed the information that had thus far been received. "The crusading army reached Beziers the day before yesterday and began to set up camp," he said. "The Bishop of Beziers approached the army apparently with a written list of some two hundred and twenty people whom he accused of being Bon Crestians. it was agreed that the town would be spared if these people were handed over, so he returned to Beziers to let the leaders know. To their credit they refused to relinquish any of their inhabitants and the noble Bishop then demanded all his brethren leave with him to save themselves; a

227

handful apparently did." He paused, and his wife poured him a cup of wine from which he took a large mouthful before continuing. "It becomes somewhat less clear after that. The townspeople barred the gates and set guards on the walls and the Crusaders resumed setting up camp for a siege. It would seem that several of the youths of the town decided to mount an expedition of their own to taunt and harass the army, which aggravated the camp followers who chased the lads. A fight ensued which attracted the attention of the routiers (mercenaries), who decided to arm themselves and storm the walls which were not as yet fully guarded. Somehow, in the disarray, the main gates were opened and the routier entered the town, rapidly followed by the knights who would not wish to be left behind. Not a person was spared, even woman and children hiding in the churches were slaughtered." Raimond was openly crying by this point but he continued. "Once all were killed the rabble began to loot, but the knights wanted the spoils for themselves so drove the scum away who in revenge then set light to everything. Beziers is just a funeral pyre now, still burning, all defiled and destroyed." He sat down heavily in the nearest chair, head in hands.

Lady Agnes was horrified, tears were sliding slowly down her face as she took in the enormity of what she had just heard, the utter brutality of slaughtering and burning an entire town was so alien a concept to her, indeed to the whole of Occitan, that it was simply too much to take in.

Grace sat silently on Guilhem's lap, his arms around her and his head resting on her shoulder. "How many people lived in Beziers?" she asked finally, the words barely audible.

Guilhem answered, "Perhaps twenty thousand, there would have been refugees as well as the usual number."

Lady Agnes retched in horror and Grace leapt from her husband's knee to find a bowl and washcloth for her mistress. "Twenty thousand souls. Dead!"

It was beyond comprehension, her modern mind knew far worse death tolls would follow in conflicts to come where technological warfare played a part, but these people met their deaths in a very personal way; a sword, bayonet, axe. Close quarters and seeing the face of their killer. They must have been terrified and then, even if the wounds hadn't killed instantly, the fire would have consumed them. Grace was trying unsuccessfully to hold back her tears, how she wished she would just wake up in her own bed in the house in the Cotswolds and away from this terror.

Chapter 29 – An Unhappy Match

Following the awful news from Beziers, which had spread through the Ciutat and the suburbs as if borne by Mercury, winged messenger of the Roman gods; the inhabitants of Carcassonne had veered between terror and a righteous anger that the citizens of Beziers, their fellow Occitanians, had met such an end. Much muttering was heard, especially amongst the young men, that the Crusaders needed to be a taught a lesson. Overhearing one such show of bravado, Guilhem had stepped in and in no uncertain terms had informed the group that it was just such behaviour had brought about the destruction of Beziers. Who knew what may have happened had the siege run its course. Beziers, like Carcassonne was well provisioned and could have withstood a lengthy siege. Somewhat chastened, that particular group of youths slunk away.

By the end of that day the wooden protective hoardings were in place all around the walls of Carcassonne and patrols of mounted soldiers were regularly scouting, on the lookout for signs of the invading army, everyone knew it was but a matter of time before they would arrive.

Grace and Guilhem made love with a fierce passion that night, both aware that time may be running out. When finally they lay spent and gleaming with perspiration, Guilhem turned to her and said, "Raimond will not surrender easily and I agree with him, but he will do whatever he can, short of sacrificing any of his people, to ensure that Carcassona will not meet the same fate as Beziers. Should something happen to me you must make your way to Minerve as soon as it is safe to do so. Keep this ring," he pulled of the gold ring inset with a cabochon ruby which he wore on the little finger of his left hand, "with you and you will be known to be my wife. I sent word with the soldiers who took our belongings that this may come to pass so you should have no difficulty gaining admittance."

Grace clung to him, tears pouring down her face.
"Nothing will happen to you, my love, we will go to Minerve when this is over - together."

"I hope so," Guilhem smiled sadly, "and if we can't be safe at Minerve, well, then we will head into the kingdom of Aragon and seek sanctuary there."

The ring Guilhem had given to Grace was far too large for her small hands, the only digit it did not immediately slide off was her thumb and she found it far too uncomfortable to keep it there, besides being terrified it would slip off and she would lose it, so the following morning she devised a way to tie the piece of jewellery to the neck cord of her underslip, it then lay hidden under the linen, nestled between her breasts and completely invisible to anyone. Guilhem approved greatly of her cunning.

Later that day, the 24th of July, whilst Grace was sitting with Lady Agnes and the younger ladies-in-waiting, they heard a terrible commotion in the passage outside the door. A woman's voice could be heard shouting and screaming, apparently demanding admittance to the room and obviously being denied.

"Go and see what's happening, Ysabella," said Lady Agnes in an exasperated tone of voice, "All that noise is giving me a headache!"

Grace dutifully made for the door and opened it to enquire what the problem was, as she did so a woman hurtled through, landing in an ungainly heap on the floor near Lady Agnes. The guards raced in, obviously intent on dragging her back out but were stopped by their mistress who recognised the intruder as Helena and motioned the guards away.

"Helena? What in the name of all that is holy are you doing here? My husband removed you from my service, you shouldn't be here!"

Helena raised her head and the other occupants of the room were shocked to see an eye so swollen it was nearly shut and what looked like marks left by strong fingers around her neck. Despite the injuries the woman appeared unbowed and went straight to the offensive.

"Yes, My Lady, as you see the husband you chose for me is not disposed to be gentle; it would seem he can only spill his seed if he is beating me. I hope you are pleased?!"

"Of course not. We had no idea he was like that. Had we done we would have rejected his suit for you! No one has ever accused him before of violence, so how could we know?"

Helena sneered, "I bet she did," she indicated Grace.

"Of course I didn't, you stupid girl!" Grace protested, "I hadn't even met him until our weddings!"

Helena looked as if she was about to attack Grace but thought better of it. Scrambling to her feet, she attempted to straighten her gown and hair.

"I am here to request my marriage be annulled," she announced. "I cannot be expected to live with such a beast."

Lady Agnes sighed, "Helena, whilst I understand how terrible your situation is, at the moment the situation facing ALL of us is more perilous, there is no one with any time to listen to your accusations and pass judgement. From what you have intimated the marriage has been consummated and will therefore be hard to nullify."

There was obviously more to say, but Helena interrupted, "Accusations! Do you think I did this to myself?!"

"No one is saying that!" Lady Agnes soothed, "but now is not the time to act, in case you haven't realised we could soon be under siege! I promise that once this is all over I will speak with MY husband and see what may be done. In the meantime, I understand you may not wish to return to the room you share with de Merlon, so you may sleep in your old quarters. If necessary, I will send word to your husband that your services are required by me for now. BUT in deference to my husband's wishes you WILL NOT come to me again. Is that understood?"

Helena drew herself up to her full height. "Perfectly!" she spat. "Thank you, My Lady. I bid you goodbye." With those words she marched out of the room practically knocking over Grace who tripped and banged her arm, hard, on the edge of the still open door.

Lady Agnes took a tremulous breath in. "That was something I really didn't need," she said, once the door was firmly closed behind Helena. "Did I do the right thing allowing her to return temporarily to her old quarters, if not my service?"

"I think so," said Grace. Peyronella and Marguerida nodded their agreement, both well aware that they would be forced to share their living space with Helena again. "I actually feel really sorry for her," said Grace rubbing her sore arm. "No one deserves such treatment from the man they marry."

"She probably had it coming," muttered Peyronella.

Grace rounded on her. "No one EVER 'has it coming', Peyronella, I don't care what she may have done, he should not have laid one finger on her!"

Peyronella, chastened and cheeks red, promptly apologised and the group of women, somewhat embarrassedly resumed the tasks interrupted by Helena's arrival; clearly the younger girls would have liked to discuss the situation but neither Lady Agnes nor Grace would be drawn into a discussion and so an awkward silence ensued, broken eventually by Favia arriving to request Grace's assistance in a household matter.

Grace jumped up with alacrity and accompanied Favia to the kitchens; en-route she told Favia of the latest development regarding Helena.

Favia tutted, "Strife follows that girl!" she said. "But I will find something for her to do to keep her occupied and away from that man."

"And I will speak to Guilhem to see if he can send de Merlon on some kind of sortie so he won't notice Helena's absence from their bed chamber," Grace added.

Alone in their bedchamber later, Grace told Guilhem about de Merlon's mistreatment of Helena, despite his obvious distaste for the woman he was horrified that her husband had used her so vilely; his own sense of honour was revolted by the concept of beating a woman and he said as much to Grace.

She hugged him and said, "Not all women are as blessed as me to have such a wonderful husband! Favia is finding work to occupy Helena but I wonder if it would be possible for you to send him away on some pretext?"

Guilhem thought for a moment. "I could ask him to return to his home to see if he could gather any more men. I doubt he will find any, his holding is small and the peasants will not leave their land to follow him here but he will be out of the way. To be honest I would be glad to see the back of him myself, he is a self-opinionated, bombastic idiot who knows little of warfare and even less about the men he would attempt to lead. To be frank he is a liability!"

Grace smiled, "It sounds like a good idea to send him away then. Has there been any more news from Beziers?"

Guilhem's face clouded, "A handful of survivors were picked up by one of the scouting parties, all were injured, a couple burned as they escaped; they confirm what we have already heard, no mercy was shown, there was no attempt to seek out the Bon Crestians it was simply an excuse for the soldiers to kill and loot - women, children. One of the men we picked up, a boy really, tells how he saw a baby ripped from his mother's arms, thrown into the air and skewered on a sword as it came down. It beggars belief that any man of the church could condone such behaviour, but it seems Armand Amaury is pleased; he feels a message has been sent."

"A message?! Twenty thousand people dead is a message? This Crusade has nothing to do with religion and everything to do with the Church of Rome and the French wanting our lands."

Grace's eyes were full of tears. An agnostic in the 21st Century, she was nevertheless aware that Ysabella had a faith, albeit not a strong one and the populace in general were deeply religious; to her modern mind the belief in a higher power, particularly one which did not seem to value women was nonsensical. What little she knew of the Bon Crestians seemed to show a more egalitarian state of affairs, Ysabella's memory provided sketchy details but her own mother was deeply involved in that church and planning to take their highest rite, the Consolamentum to enter the ranks of The Elect.

Guilhem agreed, "I want nothing further to do with the Church of Rome! It is corrupt, caring more for money and power than the spiritual welfare of its followers. I will pay lip service if it keeps us safe but how can I believe in a God that allows innocents to be slaughtered by his agents? We must say nothing of this outside this room, Ysabella, we will be safe enough here in Carcassona and before the arrival of the Crusaders probably the whole of Occitania felt the same way about the Roman religion, but now all will be afeared of the Church and fear leads to recriminations - anyone having different beliefs, or none at all, will be persecuted."

Grace nodded, she could understand that.

Chapter 30 - A Waiting Game

By the following morning it became apparent that refugees from outlying villages were flocking to Carcassonne in search of protection, the news of the terrible events at Beziers having begun to spread far and wide. The already overcrowded Ciutat began to creak at the seams and tempers, already stretched by the conditions, began to fray even further. Having volunteered to help tend to any sick or wounded, Grace suddenly found herself swamped with, mainly young men, nursing minor injuries caused by fist fights. The best she could do was clean up the cuts and scrapes using boiled water and torn off strips of the bandages she had sterilised and send the youngsters on their way with a caution to calm down...easier said than done in the heat and enforced close quarters.

Getting wearily to her feet to stretch after an entire morning of dealing with surly individuals all itching for a fight, Grace spotted Helena glaring at her across the courtyard of the castel. She shrugged her shoulders, there was nothing further to be done for the woman at the moment - her husband had been despatched on his fabricated mission this morning and she was reinstated into her former quarters...what more did she expect? 'Revenge' was the thought that popped into her mind, for one reason or another Helena blamed Ysabella and would try to find some way to harm her - Grace resolved to stay well away.

Warm hands encircled her waist and she turned to see Guilhem, he looked grim - an expression seldom far from his face the past few days. Without further preamble he said, "The men I sent to Montpellier have returned. They saw Beziers from afar, still smouldering and then headed for Narbona. As they got there they discovered the city has surrendered without a fight, I can't say as I blame them, apparently the flames from Beziers could be seen as the place burned to the ground. The Crusaders will head here next - I imagine some will arrive in the next couple of days. Raimond is prepared to negotiate but he won't roll over the way Vescomtat Aimery od Narbona has and he won't give up any of the Bon Crestian sheltering here...even if he knew who they were!"

"What should be done, husband?" Grace asked.

"Continue exactly as we have been I suppose." he replied. "We need to try to keep peace within our walls and be prepared for a siege. We will keep patrolling and will hopefully spot the army long before it arrives - my worry is they will camp by the river Aude and cut off our route to water, the wells are fine for now but with this amount of people and in this heat they won't last indefinitely. I fear you may have been right about that."

"Should we see if more water can be brought up now?" Grace mused, "Although I'm not sure what we could store it in."

Guilhem nodded, "If you can ask Favia to search for suitable containers I will find men to take them to the river to fill them. I must go now, my love." He planted a kiss on her forehead, "but I will see you this evening."

Grace went looking for Favia and eventually found her haranguing a group of youngsters who were hanging around the entrance to the kitchens, obviously hoping for a tasty titbit or two. They were children, the oldest no more than ten but they were not disposed to leave and were plainly getting in everyone's way. Out of the corner of her eye Grace spied Vescomtat Trencavel and surreptitiously moved in his direction; seeing her coming and noticing the contretemps outside the kitchen he nodded at her and moved swiftly towards the scene of the commotion whereupon with a few choice words he moved the rowdy children on.

"Losing your touch are you, Favia?" he quipped. "You used to put the fear of God in me when you shouted like that." He winked at Grace who had joined them and she smiled in return.

"Hmmmmphhh," exhaled the older woman. "Children today have no respect for their elders." Grace stifled a giggle, it would seem some things never changed through the ages she thought.

Deciding it appropriate to change the subject at this point she outlined her and Guilhem's worries about water supplies once the invading army arrived. The Vescomtat was all in favour of stockpiling what they could and left them to it.

Favia grumbled about the extra work, but helped in the sourcing of appropriate containers - many of them filled only a few days ago and now empty. Seeing how quickly what had seemed like a huge amount of water had disappeared only heightened Grace's concern and she made a note to suggest that supplies were restricted to one small bucket per family for the foreseeable future.

As the pair worked together Favia remarked, "I am proud of you, Ysabella, marriage has been the making of you - you have become a very thoughtful and responsible young woman. Your mother would be very proud of you I'm sure."

"I wish I knew how she fared," Grace, with Ysabella's memories, replied. "It must be four years since she sent me away and for several years before that she was so enamoured of the Bon Crestian path that she was seldom at home - still she is my mother and I hope she is well."

"Your mother is a very unique woman, Ysabella, strong and determined. She struggled to come to terms with being a wife and mother, she had such an enquiring mind and hated to be controlled. She met one of the Elect not long after your father passed on and was captivated. She told me the way of the Bon Crestian was her calling, that even as a woman she could have an influence. She loved and loves you deeply my child, she just wasn't very good at parenting."

Grace nodded, the strength of mind and purpose just described was not unlike her own and she could understand Ysabella's mother not wanting to be restricted to simply being a widow and mother.

The heat by midday was unbearable, Grace could feel the sweat trickling down her back and between her breasts and her hair clung in clammy tendrils around her face - she wished she could strip down to her linen shift. Removing the veil she scooped her hair up and onto the top of her head, desperate to feel some air on the back of her neck. It helped a little so she re-plaited the braids

241

and devised a way to fasten them to the top of her head, the veil and circlet held the makeshift hairstyle in place.

Water from the river, carried in whatever could be found, had been brought into the castel; it looked less than clean but since it would likely be used only for cooking; when it would be boiled; or for washing, she presumed it wouldn't add to the risk of waterborne diseases too much...at least within the castel where there was a ready supply of other things to drink. Never the less, Grace thought she would suggest that if the water were to be used to drink or for washing wounds it be boiled first. Outside of the castel it would be more difficult to control the use of the river water, she had noticed that many people seeing the steady progression of water up to the Vescomtat's residence had followed suit and collected a supply for themselves...she couldn't blame them.

Returning to Lady Agnes' chamber was a blessed relief, stone-built castles were often cold and dank in winter weather but in the height of a Midi summer the thick walls kept the heat out and provided a pleasantly cool refuge. Peyronella and Marguerida were sitting on the floor at their mistresses' feet helping her to sort and wind her silk embroidery threads. It was a peaceful scene in complete contrast to the chaos in the courtyard and Ciutat and Grace heaved a sigh of relief; the two girls were eager to hear of any news and she brought them up to date in as far as she could, whilst sparing them the grisly details the few survivors of Beziers had recounted. Within this room the unfolding disaster seemed a long way away, a tray of sweet pastries and fruit rested as usual on one of the tables together with jugs of watered wine and Lady Agnes encouraged Grace to help herself -

as she did so she wondered how long these little luxuries would remain available once the siege began.

The next few days continued in much the same vein, everyday tasks were carried out at the same time as the hoardings were patrolled and scouting parties despatched; Grace imagined it must feel like the so called 'phoney war' in 1939 when Britain had first declared war on Germany...nothing much happening other than preparation but everyone waiting for events to unfold. Soldiers reported that the army was making its way towards Carcassonne following the stop at Narbonne to accept that city's surrender, but it didn't seem to be in any hurry. People around the town muttered that if the Crusaders didn't hurry up they'd go back home - many of the permanent residents wished they would!

Then, on 28th July, came the news that everyone dreaded, yet, in a bizarre way, looked forward to as it meant, finally, that something was going to happen; an advance party of the Crusaders was spotted to the south east of the Ciutat, maybe fifty men on horseback. By mid-afternoon this group had settled near the banks of the Aude and set up an initial camp. Vescomtat Trencavel had the men closely watched but made no attempt to make contact and the following morning, presumably rested and refreshed, a party of five left the makeshift campsite. The consensus was they were going to meet the main body of the army and guide them in.

Grace asked her husband why no attempt had been made by the Vescomtat to attack these men, "After all," she reasoned as she lay in his arms, "it could slow the rest of them down if they aren't sure exactly where they should be heading."

"It would make little difference, my sweet," came the reply, "and engaging the advance force would antagonise the leaders, Arnaud Amaury and someone called Simon de Monfort, whom I gather has become rather influential. Raimond still thinks he can negotiate with them, killing their men or taking them prisoner before negotiations can even begin would not be conducive to opening talks."

"Does he really think they will negotiate in our favour?! These are the same people who slaughtered twenty thousand and burned Beziers to the ground! I hardly think it likely." Grace was bright-eyed with barely suppressed fury, of course she knew what was going to happen and there was still a part of her thought that if events could be changed, the Crusaders turned back now by force, thousands more people would be spared in the coming years.

Guilhem propped himself up on one elbow and looked down at the beautiful angry face of his young wife. She had a fire in her, he had spotted that immediately, but sometimes fire must be tempered by caution and he said, "Ysabella, do you think I do not agree that negotiations will at best be difficult? Raimond only wants what is best for everyone in Carcassona and if that means we bide our time until the leaders of this accursed army arrives, then that is what we must do. We cannot, must not, sink to the bestial level of these northern invaders. Paratge is the philosophy we live and, if necessary die by." His eyes were filled with tears as he spoke the words and he brushed her lips gently with his own. "If it should come to a battle and I do not return, know that for this short time I have loved you with all my heart." A single tear spilled, catching on his black lashes before splashing onto Grace's cheek.

The sight of such a strong and noble man crying almost broke Grace's heart and she drew his head down to rest on her shoulder, "My love, my husband," she whispered tenderly, "I know in my heart we will survive, and you and I will one day be very far from here - happy and together. We will raise a family and try to forget. We can take a different name if we need to, do as you said and travel to Aragon, find a place no one knows us and be happy there. Be brave, my heart."

A sob caught in Guilhem's throat, she painted a picture he could hold in his mind whatever came to pass, and he loved her even more for it.

Chapter 31 – The Crusaders Are Here

The invading army continued to arrive over the next five days until by 1st August, the entire area to the west of the Ciutat was covered with the accoutrements of war; brightly coloured pennants fluttered in the light wind looking like a myriad butterflies; dusty tents littered the ground and hundreds of individual campfires sent plumes of smoke into the air. The invaders were not lacking in supplies as the conquered had yielded their stocks - either by force as in the case of Beziers; willingly (in order to save themselves) as in Narbona or simply by default as villages in the path of the army had simply fled, leaving everything behind.

Guilhelm stood on the ramparts with his liege Lord Raimond Rogier Trencavel under the protection of the hastily constructed but nevertheless sturdily built hoardings; "Holy Mother of God," he blasphemed quietly, "they mean to completely destroy us!".

"Not just us but our whole way of living," Raimond agreed. "The northerners will not rest until they own our lands and we dance to their tune. This crusade against the Bon Crestian is merely an excuse to bring us all under the aegis of King Philip, he's funding Innocent's crusade because it suits him to get rid of us, not because he gives a damn about the Bon Crestian!"

"Agreed," Guilhelm responded, "but we have no choice other than to stand our ground. We have plenty of supplies within the Ciutat. Water, as my beautiful wife pointed out, may be the main issue; especially if they take St Vincent and cut off our access to the river."

"Well, we must try to ensure that doesn't happen," Raimond said firmly, "we shall post guards on the ramparts at regular intervals, the invaders will not get close to us without us knowing."

The two men descended into the castel and went their separate ways, Raimond to talk to the great and the good of Carcassonne and Guilhelm to address the soldiers. By midday the ramparts were bristling with, largely inexperienced soldiers, standing guard duties; many were obviously overwhelmed by the sight of the arriving Crusaders whilst others, the more belligerent, could be heard hurling insults in the coarse Occitan of their upbringing. Guilhelm smiled at the more inventive of the comments whilst at the same time making a note to tell them to desist...someone in the camp may understand enough of the local language to understand what was being shouted and an enraged man would fight more keenly if he felt his honour was being undermined.

Back inside the safety and relative calm of the castel, Grace was involved in a heated discussion with one of the laundry women whom she had spotted using vast quantities of their precious water stores to wash some bedlinens. "Don't you understand that we must save our water, ration it out?" she remonstrated.

The buxom laundress, red of face and with sinewy arms showing the muscle definition caused by years of hefting huge cauldrons of water and wet linens around, stood her ground. "'Tis always a Wednesday that I wash the Vescomtat's bed linen - him and the mistress like their linens fresh and clean!" she insisted, "I be seeing no reason not to do it today – 'tis Wednesday after all!"

Grace sighed, she and others had tried to insist that water be rationed but the message did not seem to be getting through, especially to some of the staff in the castel who appeared to think they were exempt from the dictat by reason of serving the Vescomtat. It was another scorchingly hot day, too hot in fact to argue with the laundress but she had to persevere, the Ciutat was full of stories of the arriving army - surely it shouldn't be difficult for the inhabitants of Carcassonne to recognise the threat they were all under? She persevered in her attempt to tell the woman that there must be no further laundry undertaken until the crusading army had been defeated; but was met with a stony-faced defiance. Finally, exasperated, she gave up trying to explain the situation, which, she thought, should be clearly evident to all but those of limited intellect. She would instead have the vats of water put under lock and key, and the well within the walls of the castel put under guard at all times. She'd like to see the argument which could result when the laundress next attempted to access a water supply!

The laundress spun on her heels and returned to her task, draping the now clean linens over a series of wooden poles set into the outer wall of the kitchen; they would be dry within an hour, so intense was the heat.

Grace meanwhile headed back indoors and made her way to Lady Agnes' chamber, relishing the relative coolness to be found within the thick stone walls of the castel. Since the last vicious encounter with Helena, the older woman had been conspicuously absent, Favia having successfully found tasks to keep her occupied. Peyronella and Marguerida were sharing quarters with her once more but reported that she had, so far, made little attempt to engage them in conversation; instead merely undressed and got into her narrow bed. It was with some disquiet therefore that Grace found herself face to face with Helena as she rounded a corner en-route to the upper floor. She decided to act in a manner befitting her 21st century name and greeted the other woman cordially and with a pleasant smile. Helena however, still sporting the mark from the split lip she had received on her unhappy wedding night, merely sneered in return and pushed roughly past Grace causing her to bang her elbow, hard, on the wall.

"I give up!" Grace muttered and made to continue on her way.

"Give up on what?" said the voice of her husband from behind her.

She turned and smiled whilst rubbing her sore elbow,

"On Helena," she answered him, "it doesn't matter how pleasant I try to be towards her, she just throws it back at me!"

"She'll likely never change her attitude towards you, my love; she is too full of jealousy to do so. Leave her be."

"I feel sorry for her," Grace countered, "She didn't want to be married to de Merlon and he's treated her appallingly."

"Indeed he has and you have a kind heart, my beloved, but she has never been a likeable individual, she is too bound up in the myth that life has treated her badly and refuses to see that it is her own actions in the main, which have brought about her unhappiness."

Grace smiled somewhat sadly, "I suppose you are right, husband, but I do so hate confrontations."

He hugged her tightly, "Well we are all facing the worst kind of confrontation, have you seen the army massing by the river? It's larger than we feared, too big for us to confront - our only option is to hope we can last a lengthy siege."

Grace paled, "I dare not look over the ramparts, even if I were allowed up there!" she added, remembering the day she had climbed up and then had fallen into his waiting arms as she attempted to climb down. "But you have reminded me; I caught one of the laundresses using huge amounts of the stored water to wash bed linen, she would not see reason and I fully expect that she will try again so I think we should lock away the barrels we collected and have a guard on the castel's well, otherwise we will run out of water very quickly if we can't access the river."

Guilhem frowned, "Silly woman! The river approach is already unsafe as the Crusaders are camped down there and I fully expect them to make raids on St Vincent before much longer which will completely cut off any approach; I'll organise for a couple of guards to stand duty by the well if you can have Favia lock away the stores."

Grace agreed to talk to Favia as soon as she could.

"Guilhem, what do you think will happen?" she asked quietly.

"I do not know, my love," he responded equally quietly. "There's too many to fight and we can only last so long under siege conditions. We just have to hope to last long enough so that those conscripted men in the Crusader army whose tenure is only 40 days, begin to pack up and head home for harvest time. Their army may then, possibly, be overturned by us, but I think it unlikely. In my opinion, the best we can hope for is that we come to terms with them and save our skins, if not Carcassona."

Grace shuddered. She knew, or at least thought she did, that the inhabitants of the Ciutat would survive, that there would be no repeat, this time, of the horrors inflicted on Beziers but what happened to the citizens once they were forced out of the town was another matter. She supposed she and Guilhem would head to his home in Minerve, but she also thought that Minerve was ultimately taken by the crusading forces; however, if as she had begun to suspect, Guilhem and Ysabella were a distant part of her familial tree, she had to believe that one or both of them would survive the upheavals in the lands of Occitania and manage to make a home somewhere else. The thought cheered her slightly and she reached on tiptoe to kiss her husband who responded by enfolding her in his strong arms and returning the kiss with interest.

Released from his hold, she bade him farewell for the moment and continued on her way to Lady Agnes, somewhat lighter of heart than she had been.

Chapter 32 – Being Strong

Lady Agnes was in a state of panic when Grace eventually arrived at her chamber; the woman had apparently decided to look out over the encamped army and had been horrified at the vista she had seen. The two young ladies-in-waiting were understandably frightened by their mistress's reaction, although they hadn't looked for themselves, and so Grace found herself entering a room occupied by three near hysterical women. The presence of Favia would no doubt have acted as a calming force, but she was currently preoccupied in ensuring the domestic affairs of the castel were running smoothly in the current crisis.

Marguerida ran to Grace, "Oh, Ysabella! What are we to do? Lady Agnes says the invaders outnumber us. How can we survive?"

Grace took a deep breath. "I haven't seen the army but yes, from what Guilhem has told me, they far outnumber us. But ladies, what is the point in expending energy and tears over something we have no control over? Our men will have to deal with the strategies of war and siege whilst we try to look after each other and the people of Carcassona."

"But we're going to die!" Peyronella sobbed, "just like the poor souls in Beziers."

Grace moved swiftly across the chamber and shook the younger woman. "I will not hear you utter another word along those lines!" She said firmly. "We are not going to die. I feel this most strongly. Your job right now is to take care of Lady Agnes, of young master Raimond and the unborn child, for they are the future of the Trencavels." Peyronella sniffed and collapsed against Grace, forcing her to hold her tightly; she was shocked to feel the younger girl shaking with fear and she spoke gently to her, "We have to be strong, Peyronella, all we have is hope and a belief that we will survive. Hold onto these and you will prevail."

Peyronella gulped back her tears and Grace could feel the shaking lessen until in a few moments the girl was able to pull away and stand on her own two feet.

Grace now turned her attention to the Lady Agnes who was sitting, ashen-faced, in the corner, cradling her swollen belly in one arm whilst the other held tightly onto her young son. So quiet was Raimond that Grace hadn't noticed his presence; he was usually a whirlwind of action so to see him so still was both unusual and disturbing. She moved over to them and dropped to her knees.

"Master Raimond," she said quietly, "try not to be afraid. You need to be strong for your mama and the new baby. Can you do that do you think?"

The young boy turned his huge brown eyes towards her and said tremulously, "I shall try very hard to look after mama and be a man."

Grace's eyes filled with tears and she reached out for the child and hugged him tightly, hiding her face in his tousled curly hair so his mother wouldn't see her emotional response. "You are a brave lad,'" she said briskly, "Now, how about Peyronella and Marguerida take you down to the kitchens to see if you can find a treat? I will take care of your mama whilst you are away, don't worry." His face brightened at the thought of food and it took little persuasion for the young ladies-in-waiting to accompany him.

Once they had departed, Raimond now chattering excitedly about what treat the kitchens could provide, Grace turned all her attention to her mistress. Lady Agnes looked wan and pale and to Grace's midwife tuned eyes there were traces of puffiness in the fine-featured face.

"Perhaps you should lie down awhile," she suggested.

Lady Agnes demurred, with none of her usual resistance which worried Grace, and tried to struggle to her feet, eventually succeeding only with the assistance of a proffered arm to haul her up.

"I'm so tired!" she said quietly, "SO very tired and so very afraid." Grace gently hugged the woman, feeling the hard roundness of the pregnant belly between them.

"Come," she said, "lie down, rest and let me examine you."

Once on the bed the mound of pregnancy looked even more pronounced and Grace could see for the first time the swollen ankles and puffy fingers. "Has the child moved much?" she asked.
Lady Agnes thought for a moment, "A little, not so much as usual but I doubt there is much room for him now,"

she patted her stomach gently and Grace could see a definite movement beneath the linen gown.

Good, if the child was still responsive then all was well, but the swelling and tiredness was a worry; her training warned of pre-eclampsia, dangerous if not treated in her time but almost certainly fatal to both mother and child in this age. She carefully felt around the bulge, it was tight as a drum and from what she could tell the child's head was fully engaged; delivery could be anytime from now, but she wondered if there was any local herbal knowledge which could possibly bring upon labour more quickly if the worrying symptoms persisted or worsened.

"Is all well?" Lady Agnes asked, a worried town in her voice. "I don't remember feeling this tired and unwell when I carried Raimond."

"All seems to be as it should," Grace replied, "I'm a little worried about the swelling in your ankles and fingers but it is extremely hot and you are very close to your time; resting with your feet raised will help - like this," she demonstrated by placing two of the bed's pillows under her mistress's feet, "and as I recall we were not facing the threat of an invading army when you birthed Raimond - surely that is contributing to your lack of well-being, My Lady."

Lady Agnes smiled wanly, "Perhaps you are right, Ysabella. I just want the child out now so I can be of more support to my husband."

"Your husband would wish you to rest and take care of yourself and that will apply just as much when the child arrives as it does now." Grace admonished her, finding it increasingly difficult not to take the woman in her arms and tell her that of all of them, her beloved husband was the one who would not make it out of Carcassone alive. "Will you be alright by yourself for a short while whilst I find Dame Balsace?" Grace asked. "I would like her to see you, she has more experience than I."

"I shall be perfectly fine," Lady Agnes replied. "Perhaps you could bring me a cool drink when you return and ask that young Raimond be kept away for a while - I love him dearly but it is difficult to rest whilst he is around!"

Grace smiled her acquiescence to both requests and left the room. She located Dame Balsace in the kitchen with Favia, much as she had expected, and informed her of Lady Agnes' condition; she still found the elderly midwife's dialect almost impenetrable but had quickly realised that the woman understood the langue d'oc as spoken by her. With Favia's translation skills Dame Balsace communicated that she agreed with Grace's concerns and would head immediately to examine the pregnant woman. She poked a bony finger into Grace's arm and with a twinkle in her black button eyes cackled something which made Favia smile as she repeated the woman's words.

"She says she knew you would be useful!" Favia laughed and with the wizened crone hanging onto one arm headed out of the kitchens, leaving Grace to organise a cool drink; something sweetened with honey for energy, she thought.

As she herself turned to leave she spotted the other two ladies-in-waiting with young Raimond and asked that they keep him entertained for the remainder of the day, before taking him to the nursery maid who would put him to bed.

"Does Mama not want to see me?" the little boy asked tearfully.

"Of course she does, but she is very tired right now and is going to bed early," Grace reassured him.

"Without supper?" he asked askance, "Has she been bad?"

Grace hid a smile, "No, my sweet, but your baby brother or sister is so big now that your mama doesn't have a lot of space in her tummy for food."

He grinned, "Yes, Mama is so fat now!" and resumed eating the sweet pastry in his hand without further questioning.

Back in Lady Agnes' chamber she found Dame Balsace had ordered the woman strip to her fine linen undershift and was busily moving her nut-brown hands over the distended stomach, chattering all the while in a reassuring, if unintelligible, fashion. Favia was attempting to convey the meaning of the babble which essentially seemed to be that all was well, that the child was strong and would be born within the week; until that time Lady Agnes was to rest and to drink a decoction of raspberry leaves, which she would prepare and bring to her, to strengthen her womb and contractions. Grace smiled inwardly, raspberry leave tea was also anecdotally said to bring on labour, Dame Balsace obviously wanted to hurry the child out as gently as possibly.

Lady Agnes seemed reassured by the attentions of the midwife and once she had sipped on the sweetened wine Grace had brought, she announced her intention to try and sleep.

"Should I tell the Vescomtat to sleep in the ante-room," Grace asked her mistress, "so he won't disturb you?"

"No," came the response, "I need to have him near me when I can." Grace nodded. "You go to your own husband now," Lady Agnes said, "Dame Balsace will stay until I fall asleep." The crone nodded and both Grace and Favia left the pair alone.

"What made you ask the Dame to see our Lady?' Favia asked as soon as the door shut behind them.

Grace thought for a moment before replying, it would be highly improbable for a young woman of Ysabella's age in this time to know about pre-eclampsia, so she needed to be careful about what she said.

"Lady Agnes seemed to me to be more tired than she should and her fingers and ankles are swollen. I remembered mama looking after a woman who showed the same symptoms - she lost the baby and almost died."

Favia nodded sagely, "I remember something similar myself many years ago, better safe than sorry eh?"

Grace nodded, "Indeed, and Dame Balsace knows more than you and I put together!"

The women parted at this point, Favia back to the kitchen and Grace to the chamber she shared with Guilhem. It was almost time for the evening meal to be served; informal as the arrangement currently was in light of the present situation, and she felt a need to splash her face and tidy her dishevelled hair before heading for the hall.

Chapter 33 – A Time To Fight

Grace awoke with a start, her head was resting against her husband's shoulder, his arm holding her against him as he slept. The noise which had awakened her came again, a determined knock at their door.

"Guilhem, Guilhem," she said softly and then, getting no response, "GUILHEM!" He sat up abruptly, he would have taken her with him had she not adroitly moved.

"What is it?" he asked sleepily.

"Someone is at the door!" she exclaimed, "and whoever it is, is more likely to want you than I."

"Oh I don't know," he replied, "A lot of men would want you, my love, if they could."

"GUILHEM, DOOR!" was the only response. He bounded out of bed, by now fully awake and headed for the door, where the person on the other side had now begun a constant drumming on the sturdy wood.

"By all the heavens, what is the matter?" he said loudly, as he opened the door to be confronted by one of the younger guards, who appeared shocked and nervous - whether because of Guilhem's nakedness or the glimpse of Grace in the bed behind it was hard to tell. A quick and low toned conversation ensued. From her position in the bed Grace could see Guilhem's shoulders stiffen, it was clear that the guard's unease was to be laid at the feet of her husband.

"Guilhem, what is it?" she asked as he finally shut the door and leaned his back against it. His face was set, the blue eyes steely and his hands were clenched into fists.

"The Crusaders have stormed St Vincent," he said quietly, "the suburb is empty of people but there is shelter and possibly food which they could utilise. It also brings them much closer to our walls."

Grace paled, "What is to be done?"

"Raimond is organising a counter offensive, I am to join him."

She flew out of bed and into his arms, tears in her eyes. "And so the fight begins," she said tremulously, "I will dress and ensure we are ready to treat any wounded."

Guilhem held her tightly and kissed her gently on the lips, "If anything happens to me, you should make your way to Minerve as soon as you can. My people there will take care of you."

Grace bit back a sob, "Nothing will happen to you! Remember? We WILL leave here and start a new life."

He kissed her again; "I shall hold that thought in my head, my love. Now help me dress."

In silence he donned his clothing, adding a padded gambeson and chain mail vest to his usual attire before drawing a surcoat over everything and tightly fastening on his sword belt.

"Should you not protect your arms, my love?" asked Grace, concerned by the sleeveless chainmail vest.

"This is the only chainmail I have with me," he shrugged, "and in any case it is too damn hot to consider more armour, I will just have to make sure I get them before they get me!" He attempted to smile but it was a poor effort and he added quickly, "For the first time I have someone to fight for - I WILL be back, my love. I promise."

Grace nodded, tears not far away, "I know you will!"

With one last kiss he turned and headed out of the door. She fell to her knees shaking. In all honesty, she didn't know if he would be back unharmed, or indeed at all; her knowledge of events was sketchy - half remembered facts from a childhood visit 800 years in the future - but she had to believe that they would both survive and go on to found her family tree. Taking a deep breath, she got to her feet and dressed; she contemplated heading to Lady Agnes but decided instead to seek out Favia and attempt to establish some sort of emergency room to receive any wounded men.

By the time she had located Favia the inner courtyard of the castel was awash with men, some armed with only farming implements and wearing their everyday clothing; others, the small garrison and Vescomtat Trenceval's personal guard including Guilhem Bastier, wore various incarnations of armour and carried swords and lances. In comparison to the vast hoard gathering by the river they were pitifully few, both in number and equipment. Grace shuddered, Carcassonne was well fortified, perhaps they should just try to sit it out - wait for the bulk of the Crusaders to begin to leave, bound for their homes and harvest time. She was not in charge though and telling Raimond Trenceval what she knew of the fate of his Ciutat would be useless. She sighed deeply and then, having spotted Favia, hurried across to the older woman.

"Favia!" she shouted, to be heard above the hubbub of the gathered men. "We should look at finding somewhere that the injured may be brought."

Favia turned, her taciturn face, even more stern than usual, broke into a brief smile when she spotted Grace. "Let us hope it won't be needed, Ysabella," she said, then added, "but looking at some of these men I fear it will be. Come, there is an empty storeroom near the kitchens which would work."

Arm in arm the two of them managed to negotiate a path through the assembled people; Grace's small, dark beauty attracting appreciative looks as they passed. The storeroom was indeed empty but also very dark and dirty. Favia managed to round up several servants who set to trying to clean up the space using minimal water, whilst she located as many candles as she could find.

"We won't light them unless we have to," she told Grace, who was busy sorting through a pile of blankets and worn bed linen.

Any injured would have to sit or lie on the, mercifully now swept clean, floor, the bedding, worn as it was, would afford at least some small amount of comfort. Although training in midwifery in her own time, she was also a qualified first aider and was racking her brains to remember some of the information she had acquired. Minor injuries shouldn't be a problem she thought, provided they were at least cleaned properly, but with no antibiotics or antiseptics anything more major would likely be fatal. She would have to attempt some kind of triage, no point treating someone if they were unlikely to survive - harsh but true.

A sudden thought struck her, "Favia, are there any strong spirits, errr aqua vitae, anywhere in the castel? Mama told me cleaning wounds with the stuff seemed to help them heal without putrefaction."

Favia looked a little bewildered but nodded and disappeared, returning momentarily with a number of flagons. Grace opened one of them and sniffed the contents gingerly, a distinct alcoholic aroma assailed her nostril.

"This should do," she smiled, "it's made my nose hair curl so it must be good and strong!"

Favia chuckled, "Your mother has some strange notions, but I have to say she is one of the best healers I know - if she says this helps then so be it! Have you broken your fast yet, my girl? Can't have you passing out once we have a room full of men to tend to." Grace shook her head and, as if mention of potential food had triggered a response, her stomach chose that moment to growl loudly in protestation of its empty state. "I take that as a no." Favia grinned, "Come, we have done all we can here, let us go and see what we can find to quieten that stomach of yours!"

In the kitchens Favia arranged for some breads, figs and honey sweetened wine to be brought to them. They sat companionably munching, talking little, each wondering what the next few hours may bring.

A sudden commotion made them jump to their feet. "What is it?" Grace asked fearfully.

A passing servant overheard and replied, "The soldiers are coming back!" before rushing away intent on his own business.

"Come!" said Favia. "I fear we may have work to do."

Chapter 34 – Triage

As they rose to leave the kitchen, Favia managed to collar a young boy, asking him to make his way to where the retreating band of fighters were entering the Ciutat and to tell the leaders to send any injured men to the storeroom. By the time the two women reached the room, a matter of minutes later, several wounded men had already arrived; walking wounded to be sure but spilling a fair amount of blood between them. Grace grimaced, this was going to take more than the two of them. Favia had obviously reached the same conclusion and was already instructing one of the ever-present young boys, this one besides himself with excitement, to carry a message to the kitchens asking for assistance.

Grace began to assess the injured; all had flesh wounds, the worst being what appeared to be a sword cut to the side of one of the men; he was wearing no armour of any kind, so she assumed he wasn't one of the guards or soldiers, which had lifted a large flap of skin and was bleeding profusely. So far as she could see it was a clean cut, the blade which had inflicted the damage was obviously sharp. The others sported numerous cuts and grazes, none were life threatening.

"We should treat only the most badly injured inside," she said in an undertone to Favia. "Any with just cuts and scrapes, like most of these, we can clean up just as well outside where there is more light." Favia nodded her agreement.

A number of women approached from the kitchen, the help Favia had asked for, and Grace began to instruct them on how to clean the wounds using a mixture of the aqua vitae and boiled water. They grumbled at the notion of actually cleansing a wound but one look from Favia quelled their protests.

Grace led the man with the side wound inside and began to wash out the deep gash, he swore loudly in Occitan and then, blushing deeply, apologised, "Begging your pardon but that hurts more than the blade did!" he said gritting his teeth.

Grace smiled at him, "I'm sure it does but cleaning it well means it will heal well." He nodded and managed to stay both quiet and still as she finished her ministrations and then wrapped the deep cut using one of the bandages she had insisted be boiled. "You're done" she said at last, "stay here for a while whilst you recover."

"I'd rather leave and let my wife know I'm in one piece," he said, adding, "If that's all the same to you, dòna?"

She nodded and he got gingerly to his feet.

As he reached the door she suddenly said, "Is it very bad?"

He nodded, "There's too many of them, dòna, we can't fight them all." Grace nodded and he went on his way, leaving her to rinse her hands in a bowl of neat alcohol. From what the man had just said they should be prepared to accept more casualties.

For the next hour or so a constant stream of wounded arrived to be triaged by Grace, the vast majority were cleaned up, bandaged and sent on their way but a few had been led or carried into the storeroom, their wounds requiring more than mere patching up. With a start Grace recognised one of the injured as being one of Guilhem's men from Minerve; a young knight, no more than seventeen, with the first sparse sproutings of beard visible on his chin. He bore several slash marks to both arms which had obviously bled heavily and were now crusted over, but of more concern to her was a deep wound at the juncture of his neck and left shoulder, the result, by the looks of it, of a vicious downward slashing movement. The boy was barely conscious, and blood soaked his surcoat, turning the light blue fabric into a deathly shade of purple. On closer inspection Grace could see that the padded gambeson was also sodden with blood. The boy's life was draining from him and there was little she could do but ease him as he slipped away. Her eyes filled with helpless tears, but she spoke quietly to the lad without letting her voice betray her emotions and held onto his hand until he exhaled one final tremulous time. Her tears dripped onto the poor boy as she got to her feet after covering his face with a corner of the old linen sheet on which he lay.

After taking a deep breath she turned resolutely towards the next of the wounded, but her eyes were drawn towards the doorway where yet another injured soldier was being helped in; he was on his feet - just - but was obviously struggling to stay upright. To her horror she saw it was Guilhem, his face grey underneath the blood splatter and dirt and his left arm hanging uselessly by his side, blood dripping in a regular patter from his fingertips. Heedless of anyone else in need she flew to his side and he attempted a smile.

"Set him down here," she instructed the two men assisting him, "carefully!" she added.

Guilhem sank to the floor, the last of the strength in his legs obviously deserting him and Grace fell to her knees at his side. "Oh what have you done to yourself, my love?" she asked, gently brushing back the black hair which had fallen over his face.

Guilhem swallowed, "It looks like I needed my other chainmail after all, eh?"

She nodded and used a small, sharp knife she had acquired to cut through the fabric of his surcoat to reveal a bone deep cut to his upper left arm, clean through the bicep but fortunately, on first inspection at least, there appeared to be no damage to the humerus.

"Is it bad?" he asked.

"Bad enough, but it could be worse I think. Can you still move your fingers?" He waggled the digits in response. "Good. It's nasty, but it will mend in time IF we can keep your arm still whilst the muscle heals. It needs to be cleaned out with aqua vitae before I strap it, it will hurt, a lot, and I'm not sure that I can do that to you. Could I ask Favia? Please?"

Guilhem nodded, "but I want you to bind the wound afterwards." His eyes pleaded with her and she acquiesced, dropping a kiss on his head as she got to her feet to summon Favia.

Favia listened carefully as Grace told her what to do, including swilling her hands in the neat alcohol before beginning the cleaning process and then set to; smothering Guilhem's protestations of pain with clucks of disapproval. Grace smiled inwardly, Favia was a matron-like figure who brooked no argument, she would have made a great ward sister in her time she thought. Guilhem being in safe hands she turned her attention to the three other men in the storeroom, one was clearly well past help, the breath rattling stertorously in his chest, causing frothy pink bubbles to appear on his lips - a sure sign of damage to the lungs. He was, mercifully, unconscious however, unlike the next patient who was propped, half sitting against the wall and demanding a drink. Grace didn't need to look too closely to see the man had suffered a devastating stomach wound; the smell alone alerted her to the fact that his intestines had been punctured. He would die an agonisingly slow death yet seemed unaware of his situation. She could only suppose that shock was preventing the pain signals from kicking in but they undoubtedly would and there was nothing she would be able to do to assuage his suffering. She gulped and moved towards him, offering him the barest sip of water - just enough to wet his lips. He begged for more but she would not relent - simply promised to return to him soon. The third man had a head wound which looked much more serious than it was, lots of blood and a deep cut but no sign that the blade had cracked his skull. She spoke soothingly to him as she cleaned and dressed the wound, offering a swig of the aqua vitae to take the edge off the pain.

"I've finished," she said securing the bandage in place by tucking the loose end in as firmly as she could. The cut

had stopped bleeding and she thought it would heal well, although he would likely be left with a thick scar.
"Stay here a few minutes to rest but you may leave when you feel able."

The man with the stomach wound obviously overheard this comment as he piped up to protest that he wished to leave too.

"Not yet you don't!" Grace said as she turned to face him. His face was now an ashen colour, he was probably bleeding internally and she thought it wouldn't be long before the blood loss would cause him to pass out. He still appeared to not be in any pain and she wondered again how long that could last and what to do when the agony began. "I just need to bind his arm," she said finally, indicating Guilhem, "and then you are next on my list". The man nodded, the bullishness was leaving him in stages and he sat quietly as she walked to her husband.

"How does it feel?" she asked tenderly, inspecting the gash on his arm.

"Sore!" he responded, "I swear it didn't hurt this much when I came in."

"It probably didn't," she responded, "the body seems to temporarily shut down the pain response, I think it must be to let people move to safety, but once the person is in a safe place the pain comes crashing in. It's a good sign though," she dropped her voice to a mere whisper, "the man across there still feels little despite a sword wound which has punctured his guts." Guilhem looked concerned, a dark shadow in his blue eyes.

271

"He won't make it, will he?" he asked equally quietly.

Looking him straight in the eye she said, "No. I only hope he falls unconscious soon, I have nothing to give him to ease the pain when it starts."

Guilhem frowned, "Dying of a gut wound can take time, I've seen it before. Once my arm is bound I will sit with him. He is a soldier and should be given the chance to die well."

Grace looked appalled as the meaning of what he had said hit her, "You mean kill him?" she hissed.

"I do, although maybe someone else will have to do it, I doubt I would have the strength at the moment."

"Guilhem, you can't! That would be murder."

"He is going to die anyway, my love, you said it yourself. At least let him have the choice to die slowly and in agony or quickly at the hands of a colleague. A sharp blade across the throat could be a mercy for him."

White-faced at the thought, Grace could at least understand what Guilhem was saying, he had been a soldier since childhood and had probably seen many men die of their wounds - given the choice she thought he would opt for the blade of a friend too.

She nodded, "Fine, sit with him, talk with him, it will be his decision." With his good arm he cupped her cheek.

"I love you," he mouthed.

Binding his arm was straightforward enough although he protested at the need to strap the arm to his side and support the lower arm with a sling. "It will stop you moving it!" she insisted, "the muscles won't knit together if you don't keep it still!"

He pulled a face but was in no position to challenge her assertions, and as soon as she was done he asked for help to get to his feet and cross to the man with the stomach injury. "I take it the other man is beyond aid too?" he asked sotto voce.

"I think his lungs are damaged, it's only a matter of time for him but at least he isn't conscious."

Guilhem nodded, "Now go outside, my love, take a rest and some air, leave the soldier to me." Grace wanted to protest but she did feel the need to escape the sickly metallic stench of blood overlaid with the foetid smell of the man's damaged guts and once Guilhem was seated next to the other man she fled outdoors with some relief.

It was a scene of carnage in the courtyard; there were too many walking wounded to be counted and, against one of the walls, lay several men who obviously hadn't arrived at the makeshift hospital under their own steam. The covered faces indicating that there would be no battle to save those particular lives. Favia and her team were doing a sterling job in wiping away blood and cleaning the cuts and scrapes, Grace made her way over to where Favia was dealing with one of the professional soldiers who, in addition to a broken nose and black eye, was sporting a number of slashes to both his surcoat and the flesh of his arms; none of the wounds were

273

particularly deep but he was complaining fiercely at the sting of alcohol. Favia was stoically ignoring the curses as she worked but as soon as she was finished she returned fire with a volley of expletives over his behaviour which made the man blush and those around burst into laughter.

Grace smiled herself, despite the awfulness of the situation; the broken bodies and sounds of men in pain.

"Are there anymore badly injured do you know?" she asked Favia.

"No, this is it," the older woman replied. "There are several more bodies in St Vincent, I'm told, but they had to leave them there as they retreated. How is Guilhem?"

"The cut is through the bicep and down to the bone but it should heal, as long as he doesn't try to use that arm." Grace replied. "Retreat, you said. One of the men I treated said there were too many to fight. I take it we have lost this particular battle then?"

"It would appear so," Favia said grimly. "The Crusaders lost men too, a bloody battle and nothing really gained for either side. They have an empty suburb but are no closer to taking Carcassona and we have lost good men."

"You forget," Grace interjected, "any chance of accessing the river is now gone, we only have the water in the Ciutat to rely on and that won't last much longer."

Favia frowned, "I hadn't thought of that! On the plus side the Vescomtat is in one piece; he is in discussion with his advisors I believe."

"Some good news then," Grace said drily. "I should go back in soon. I left Guilhem, at his request, talking to a soldier with a stomach wound, a deep one which has punctured the intestines, he thinks the man should be given the chance to 'die well' as he put it rather than linger in pain."

"He is right, you know," Favia said gently.

"I suppose so," was the only response Grace could muster.

Grace returned disconsolately to the storeroom and upon arrival saw that the injured man had indeed opted for the quicker death, his head was pillowed on Guilhem's thighs, his right hand on the hilt of a dagger which was embedded in his heart; Guilhem's hand covered the man's and had obviously provided the required force. Her husband's eyes were full of tears as he raised his head to look at her. "I had to," was all he said.

Moving to his side she put her arms around him, careful to avoid the injured side. "I know, my love, I know." Guilhem sobbed silently for a few moments and then, composing himself, asked her to help him stand. She gently lifted the dead man's head from her husband's lap so he could extricate himself and together they removed the dagger from his chest and cleaned the blade before

275

Grace placed a clean, but worn, piece of linen over his face.

"The knife is his," Guilhem said, "he insisted we use it rather than mine." Almost reverently he put the small sharp blade on the dead man's chest. "Is there anything further you can do here?" he asked, "because if not then I would really like to return to our chamber and escape this stench and this - this - this…" he struggled for composure before continuing, "this utter futility and senseless waste of good men!"

Grace checked the one remaining patient; at some point between her leaving the storeroom and returning to the sight of her husband cradling a dead man, he had breathed his last, quietly and without any fuss.

She shook her head at Guilhem, "No my love - I am not needed here anymore. Let's get you away."

Hand in hand they made their way into the chaos outside and thence to the quiet and privacy of their own chamber.

Chapter 35 – A Responsible Man

After helping her husband, with some difficulty due to the arm injury, out of his chainmail vest and gambeson, Grace used a little water from the jug in their room and a piece of fabric torn from his ruined surcoat to wipe his dirty and bloody face and hands. He was unusually quiet and compliant which worried her, but she supposed the scenes he had just witnessed would be playing in a loop in his head.

This was confirmed when after several minutes of her ministrations he suddenly pushed her hand away, "Stop it woman!" he said harshly, "I'm clean enough!" Grace chose not to rise to the tone of his voice but rather moved away and sat quietly at the end of the bed. "I'm sorry," he said, voice breaking. "I can't stop seeing the sword as it sliced my arm; the look in the soldier's eye as he tried to kill me. I wonder if my face had the same look of intent, hate even? I've fought before but never to protect something, someone that means so much to me. I've seen men die before; killed some too, too many in fact, but I've always before fought with soldiers who are being paid to do battle. Today I fought next to farmers and peasants, watched them die for want of armour and a sharp blade of their own. I wanted to shout to Raimond, tell him to fall back; that we could never win - but I didn't and now I wonder if I could have saved some of those who died..." His voice tailed off.

That was probably the longest speech she had heard him make and it was clear he was feeling a weight of responsibility which should not by right belong to him.

"Guilhem," she said in a measured tone, choosing her words carefully. "You are a vassal of the Trencavels, as am I and indeed everyone in Carcassona. We do as we are bade, to the best of our ability, we may advise but cannot command. I understand how much you wish you could make things right for us all but you must not allow yourself to believe that you can defend everyone. My love, you are strong, brave and kind but you can't bear the woes of us all." She moved beside him and stroked his hair. "No matter how much you think you should."

His eyes filled with tears, one single drop daring to overflow and spill onto his cheek. "I love you," was all he could manage to say.

"I know," she said in return. "Now rest, my husband. I need to visit Lady Agnes, I haven't seen her today, she will have had Peyronella and Marguerida with her, but they know nothing of child bearing and she worries so!"

He reached for her with his good hand, "Stay with me a while, please, I will sleep if you sit with me I think."

Grace kissed him gently, "Then lay down, my love." He obeyed, and she pulled a thin blanket over him despite his protests. "Hush!" she said, stroking his forehead in a rhythmical fashion, "rest."

Grace had no idea how long she sat next to him, stroking his head and cheeks whilst repeating soothing words in a quiet voice, but eventually the effects of the fighting, his wound and overwrought emotions caught up with him and he succumbed to sleep. She remained by his side a little while longer, not wanting to leave him alone but knowing she must, before reluctantly rising and heading for the door. He muttered something incoherent as she moved away but didn't move or wake. She opened the door and slipped through, closing it behind her as quietly as she could.

Minutes later she was at Lady Agnes' chambers and was admitted by one of the guards who raised a quizzical eyebrow as she passed. She had no idea why until she entered the room and was greeted by a volley of exclamations from the occupants.

"Oh, my dear!" Lady Agnes said, struggling to her feet, "what have you been doing?"

Grace was startled, "Favia and I were helping the injured - why do you ask?"

"Because you are covered with dirt and what looks like blood! And your hair is all over the place," Peyronella said, looking a little queasy.

Grace looked down at her gown, the front was indeed splashed with blood and probably other bodily fluids; in the heat of the moment she hadn't noticed. Closer inspection revealed her hands were none too clean either and now it had been mentioned she could feel that her hair had broken free of its bindings and was curling around her face. The shock of what she had experienced began to set in and her knees suddenly and unexpectedly buckled beneath her; she would have fallen had Peyronella not reached her in time and led her to one of the low chairs.

"Sit for a moment," Lady Agnes said. "Have you eaten or drunk anything today?"

"Not since early this morning," Grace replied, her teeth chattering for some reason.

"Marguerida, please go and find someone to bring some honeyed wine and a selection of food up here...enough for us all. Ysabella, let us get you out of that gown and cleaned up."

Grace got to her feet again and allowed Peyronella to help her out of her stained and frankly rather smelly gown. Clad only in her thin linen shift she shivered, hot as it was outdoors somehow the inside of the castel rarely felt warm. She stood patiently as Lady Agnes instructed the young lady-in-waiting to wash her face and hands and comb out and re-plait her dishevelled hair; a warm blanket from the bed was then draped around her shoulders and she gratefully sat down once more.

"Is it truly awful? How many are hurt? Are there many dead?" Peyronella fired the questions at her until hushed by her mistress who interjected.

"Peyronella, give Ysabella some time!" She turned to Grace, who was beginning to feel less wobbly now she was clean and warm, "Is there much you can tell us, my dear? Did you see Raimond? Is Guilhem alright?"

Grace's eyes filled with tears but she answered, "I haven't seen your husband, but Guilhem told me he was unharmed. A lot of our men have been injured, several have died. There were too many of the Crusaders, they vastly outnumber us and some of our men are more used to carrying a scythe than a sword. I have seen men die today and more blood than I care to remember. I even had to bind the wounds of my own husband."

"Guilhem is hurt?!" Lady Agnes asked in consternation. "How badly?"

"A deep sword wound on his left arm, down through the muscle to the bone. He should heal but shouldn't fight again until it does. For this at least I am grateful."

At that moment Marguerida reappeared with a kitchen servant bearing food and drink and so Grace was spared any further discussion of her experiences of the day, at least for a short while. She managed to force a little food down and, finding that she was indeed hungry, took further bites of the sweetened bread and a large swallow of the honeyed wine, before she said anything further. Eventually, starting to feel a little more like herself she continued with her narrative.

"We were forced to retreat I am told, leaving our dead still on the ground and St Vincent to the Crusaders who have now blocked all access to the river. I fear that the wells will run dry before the fighting is over; I see no way Carcassona can prevail." The other women looked aghast and Lady Agnes held her belly protectively.

"Raimond will find a way!" she said. "He promised."

The door flew open at this point revealing Raimond Rogier Trencavel, almost as blood splattered as Grace had been and wearing a look of desperation.

"I see Ysabella had told you of the day's failure?" he said quietly. "I have tried to negotiate via messenger but they will have none of it! Other than to tell me King Peter of Aragon is interceding on our part and will be arriving here soon."

"Well that is something at least," his wife replied, "Surely they will listen to him?"

"I doubt it but I shall remain hopeful, My Lady," was his measured response. "Ysabella, how is Guilhem? I saw him being helped from the field."

"He will mend, My Lord. A nasty deep wound to his arm, he won't be able to fight again without risking losing the use of it."

Raimond nodded, "I would not expect a badly injured man to fight by my side, but I will miss his presence." Grace breathed an inward sigh of relief, she had worried that Guilhem would be expected to fight on despite his damaged arm.

"My love, I must go now," the Vescomtat addressed his wife. "I just needed you to see I was in one piece." He hugged her tightly and kissed her fiercely on the lips then, before she could protest, turned and headed out the door.

Lady Agnes sank onto her chair, she knew little of battles but she did know her husband, and his despair was very evident to her. Grace could see that the woman was concerned but this time could do nothing to reassure her; the food and drink, not to mention removing the blood-stained gown had revived her and she felt it was time to return to check on her own husband. She voiced this out loud and her mistress agreed but before letting her go she insisted on lending Grace one of her own gowns and taking the remains of the food and drink with her for Guilhem.

"You can't walk through the castel in only your shift and a blanket, and taking the food will mean you don't have to head to the hall later looking for something for him!" she exclaimed.

The chosen gown was very plain, and a little too tight in places but was nevertheless very serviceable and Grace thanked the woman profusely before taking her leave.

Arriving back at her own chamber she carefully opened the door, struggling to balance the heavy tray of vittals as she did so, eventually having to place it on the floor in order to gain access. Guilhem appeared to still be sleeping so she tiptoed across the room, depositing the tray on a shelf before quietly closing the door and climbing onto the bed besides him. She was asleep within moments, curled on her side with her face near to his.

Chapter 36 – Wounded Soldier

Exhausted as they both were by the day they had experienced, the pair of them slept soundly until the early hours of the morning, just before dawn, when the sun would sneak in, gilding the land with a rosy gold hue.

Guilhem stirred first, he rolled onto his injured arm which sent a frisson of pain shooting through him. His muffled expletive roused Grace and she sat up quickly - too quickly, her head span with the sudden movement, causing her to collapse back again.

"Urghh," She said, "I shouldn't have done that! Are you in pain, my love?"

"A little," Guilhem answered, "I just rolled onto the arm, that hasn't helped."

Grace sat, more cautiously this time. It was very dark in the room, the only light coming from the un-shuttered window, she could make out his face as a paler blur against the coverlet but that was all. Getting to her feet she stumbled to the shelf which held the candle and then realised she had no means of lighting it as there was no fire lit in the small hearth in the room.

She cursed under her breath but Guilhem obviously made out the sentiment, if not the words themselves as he sat up himself and said, "Look to my things over there," he gestured to the shelf where she had placed the tray of food the previous night, "there is a fire starting pouch there. If you can catch a spark on the charcloth you should be able to light the candle."

It took several attempts, a grazed knuckle and much cursing before Grace managed to direct a strong enough spark from the flint and steel onto the blackened cloth and thence to the candle - she held her breath as the tallow candle spluttered before the flame steadied, casting a faint light around the room.

In the yellow glow of the single flame Guilhem looked an unhealthy colour but after feeling his head and the injured arm (without removing the bandage) she could feel no trace of fever or heat which could indicate incipient infection.

"Are you hungry?" she asked him. "I brought some food in with me when I returned earlier but you were asleep and I didn't want to wake you."

"I am," he said, "also thirsty and need to relieve myself - which will be difficult with one hand."

"Surely you don't need both hands to hold it steady?" she quipped.

He smiled in return, "No but it will be difficult to unfasten the braies and hose one-handed."

Grace laughed, relieved that his sense of humour was still present. "Well that I can help you with – come, stand up." He did as she asked and she untied the knots in the cord to the hose, essentially just tubes of woollen fabric which ended at groin level on the inner leg and hip level on the outer and were tied to fastenings on the linen braies undergarment. The hose puddled to the floor and he stepped out of them, allowing her to loosen the tie to the braies so he could extract himself to urinate. "Really? Now?!" Grace laughed as the member thickened and stiffened.

He smiled sheepishly, "No, I doubt it, my love, but this is too stupid to know any better!" he wiggled his cock at her, making her giggle as she slid their waste bucket towards him.

Whilst he peed, with obvious relief if his deep sigh was anything to go by, Grace set about examining the tray of food. She had had the forethought to cover everything with a cloth before bringing the tray to their room and so the bread, although a little dry was perfectly edible. The soft cheeses were by now trying to escape from the platter on which they had been served but again were fine to eat and the honeyed wine, although not as cold as she herself would have liked was fine to drink. She poured a good measure of the drink into one of the goblets on the tray and handed it to Guilhem, who was by now seated on the bed. He drained it in one go and without saying anything she refilled it and handed it back; this time he sipped rather than quaffed.

"Can you manage some food?"

"Well my belly thinks my throat has been cut," he responded, "not that that is perhaps the best sentiment to express given current circumstances!"
Grace smiled thinly and put the laden tray on the bed between them, "No, perhaps not the best comparison, my husband!"

They nibbled companionably for a while, Guilhem consuming the majority of the food. Once he declared he had partaken of enough, Grace brought the candle over to the bed, the better to take a look at him. He was still quite pale and had dark circles under his eyes but in truth looked much better than when she had first lit the candle.

"You look better for eating," was all she said.

"I feel it," he confirmed in response to her. "The arm hurts, a lot actually, but that is good. When it first happened I didn't feel a thing, an old soldier once told me that once it starts to hurt it's healing - hopefully he was correct."

"We shall see," said Grace cautiously. "As long as the skin and muscle can knit together you should be fine. That does mean, as I said earlier, that you must keep the arm as still as possible. Raimond has already said you are not to fight again - thank God!"

Guilhem drew his black brows together in a frown, "We shall see about that!"

"Indeed we will," she retorted, "he has already said it, I heard it and I am not about to forget! Guilhem, you will be of little use, we will need to keep the arm strapped to your side if it is ever to heal and frankly, even if every man we have - and the women too - were to take up arms, there still wouldn't be enough of us to defeat the Pope's army! What, therefore, is the point?! Surely you can see that?"

He frowned again, "I do, but I know Raimond, he is a hot head and will insist on leading more missions. I will feel useless if I don't take part."

"You will be more useless to me dead or maimed for life!" Grace retorted, eyes full of angry tears. "Do as he has already said, my love, let the arm mend."

Guilhem looked mutinous, but the tears in her eyes moved him and he pursued the matter no further, instead suggesting that they try and sleep a little more before the sunrise. He didn't consider the issue closed however and planned to tackle his liege Lord on the morrow.

Chapter 37 – Dark Days

Guilhem awoke first this time and looked across at his wife, who lay on her back clad only in a linen shift, dark curls tumbled on the pillow and one arm was flung back above her head accentuating the curve of her breasts, dark nipples just visible through the thin fabric. He felt his desire rise but common sense, and a dull but insistent and painful throb in his arm, dictated that his passion would not be slaked – not this morning at least. He got carefully from the bed and used the waste bucket, managing to loosen the braies by himself, then looked to see if there was any of the honeyed wine left; there was but only a little and he drained it straight from the jug - it barely wet his lips.

Grace came awake to the sight of her husband clad only in braies, which were on the brink of falling down as he hadn't managed to retie the cord, shaking the jug as if more drink would magically appear. She burst out laughing at the sight, which made him smile in return.

"I take it you are thirsty, husband?"

"My mouth is as dry as a nun's..." he started to say and then, realising that his chosen analogy perhaps wasn't the best to share with his young wife, he quickly added, "...as a nun's habit".

Grace knew perfectly well what he had originally intended to say but thought better of letting him know that. "Well I shall help you to dress and we will head out to see what we can find to wet the, err, habit. Unless you would rather stay here and let me go alone?"

"No, we shall go together," he said, hoisting up his braies, "For the love of God, tie these up for me, woman, before they end up around my ankles!"

She laughed again but rose obligingly to assist him. It took some time to manoeuvre him into his clothes, hampered as they were by his bad arm, but they managed eventually and Grace even devised a sling of sorts in an attempt to keep the arm immobile. By the time they had finished Guilhem was sweating and grey of face; he began to realise just how difficult it would be to fight one-handed, when the pain caused by simply getting dressed was enough to make him feel sick. Grace wisely said nothing but instead pulled the dress Lady Agnes had provided over her head and fastened the ties at the side, before tending to her hair and placing the fine linen veil on her head. She was deliberately slow in her actions in order to give him time to recover.

Finally, she declared herself ready to face the world and was pleased to see that the brief respite she had provided had enabled Guilhem to gather himself, his face had lost the grey hue and he had mopped the beads of sweat from his face.

"Come," she said, opening the door, "let's go to the Hall first of all to see if anyone has laid out food."

They walked, her arm linked through his good one, at a steady pace until they reached the Great Hall, where the noise of people talking could be clearly heard, indicating that their quest for sustenance may be realised. The space was busy with people and a simple repast, the usual breads, soft cheeses and some over ripe figs, was laid out for anyone who wanted it. Grace motioned Guilhem to one of the bench seats and busied herself collecting a selection of items for them both. The only drink appeared to be wine, albeit watered, so she located a couple of goblets and a half full jug and managed to carry the whole lot back to Guilhem without tripping or dropping anything.

"It's nice to see your balance is restored," a voice said behind them as Grace deposited her gains on the table in front of her husband.

Guilhem looked behind him, it was one of the men he had been seated with the night his now wife had prostrated herself at his feet en-route to her seat in the Hall.

He laughed, "Yes, now she has captured my heart she has no need to fall at my feet!" The other man laughed in return and Grace blushed furiously but said nothing.

"You are wounded I see," the man said, "Still, you have your life AND your arm apparently, which is more than some."

Guilhem's face darkened. "A bad day for us!" he said vehemently.

"Aye, and I think there'll be more! We are too few to face down that hoard. The Vescomtat should talk terms so we don't end up like Beziers."
Guilhem held his tongue, not wanting to get involved in an argument and after a few pleasantries the man moved on.

"Do you think he's right?" Grace asked as soon as he was out of earshot. "Should we surrender now?"

"Aye, maybe we should - perhaps it would spare us further casualties but after Beziers, who can say they would want to talk terms? Unless of course those terms involved complete capitulation on our part and I doubt very much Raimond would ever accept that. This is his birth right and young Raimond after him. He will very much want to hold onto it!"

Grace nodded, wishing she could remember the dates she heard when visiting the Ciutat in the 21st Century, not that it would help she thought bleakly.

Guilhem applied himself to eating and drinking. He was young and strong and, as far as Grace could tell, there was no sign that his wound had become infected. *I'll check it later* she thought to herself as she demolished a bread roll with a curd-like cheese squished on top.

Guilhem grinned at her through a mouthful of food. "You don't hold back on eating, do you wife?!" he said once the mouthful was swallowed.

Grace laughed and was about to reply when Helena's acid tones interjected.

"I don't know what you two lovebirds have to laugh about," she sneered. "The world is going to hell and you two heretics are laughing! Perhaps the crusade is right in going after the Bon Crestian after all."

Before either of the stunned recipients of the vituperative comments could respond, the woman, head held high, flounced past to deposit a further tray of bread on the food table. Favia had obviously relegated her to kitchen duty in order to keep her away from Lady Agnes.

"Well!" someone said, "she certainly hasn't become any sweeter since her marriage. Where is De Merlon, by the way?"

Another voice replied, "Sent off to check the far reaches of the Vescomtat's lands. Probably glad to get away from her! Don't mind her, you two," the owner of the voice nodded in Guilhem and Grace's general direction, "she is a sour-faced wench whom nobody wanted, but she can do you no harm."

Guilhem raised his goblet in acknowledgement but said nothing. Meanwhile out of sight but not earshot, Helena overheard every word and bristled with indignation, she would find a way to bring Guilhem and the upstart Ysabella down, if it was the last thing she did!

Grace looked at her husband, "I wish I knew why she hated me so!"

He hugged her briefly with his good arm, "You are all she isn't," was all he said.

About to reply, Grace's words were halted by a commotion of raised voices and the sound of running feet.

"They're in St Michel!" someone said.

Guilhem rose to his feet, "We must find Raimond!"

"Husband, someone will already have called for him, you know that."

Guilhem looked crestfallen. "I would speak to him though," he said.

Grace nodded and they made their way, with some difficulty, through the throng of excited people. Spotting Raimond through the crowd, Guilhem called to him.

"Cousin! A word?"

Raimond Rogier beckoned him forward. "How is your arm?" he enquired solicitously. "Ysabella told me it is a bad injury but should heal with time."

"It hurts, but from what I could see it was a clean cut, it was even cleaner once this one had Favia wash it out with aqua vitae! Cousin, what are we to do now? What is happening with St Michel? Have they really taken it so easily? Did we not resist?"

The Vescomtat looked harried. "So many questions! I don't know the answer to most of them myself. You are welcome to join me as I meet with the council BUT you will not take part in any further fighting. You would be a liability with your injury, and in any case I fear Ysabella may damage me if you attain any more wounds!" He was smiling as he said that, trying to make light of the fact that he didn't want Guilhem to fight, but Grace could feel the tension in her husband and see the set lines in his face. His cousin obviously spotted this too for he added, "You will be of greater use to me here in the Ciutat ensuring the guards are doing their jobs. It would appear that they were sleeping in the dawn hours and therefore didn't see the invaders until St Michel was already occupied!"

Guilhem appeared slightly mollified at the thought of still being of use, even if he wasn't in the thick of the action. "Will they be punished? The guardsmen that is?"

Raimond shook his head, "We need all the men we have, they will be reprimanded of course, perhaps you could do that, I know the men respect you, but we can't afford to lose them. Come. The council awaits. By your leave, My Lady?"

He bowed his head at Grace who nodded, and the two men set off towards the painted hall, leaving her to wonder what she should do next; attend Lady Agnes she supposed and, mind made up, she headed out of the Hall.

Lady Agnes, together with Peyronella and Marguerida, were, as Grace had half suspected, in a state of mild hysteria, not helped by young Raimond charging around the relatively small space wielding a wooden sword. Unlike Grace herself they were very much contained inside and had to rely on information from visitors, of which there had been few. The young ladies-in-waiting flew to Grace's side as she entered the room, twittering and fluttering rather like baby birds but demanding information rather than a tasty worm.

"Girls! Hush!" Lady Agnes implored. "Let Ysabella at least shut the door!"

The two girls backed away a little allowing Grace fully into the room, whereupon young Raimond ran at her with his wooden sword demanding she surrender to him. She smiled, at that moment he looked very much like his father, the smile faded however as she recalled the Vescomtat's fate.

"Here," she said to the small boy, proffering a sweet roll she had stuffed in the pocket of her gown in case she was hungry later. "Sit quietly and eat this so I may talk to your mama and the ladies."

Ravenous, as usual, he took the roll with glee and promptly fell to the floor where he began to munch away.

"What news?" Lady Agnes said.

"None good I fear, Guilhem has gone with Raimond to meet with the council but it appears that St Michel was taken early this morning, the guards were asleep and didn't sound the alarm," Grace replied.

"And Guilhem, his arm? how is that?"
"Hurting he says, and Raimond Rogier has forbade him to fight any further which has mightily displeased him!"

"I can imagine," Lady Agnes said with a sad smile. "What is it with men and fighting? Even the little one feels the need to carry his sword. The world would be a more peaceful place I think if the men bore the children and the women ruled!"

"Agreed," said Grace, as the two younger women laughed at the idea of women being in charge and men being pregnant. "Now, for the moment we can do nothing about what is happening outside the walls, our menfolk will have to remain in charge. There is no point in you worrying about something you can't change, it isn't good for the baby. How are you feeling now, is the child still moving, are your legs or fingers still swollen?" As she was asking the questions Grace was surreptitiously examining the pregnant woman, who was seated but had her legs raised on a small padded stool; aside from dark circles under the eyes she actually looked better than she had for a few days, the puffiness was not so apparent.

"He or she is moving but not wriggling so much, Dame Balsace said yesterday that it was because it had moved into the right position for birthing, so I may be nearly ready to deliver."

"Let me see, stand up for me," Grace said, moving to help the woman to her feet. Standing, it did appear as if the pregnant belly had lost its round high shape and had dropped lower; with her lady's approval, she moved her hands over the stomach, pressing gently and being rewarded by the child inside pushing back strongly. From what she could feel the child had indeed moved into a head down position, but she suspected that it was still 'facing' the wrong way - the back of the skull against the woman's pelvic bone, which would make for a painful delivery. Still it was better than breach. "Do you feel any pressure here?" she indicated the pelvic floor.

"Yes indeed," came the reply. "I can barely walk to be honest and my back is hurting."

"I think you are very near delivery," Grace said soothingly, "and all you can do is wait and be calm. If your back is painful, try to lay on your side on the bed and have one of us rub the base of your spine. Here, let me show you and the girls." She led the woman to the bed and observed the slow waddling gait so common in the last stages of pregnancy; once lying on the bed Grace showed the two younger women how to massage the base of the back, firmly but not too hard and the Lady Agnes groaned in delight.

"That feels so good, Ysabella. However do you know such things at your age?"

"From her mother," came a voice at the door. "She is a skilled healer and Ysabella takes after her." Favia entered the room, "I came to see if anything is needed in here?"

"Drinks perhaps," was the response from Peyronella, "We have very little to keep our thirsts quenched."
"I'll see what I can do, water is very scarce now the wells are almost dry but we still have wine and beer in the castel."

Grace looked round on hearing this; "What about the water we fetched from the river? Has that all gone? It should have lasted a while longer yet!"

"Indeed it should, Ysabella, except some in the kitchens paid no heed to the idea of conserving what we have and have carried on as usual - including washing linens on a daily basis, despite the water being locked away!" Favia replied caustically.

"Unbelievable!" was all Grace could think to say. "Well wine and beer it will have to be then. Perhaps honey in the wine for Lady Agnes?"

"As I said, I will see what I can do!" Favia said crossly, the strain of the current situation was obviously getting to her.

"Thank you," Lady Agnes said soothingly. "I'm sure you will do your very best, you always do."

Slightly mollified by the praise, Favia went about her business and Grace also took her leave of the three women, taking young Raimond off to his nursery maid as she left. The little boy chattered incessantly as they walked along, he was as bright as a button and very curious - particularly about Guilhem's arm injury - wanting to know all about it. Grace stopped and dropped to her knees.

"It is a horrible cut, right here," she drew a finger across the little one's chubby upper arm, "I could see right down to his bone. Any harder a blow and his arm would have been cut off. Fighting is a horrid thing, Master Raimond, full of blood and gore - it is not glamorous and the right side doesn't always win!"

The boy's lips quivered and his eyes filled with tears.

"My papa will win," he said defiantly, "just you wait and see!"

Grace made no response, simply standing and setting off walking again, but she noticed the small chubby hand that reached for hers clung on more tightly than it had before.

It was late that evening before Grace saw Guilhem again and she had already retired to their room wondering where on earth he may be. Just as she was about to get into bed the door opened and he entered looking tired and dishevelled, the grey pallor had returned and she could tell the injury was paining him from the thin drawn set of his lips. She flew to his side and, taking his face in her hands, kissed him gently on the lips; his good arm went around her waist and he returned the kiss, followed by a deep sigh as he released her.

"I needed that," he said, "needed to be reminded that there is goodness in this world."

Grace drew her husband to the bed and he sat down with obvious relief. "I need to change that bandage and check the wound," she said. "Let me do it now, I found more candles so there's enough light for me to see well enough."

He nodded his assent and she helped him to remove surcoat and shirt before carefully unwinding the bandage. There was no sickly smell of infection obvious and she could detect no abnormal heat in the arm; good, she thought as she unwound the final strip exposing the gash. It had begun to crust over already and she had spotted only a small amount of blood on the bandages; both signs that the wound was knitting together. Guilhem craned his neck to look at the arm.

"How is it?" he asked.

"Healing nicely, I'm going to clean it again with the aqua vitae and rewrap it."

He sat stoically whilst she ministered to him and she said nothing further until the arm was neatly re-bandaged and fastened once more to his chest.

"What has been happening today?" she asked finally.

"Everything and yet nothing," he replied. "Raimond is convinced we can hold out, that the Crusaders will simply fade away the longer the siege lasts, and he may be right but I can't help thinking that even if they don't conquer us this time that they will be back again, the next time perhaps with even more men!"

"Water is running out you know," she told him, "According to Favia much of the river water we stored has been wasted by the castel's kitchen staff and a couple of wells are almost dry too. Sickness will soon start to spread."

Guilhem looked bleak. "It may have already started. I overheard a couple of men saying that they had heard of the bloody flux running riot in parts of the Ciutat."

It was Grace's turn to look bleak now; she was aware that the term bloody flux was a reference to dysentery or

301

typhus, both of which would be fatal without proper means of rehydrating the patient, and with no water to do so and no way of keeping a patient clean, the disease could spread like wildfire amongst the populace.

"He has to agree a surrender!" she said, "Surely it will be better than watching people die in the streets!"

"I tend to agree, my love, but it isn't our decision to make. I hear that Peter of Aragon is on his way here to intercede on Carcassona's behalf, Raimond will do nothing until he has met with him."

"Let us hope the King can talk some sense into someone!" Grace exclaimed, "It is clear that the Crusaders are hell bent on destroying our way of life and want our land - but what is land without people to tend it? If they drive us all away or kill us all then who will they have left to sow the seeds and reap the harvests. Short sighted avarice appears to be in charge - not the will of God!"

"You are right, my love, God's will has little to do with this, the Pope and his envoys are simply jealous that the riches of this land do not fill the coffers of the Catholic Church; the crusading army is a motley band of mercenary Northerners, second sons, out to make a name for themselves and steal a castle in the doing so."

On this note the two of them extinguished the candles and retired to bed. Grace snuggled as close to her husband as she could with care for his injury.

"I wish I could take you, right now," Guilhem whispered to her, "but I fear my arm will not stand for such exertions."

Grace's eyes twinkled in the darkened room, "How about from behind - you could stand at the edge of the bed."

"And you could bend over!" he replied before she could finish. "Ysabella, you are a wanton and I love you for it!"

Within a matter of minutes they were in position, Grace shivered with anticipatory desire as his long fingers felt between her legs.

"Gods woman! You're as ready as I am!" he exclaimed.

"Why should I not be?" she enquired and then gasped as he entered her with one strong thrust.

She pushed up and back welcoming him in and felt his good hand grasp her hip.

"Steady," he said, "or this will be over too quickly."

He began to surge in and out, varying the rhythm and depth of penetration, hearing her moans of pleasure build until it was too much for him and he let go; a cry of exultation left his lips, seconds later she joined him in release.

Panting and rueing the fact that he couldn't simply collapse on her back for a moment, Guilhem withdrew; his legs were trembling and he tottered unsteadily round to his side of the bed and got in. Grace lay as she was for a moment, before dragging herself up the bed next to him.

"We should try that again," she said.

He laughed, "Perhaps not straight away though, eh?! Sleep now, wife."

And sleep they both did until the dawn light began to leach through the partly closed shutters.

Chapter 38 – Besieged

The 4th of August was as stiflingly hot as the rest of the summer had been; Grace wiped a weary hand across her sweat-soaked forehead and plucked at the neck of her gown in a vain attempt to allow some air to her body; perspiration was trickling between her breasts and her hair was plastered to the back of her neck - she couldn't recall ever feeling so uncomfortably sticky. Of course, standing over a vat of boiling water didn't help but she had offered to take charge of sterilising, not that she had called it that, the remaining river water in order to ensure the castel, in particular Lady Agnes, had at least some clean water at hand. She had first of all insisted that the water be strained through some fine muslin, which had greatly amused the kitchen staff until, that is, they saw the grit and other detritus caught in the cloth. Now she was keeping guard until the water had boiled for at least 30 minutes - of course she had no way of timing this accurately but she was resolutely counting 1 to 60 in her head and making a charcoal mark on the wall each time she did so; by this rough and ready reckoning she thought the requisite time had been reached but she was determined not to leave the precious water unattended. She called for two of the servants to damp down the fire under the huge pot which was too heavy to be hung from one of the kitchens sturdy iron stands and so had been placed on a large flat stone directly on the fire itself. Once the fire had died down and the pot was cool enough to move, she intended to have it moved to a small store room - one that only Favia had the key to.

"Oof!" She said to no one in particular, "I am hotter than the hottest hot thing!" One of the servant boys who had helped put the fire out giggled at her inane comment and she grinned at him. "I need to cool down a little," she addressed the lad directly, "would you please stand guard until I return? If anyone tries to help themselves to this water tell them it is intended for the Lady Agnes in her lying in by orders of the Vescomtat."

The boy stood tall proud to be selected for such an important job, "Yes Madona!" he responded eagerly.

The air outside the kitchen's courtyard was little cooler than within but at least she wasn't also enveloped in steam. She fanned her face with hands looking for a shady place to sit and spied somewhere under one of the twin elm trees. Just as she was about to sink to the ground, shouting from the hoardings which overlooked the suburb of Castellare to the south of the Ciutat caused a sudden rush of guards and soldiers into the castel's enclosed courtyard. Grace pushed herself back against the tree and amidst the confusion managed to gather that the Crusaders were trying to occupy Castellare, Carcassonne's one remaining suburb, well-fortified in comparison to St Michel, but still vulnerable. Amongst the crowd she spotted Guilhem and began to push her way towards him, the men moved out of her way without too much of a struggle; knowledge of her healing skills had spread and Guilhem was a well-respected fellow soldier.

"Guilhem!" she cried as she got nearer.

His head raised and he made his way towards her.

"What are you doing out here, my love?" he questioned.

"Would you believe me if I said I was trying to cool down?" she said.

"I'd believe whatever you told me." he smiled. "You do look very hot. What have you been doing?"

She grinned, "Boiling water to make it safe for Lady Agnes - the child will be born soon, and I wanted to make sure there was clean water. The wells are almost dry so I've used the last of the river water. Favia will keep it under lock and key for me."

He frowned, "The sickness is spreading too. It would be best if you keep within the walls of the castel my sweet, bringing the sickness to my cousin's wife and child would not be a good idea!"

Grace nodded her head. "What is happening in Castellare? Will they take it?"

Guilhem sighed, "Probably, but not without a fight. Castellare has better defences and as far as I understand we will employ the archers to shoot down into the bourg to prevent the invaders getting close to the walls of the Ciutat before we send men in to fight."

"Tell me you won't try to join in?!" Grace implored him.

"I won't. I can't draw a bow with this arm in any case, but I will support my men by standing in the hoardings. I'll be careful, my love, I promise. Now kiss me as I'd better go."

Grace kissed him on the lips and watched as he headed out of the castel and over the bridge into the Ciutat. Sighing, she turned back to the kitchen courtyard; the water would be too hot to move still but she could at least take a couple of large jugs of it up to Lady Agnes' domain.

Sounds of fighting could be heard through most of that day, much to the consternation of the women gathered with Lady Agnes, Dame Balsace had effectively now taken up residence in the chambers as the birth grew imminent and perched like a wizened crow in the corner of the room. Lady Agnes was visibly upset, as she had received no word of her husband's well-being and the two younger women were becoming more and more frightened by the protracted siege. Grace was glad to get away on the pretext of having to assist with any possible wounded. The atmosphere in the Lady's chamber was claustrophobic and unsettling and the pregnant woman now had the experienced midwife with her.

Castellare didn't fall that day and, according to Guilhem as they lay side by side in bed that evening, the Crusaders suffered heavy losses as a result of the arrow bombardment. He smiled as he recounted the younger elements of the defensive operation pelting the attackers with whatever they could lay their hands on; rotten fruit and vegetables, stones, rocks and even horse manure.

"Some of those knights will not be fragrant this evening!" he laughed but then said quietly, "They'll be back though." Knowing it to be true, Grace simply squeezed his good hand.

Back they were, but not for some three days when they changed tactics by utilising siege engines which bombarded the walls of the suburb with rocks. The troops of the Ciutat responded by literally throwing everything they had at the invaders, including despatching burning, pitch-soaked rags, one of which destroyed the canvas covering on what turned out to be a shelter for a group of soldiers who, unbeknown to the defenders, had set a mine at the base of a wall.

To the inhabitants of the Ciutat, the constant pounding of the missiles hitting the walls was yet another misery to endure. All but one of the wells was now dry and sickness was running rampant through the population; this together with the heat and close quarters resulted in a stench which could be smelled from the castel. Peyronella wrinkled her nose; even in Lady Agnes' chamber and with sweet smelling herbs strewn around, the odour was apparent. She opened her mouth to say something but thought better of it. If it was bad in here what must it be like in the Ciutat? The relief felt when the relentless pounding stopped was palpable and they all began to believe that Carcassonne was indeed invulnerable, a lightness of spirit filled the Ciutat that evening.

The relief was short lived however, at dawn the following day Guilhem, Grace and everyone else was awoken abruptly from sleep by the sound of an explosion; the mine, set previously, had been fired.

"Holy Mother!" Guilhem blasphemed and leapt out of bed, causing a white-hot bolt of pain to shoot through his arm. "Aaaaaargh!" he exclaimed, "I keep forgetting about this damned injury!"

Grace rolled bleary-eyed out of the bed to join him, there was no sign of blood seeping through the bandages which she had changed again the previous evening, it had likely simply been the jarring action as he landed which had caused the pain.

"What was that noise?" she asked, almost afraid to hear the answer.

"I would guess a mine being set off," he replied. "Which would explain the shelter some of the lads mentioned burning; it was used as a cover to get closer to the walls. I must go, my love, to see what is happening. Meet me in the Hall at midday?"

Grace was too tired and too thirsty to protest at him leaving; she had been restricting her fluid intake to try and conserve the remaining water but the lack of it was beginning to make her feel dizzy and have a permanent mild but persistent headache. After helping him dress and insisting he take a long drink of their precious water mixed with a sweet wine, she herself took a goblet, the temptation was strong to fill it to the brim and drain it, but she contented herself with merely swilling her mouth round with a couple of mouthfuls.

With little to do and not daring to venture outside the walls of the castel, Grace decided she should attend Lady Agnes. She was even more lightheaded when she arrived there to be greeted by Marguerida, who rolled her eyes as if to say, 'nothing has changed here!' The bedchamber was stuffy and uncomfortably hot, Grace felt pin pricks of sweat break her forehead.

"Why is it so warm in here?" she asked, moving over to one of the firmly closed shutters. "This isn't healthy for you, My Lady." She swung the shutters wide, allowing a draft of dawn air into the foetid space.

Peyronella raced to her side. "We must keep them closed, Dame Balsace says so, she says the sickness will come in if we let air in."

Grace shook her head, "The sickness is caused by the dirty water which is all the people in the Ciutat have to drink. You have clean water, I boiled all of the supply for here myself and it is kept under lock and key. The heat in here and the lack of air is more likely to make our Lady ill."

Lady Agnes, who was lying on her side on the bed, weakly said, "It does feel a little better now - leave the shutters be, I will tell Dame Balsace I prefer it so. Ysabella, what was the loud noise earlier?"

Grace moved across the room. "Guilhem seems to think they have mined the walls at Castellare, he's gone to see for himself. How are you, My Lady, any signs yet that the baby is coming?"
Lady Agnes shook her head ruefully, "None and I wish it would hurry up."

Dame Balsace chose that moment to hobble into the chamber, she began to gesture at the open shutter and chatter away in her thick dialect.

"It stays open!" insisted her patient, "I already feel better."

The old crone "hmmphed" and looked accusingly at Grace who said soothingly, "It's alright, the sickness won't come in."

Dama Balsace merely glared, took up her seat by the side of the bed and was soon drowsing, her almost toothless mouth wide open emitting snuffling snores.

This time it was Lady Agnes who rolled her eyes and spoke to her pregnant belly, "Child, please come out so I may have some peace!"

Grace and the other two ladies-in-waiting giggled whilst the old lady continued to snuffle. The round belly visibly tightened and Lady Agnes caught her breath.

"A contraction?" asked Grace.

"Maybe, but a small one if so - still it is a sign something may be happening at last!" came the response.

"Let us hope so," Grace smiled. "Now, if there is nothing useful I can do here, should I leave and try to find out what is happening?"

The pregnant woman nodded, "Yes please, Ysabella, as you can see I have enough assistance at the moment." She smiled as she looked over to the soundly sleeping midwife and beckoned Grace out of the door.

It took some time for Grace to find anyone willing to speak to her until finally, a soldier she recognised as one of Guilhem's own men was able to give her the news that the Crusaders had indeed broken through the walls of Castellare and had proceeded, "In a noisy fashion, Mistress!" he had exclaimed with some contempt, to take control of the suburb, "not that they will find much to help them," he added, "as the residents brought all their edibles into the Ciutat."

Grace thanked him for the information and then asked, "What happens now then?"

The man shrugged his shoulders, how was he supposed to know the gesture implied. She debated whether it was worth imparting this further piece of bad news to Lady Agnes but decided she would want to know, so set off back to her Chamber. As expected, the pregnant woman was none too happy to hear of further misfortune but she thanked Grace for the update. The contractions had not returned and Grace suspected they were what in her training was referred to as Braxton Hicks - practice contractions. The birth was still not imminent.

The day dragged on, the heat increasing and with it the stench; it was impossible to escape the smell even within the castel itself and even Grace, well known for her appetite, found the idea of eating sickened her. Guilhem shot her a worried look as they sat side by side in the Hall during an early supper.

"It's not like you to leave food," he commented, "Are you feeling unwell?"

She sighed, "It's just the heat and the stench from the Ciutat turning my stomach."

He kissed her gently on the cheek, "Ah, my love, I wish I had sent you away to Minerve."

She smiled, "Do you really think I would have gone?"

Guilhem laughed, "No, I suppose not, and I am glad you were here to look after my arm - I fear that without your brutal cleansing I could already be suffering from the fever and on the way to losing it."

"Well I'm glad you finally agree that the extra pain was worth it. I wish I had stitched the wound too, in fact I may yet depending on how it seems to heal!"

Guilhem was about to say something when a sudden commotion stopped him in his tracks. Leaving her sitting disconsolately alone Guilhem went on his way; she didn't want to return to Lady Agnes and it was too early to go to her own chamber. Fortunately, she wasn't alone long, Guilhem returned with the news that the occupation of Castellare had ended; the invaders had foolishly left only a handful of men to guard the suburb whilst the majority withdrew to camp. The soldiers watching over the suburb from the safety of Carcassonne's ramparts had seen the departure and had rapidly organised a sortie, during which the few Crusaders left within had been annihilated and the suburb set to the torch to deny the besiegers the shelter of the houses set beneath the walls of the Ciutat itself. He offered to help Grace up into one of the watchtowers so she could see the flames. It was on the tip of her tongue to ask why it was acceptable for him to accompany her whereas he had been none too happy when she had ventured up alone, but she thought better of it and allowed him to help her up the rough wooden ladder. From the shelter and safety of the tower the couple were able to look out not only over Castellare but at the assembled army. Grace caught her breath at the sheer numbers of men, tents and equipment spread out amongst the trees and along the river; they at least had ready access to water and she could see a group of horses being led down to drink.

"We don't have a chance, do we?" she said to her husband who sighed deeply.

"No, I don't think we do, my love." He suddenly pointed at the encampment, "I do believe King Peter has arrived. See the large tent over there flying the standard of Toulouse — red with the golden cross?" She nodded. "Next to that can you see another pennant with red and gold stripes?" She nodded again. "That is the standard of Aragon, I suppose we can expect him soon then."

Almost as he uttered those words a single messenger could be seen approaching the main gate of the Ciutat and a parchment was passed to the guard. From their lofty vantage point they could see this scrap of paper being passed to the hands of another, younger guard, who began to race through the buildings and people within the Ciutat towards the castel.

"We should go down now," Guilhem suggested, "I need to be with Raimond once the King arrives."

He began to descend the ladder and beckoned her to join him so his body, one armed as he was, could shield and protect her. Once on the ground he hurried her into the castel, telling her to go to Lady Agnes. She began to argue that she should go with him, but he stilled her protestations with a kiss and sent her on her way.

Lady Agnes was pacing, in so far as a heavily pregnant woman could pace; back and forth across her chamber. News that King Peter had arrived had obviously been communicated to her and she felt her place to be next to her husband. Raimond Rogier had however vetoed her presence and she was obviously not best pleased at being excluded.

"But, My Lady!" Marguerida was saying in a soothing placatory tone as Grace arrived, "You would not normally be included in such counsel."

Although this was true, it didn't improve Lady Agnes' mood and she rounded on Grace as she entered the room.

"I suppose you know what's happening?" she snapped.

Taken aback by the tone of voice Grace said quietly, "Our soldiers recaptured Castellare and burned it to the ground, and King Peter has arrived – other than that I know no more than you. Guilhem sent me away before the King arrived."

Lady Agnes seemed slightly mollified once she heard that Grace had been excluded too and was persuaded to lay on the bed for a while. Her son was brought in for a brief while before his bedtime and the youngster's boisterous good humour appeared to boost her mood still further, although to anyone who knew her there was a wary look in the pale eyes that spoke of her disquiet.

Grace stayed in the chamber, chatting and helping keep her mistress calm until the darkening sky forced them to light the beeswax candles in the sconces, but still no word came about the outcome of King Peter's visit. Finally, just as the Lady Agnes was about to drift into a fitful sleep and the two younger ladies-in-waiting plus the ever-present Dame Balsace had already succumbed to slumber in their chairs, the door opened to reveal both Raimond Rogier and Guilhem.

Grace ran and embraced her husband, a questioning look in her eyes, he shook his head at her unspoken query leaving his Lord to explain to his now wide awake wife.

"The King has gone, he couldn't or wouldn't help other than to offer the terms that Arnaud Amaury made – that is, I would be allowed to leave Carcassona with eleven companions and as many of our possessions as we could carry. The Crusaders would then occupy the Ciutat. There was no mention of protection for our citizens, nothing said about would happen to them if I left, so naturally I could not accept."

Tears ran silently down Lady Agnes' face. "So this goes on then, husband? We stay here like rats in a trap whilst the water runs out and the people die of sickness and thirst!"

The Vescomtat was obviously surprised at his wife's vehement words but could not refute them; instead he chose only to brush a kiss on the top of her head and then leave.

Guilhem asked permission to retire with his wife and Lady Agnes merely nodded her head as Dame Balsace fussed around her.

Chapter 39 – Beginnings And Endings

The days following the refusal of the Crusaders' terms descended into a nightmare of sickness and death for the ordinary people of Carcassonne, the last of the wells dried up and the acrid smell of smoke from the burning of Castellare added to the appalling smells of decay and illness that hung over the town.

The Crusaders meanwhile had space, food aplenty from gathering in early harvests and plenty of river water; they were however unable to make any progress in breaching the Ciutat's walls and men were beginning to drift quietly away to attend to their own families and property.

Three days after the King's departure Lady Agnes finally went into labour; her waters broke early in the morning and Marguerida was sent to fetch Grace – the two younger ladies-in-waiting were allowed to stay with their mistress, but as unmarried girls were not to be present during the actual birth. It was yet another hot day and Grace felt for the woman as the labour progressed slowly but inexorably. Favia was called to act as a translator for Dame Balsace and, much to their own relief, Peyronella and Marguerida were sent away.

The long day dragged on with little evidence that the birth was imminent, Lady Agnes seemed to be in an extraordinary amount of pain, complaining that her back was breaking. Grace wished for the gas and air and epidurals of a 21st century delivery room but with none to hand she thought quickly; during one of the deliveries she had been present at, the baby's head had been the wrong way around, the hard back of the skull pressing against the mother's spine; with no way of confirming this to be the case in this instance she decided to act on her intuition and via Favia told the wizened Dame Balsace of her suspicion.

The old crone nodded and said something which was translated as, "You may be right, let us see if she is still strong enough to get onto her hands and knees."

Grace nodded, it was what she would have suggested. The three women helped the tired woman to get onto her knees, she protested at the idea but the relief of pressure on her back was immediately obvious. The elderly midwife lifted the pregnant woman's shift and peered between her legs, beckoning Grace to look too – the child's head was finally crowning.

"I see the child," Grace said encouragingly, "A few more pushes and he will be out!"

Lady Agnes took her weight on her elbows, bottom raised and pushed with the next few contractions until the head emerged.

"Now pant," said Grace demonstrating what she meant.

With the next contraction the baby was delivered into her waiting hands whilst Dame Balsace looked on approvingly. The child was a healthy size and a girl; the old midwife cut the cord with a sharp knife she had passed several times through a candle flame whilst Grace rubbed the baby with a piece of linen to both clean her and illicit a cry. The child emitted a lusty screech and Lady

Agnes smiled as she turned onto her back and allowed the midwife to assist with the delivery of the afterbirth.

"So, do I have another son to take up arms, or a daughter to stay by my side?"

"You have a beautiful daughter," Grace replied passing her the baby, now wrapped in a clean linen towel.

The little girl was already sucking on her own fist and rooted for the breast as soon as she was placed in her mother's waiting arms. There was no suitable wet nurse for this child as the woman chosen to fulfil the role had been one of the few to flee the Ciutat when news of the Crusaders approach had come and Lady Agnes had already accepted that unlike when her son was born, she would have to feed this child herself, at least until another wet nurse could be found. Dame Balsace helped the newborn find the nipple and her mother's eyes opened wide with surprise as the child latched on immediately.

"Oooh!" she exclaimed, "I didn't think it would feel like that! She's so strong!"

Grace and the old midwife worked together to clean the new mother and restore the bed chamber to a state of neatness whilst the baby fed industriously. Just as they had finished the task there was a tentative knock and Raimond Rogier poked his head around the door.

"Is all well? Do I have another son?"

"A beautiful daughter," his wife replied from the bed, "Come and see."

He crossed the room in a few long strides and perched on the bed, his eyes filled with love as he watched his new daughter and wife.

"She is beautiful, just like her mother," he said. "What should we name her?"

Lady Agnes looked up from her daughter, "Alaís, for your mother."

He smiled. "A good name."

Grace chose this moment to leave the family alone, Dame Balsace and Favia would be able to manage without her and she needed desperately to be with Guilhem.

By the time she reached their chamber it was very late and Guilhem was already sound asleep. As noiselessly as possible she shed her dress and shoes and climbed on the bed next to him, she was thirsty and hungry but wanted nothing more than to be close to him as he slept. He stirred briefly and tried to roll onto his side but the bandaged arm was in the way; Grace stroked his head gently and he drifted back into sleep, she placed her hand on his uninjured arm and eventually sleep claimed her too.

The sporadic attacks on the walls of the Ciutat continued to no avail over the following five days, during which time Lady Agnes and baby Alaís thrived whilst the general population sank into an apathy born of hunger, thirst and increasing pessimism. Guilhem moved amongst the people, careful always to avoid personal contact, and reported to Raimond that they couldn't hold out much longer. Raimond himself had sunk into a deep depression despite, or perhaps because of, the new arrival to his family, he held himself responsible for the dire straits in which they found themselves.

The receipt of a message from Arnaud Armaury did little to lighten his mood; the brief and to the point missive offered new terms to the people of Carcassonne.

"Ha!" the Vescomtat exclaimed, "He will now let us all leave but wearing only our under garments and carrying no belongings. Offers me and nine of my men safe conduct to further discuss this!"

The young man marched around his council chamber clearly in no mind to accept these new terms.

"Cousin," Guilhem implored, "Think of your children, man! At least this way they will live; if this siege goes on for very much longer the bloody flux will spread within the castel – and we have no water as it is!"

Raimond looked as if he was going to argue but he suddenly slumped, defeated, into his chair.

"There is no choice, is there?" One by one the men in the room shook their heads. "Guilhem, I would have you remain here whilst I visit the cleric." He then named the men who would accompany him and left the room to visit his wife and children.

323

Guilhem waited impatiently for his cousin to return and was soon joined by Grace. A matter of minutes after she arrived there was a sound of raised voices and running feet; Bernard Pujol, one of the knights who had set off with the Vescomtat burst into the room in obvious distress.

"They lied to us!" he shouted, "the moment we entered their camp they fell upon us and took the Vescomtat away in chains!"

There was uproar amongst the assembled – honour was unspoken amongst their people – to break terms in such a way was an anathema.

"Did they say what would happen to the rest of us?" asked one of the older men.

"We can leave tomorrow as per their original terms; they say they will hold Raimond Rogier until we have all left the Ciutat."

Only Grace amongst them knew that Vescomtat Trencavel would never be freed and she held her head in her hands.

"Guilhem," she whispered, "I should go to Lady Agnes and tell her what has happened. Assuming we have no choice but to leave tomorrow, would you find some way of asking if she at least may leave in a cart or some such? Surely a good Christian," and here she deliberately mocked the Catholic Arnaud Amaury, "will let a newly delivered noblewoman maintain some dignity, especially as they are holding her husband in chains!"

He nodded but said nothing as the debate whirled around the room and Grace fled to tell her mistress of the plight which had befallen them.

Surprisingly Lady Agnes was more sanguine than Grace would have thought possible, but then again, she had the unshakeable belief of the region that a word once given would not be retracted – she obviously firmly believed that her husband would be released once Carcassonne was emptied.

It was a long and sad night for the people of the Ciutat, Guilhem had spoken in front of as many of the townspeople as possible to tell them that at first light tomorrow they must leave through the main southern gate, that they should wear only their braies and undershirt in the case of the men and a shift for the women; that they should attempt to carry none of their possessions with them for fear of confiscation at the least, death at the worst, and that they should leave quietly and with dignity.

"Remember we are still undefeated, these proud walls have not fallen!" he thundered.

He and Grace slept not at all that night and they suspected no one other than children did so either. By dawn's first light the main gate was opened and a farmer's cart filled with hay which was covered by a rough blanket, was driven through.

"For the Lady Agnes, her children and ladies-in-waiting," said the driver brusquely but not unkindly and then sat to wait until the evacuation began.

In the privacy of their chamber Grace clung to Guilhem, reluctant to leave; this may not be her life but she was living every moment of it in a very visceral way. There was a rap on the door, Guilhem opened it to a young soldier with reddened eyes who informed him of the arrangements for the Lady Agnes. Shutting the door once more, Guilhem turned to his wife of less than a month.

"Dearest one," he said, finding it difficult to speak through a thickening in his throat, "I want you to go with your mistress, she will need you and I believe you will be safer. I will find you as soon as I can, but I want you to leave with her in the cart they have sent and get all of you as far away as possible. Do you understand?"

"Yes, but…" she stuttered through tears which had sprung unbidden and were rolling down her face.

"There are no buts," he said tenderly, wiping the tears away with his one good hand. "I would know you safe, my beloved. I will find you and we will be together. That I swear. Now go to your mistress."

He kissed her deeply, opened the door and pushed her out. She fled wearing just her shift as commanded but with the heavy weight of his ruby ring banging against her rib cage – she would not part with that, no matter what the Crusaders said and unless she was stripped naked the ring would not be visible.

Lady Agnes was silent as the small entourage made their way out of the castel and across the bridge to the waiting cart. She accepted the assistance of the driver with a small dignified smile and nestled amongst the blankets whilst baby Alaís was handed to her.

"It's perfectly comfortable," she reassured her scared son as he was lifted in next to her.

Peyronella, Marguerida and finally Grace clambered on board and with no further ceremony the driver turned the cart and headed for the Porta Narbona. Grace scanned the crowds for her husband and when she found him she locked eyes for as long as she could…if it were to be the last time she saw him, she was determined to remember what he looked like.

The cart and its occupants led the way out of the Ciutat and though the enemy encampment, a few jeers, but not many, could be heard from the soldiers. Grace held her head high and looked straight ahead as did Lady Agnes; she didn't therefore see the venomous look Helena shot her way, didn't see the woman split away from the rest of the procession and intercept a couple of soldiers, pointing at the cart as she spoke to them. They passed safely though the occupying army and the driver informed them that they were heading for Toulouse where they would be able to rest at the invitation of the Count until Lady Agnes was recovered enough to travel on to Montpellier.

"My husband will join us there, I assume," she said regally but the driver did not reply, simply looked ahead and urged the horse on.

Back at the Ciutat, Guilhem stayed until he was sure everyone had left and slowly made his own way out. He had a suspicion that Lady Agnes would be driven to Toulouse, he would make his way there but via the trails and hidden paths, not the main track which the cart had taken. As he passed by the river he heard a scream but didn't stop, simply bent his head and marched doggedly on.

It was as well he didn't stop, for the scream had belonged to Helena and much as he disliked the woman he would have felt duty bound to help her. In her quest for vengeance against Grace, the bitter woman had tried to tell a group of mercenaries that the cart they had allowed past without inspection contained one of the heretics they apparently so despised. They had given every appearance of listening to her and had suggested she follow them to one of the senior officers. Filled with hubris she had allowed herself to be taken into a tree shrouded clearing. She had no sense of danger until one of the three men had brutally ripped the linen shift from her body, leaving her naked.

"Skinny bitch, isn't she?" one of the men said laughingly.

"Not much to go around!" another said, squeezing her small breasts.

"She still has three holes, doesn't she?" the third joined in.

"Three?" questioned one of them. "Oh yeah!"

All three men laughed and set about the now terrified woman. When they had finished with her she was bloody and broken, barely alive. They tossed her shift at her and then went about their business. The last thing Helena saw before unconsciousness and then death took her was the bright blue of the Midi sky.

Chapter 40 – And So To Leave

The cart containing Lady Agnes and her retinue wound its way towards Toulouse, the terrain was rough and the pitching swaying motion of the cart quickly made Grace feel unwell so, despite the fact she was wearing only a linen undershift and her soft soled leather slippers, she begged the old man to halt temporarily in order to hop over the side. Young Raimond, fed up as he was of having to remain seated, elected to join her and the two walked companionably behind the cart as trundled along.

The day grew hotter as they made their slow process, baby Alais cried and was rapidly silenced by her mother's breast. Raimond began to whine, he was thirsty and hungry, but they had not been allowed to bring any provisions with them. After several hours and nearing midday the party stopped at Bram, an ancient circular town, seeking respite from the heat and hopefully some refreshment. The townspeople treated them with initial suspicion but once they realised who Lady Agnes was, they were made welcome and food and drink, albeit meagre, was proffered.

Grace looked around, the cart had meant they had been able to travel at a faster pace than had the party been on foot. Lady Agnes, newly delivered as she was and little Raimond would have been hard pressed to maintain a reasonable turn of speed and the two younger ladies-in-waiting would also have struggled. She wondered where Favia was but remembered the older woman saying she had kin near Perpignan so assumed she had headed south from Carcassonne rather than the westerly route they were taking. She struggled to picture a map of the region but thought that her ultimate destination was back in an easterly direction and half wondered if she should leave the party and make her way, somehow, to Minerve, but the thought of Guilhem heading towards Toulouse and his fury if she set off on her own, put paid to that idea.

The group resumed their north-westerly trek in the late afternoon, little Raimond now sleeping in the cart next to his mother and baby sister; Grace decided to remain on foot. The driver had decreed that the small party would overnight in Castelnaudary which was still several hours walk away, but the space in the cart was limited and she reasoned, in any case, they were travelling no faster than her usual walking pace and, freed of a cumbersome floor length dress, she was actually enjoying the exercise. The people of Bram had provided skins of water and a little fruit to tide them over until they stopped again; somehow the journey had become, to Grace anyway, a mere excursion.

This notion was disabused when some time later, and only a few miles from Castelnaudary, a group of men on horseback galloped up to the group. Jeering and heckling they harried the party, Alais shrieked in indignation upon being roused from slumber, Marguerida and Peyronella clung to each other and to little Raimond in terror. Lady Agnes attempted to explain the situation, but it was clear that the men, although now well aware of who she was and where she was going, were hoping that she had some goods secreted within the straw padding of the cart. In vain, the driver tried to explain that the women had brought nothing with them, that he had personally laid the straw and that there had been no opportunity for them to hide anything. The men were insistent though and forced the passengers to alight before tossing the blankets and straw to the ground.

Grace was furious and didn't attempt to hide the fact, she rounded on the ringleader, remonstrating at the treatment of the noble woman. The man, small and dark with a feral look about him turned to her and licked his lips.

"Perhaps you have something other than loot to offer us then, eh?" he leered.

Grace blanched and took a step back as the man made a grab for her. Lady Agnes screamed.

"I am still a noblewoman and my relatives will not be pleased when they find out that men of the Pope's army have defiled my women!"

The man smirked and reached for Grace again, she stepped back once more and tripped over a rock on the path causing her to fall backwards slamming her head onto the ground.

In a panic the horsemen remounted, they had no wish to be cited in the injury of a noblewoman's servant; if truth be known they had merely been after a little sport after the peaceful end to the siege at Carcassonne and had initially been unaware of the identity of the women in the cart. They wheeled around, looking for easier prey, leaving Grace semi-conscious on the ground, surrounded by Lady Agnes, Marguerida and Peyronella.

Guilhem Bastier had made quicker progress than the women, even though he had stayed to the hidden paths and at that instant happened to be a little ahead of them and on slightly higher ground. He had heard the scream Lady Agnes had emitted and decided to investigate the source. Wincing slightly at the pain in his injured arm he jogged along the main path until the party came into view. Recognising the cart immediately and seeing the women gathered around a prone body, he increased his speed. To his horror, as he drew closer he recognised the body on the ground as his wife.

"YSABELLA!" he shouted. "I'M HERE."

Kneeling he tenderly lifted her until she lay propped in his arms. "Ysabella, my wife, my life. I am here I found you. Wake up my sweet."

Grace opened her eyes and met his blue eyes, full of love and concern – smiling she reached out her hand and caressed his face.

Chapter 41 – Home Is Best

"Mr Minter, she's here," Adam shouted, as he covered the space between the attic door and where Grace lay unconscious and unmoving on the floor, "In the attic."

Kneeling by her side he gathered her up in his arms, pausing briefly to note the rags she wore, which barely covered her so threadbare were they; the smell of lavender still emanating from the clothes reminded him of something, he knew not what. He heard a small sound as something dropped to the floor – a heavy ring set with a red stone – but all his energy was focussed on Grace.

As his arms enfolded her Grace began to stir, she took a deep ragged breath and opened her eyes, looking straight into Adam's concerned face. "It's OK," he said, "I found you."

Grace sighed deeply and reached up one hand to caress his face, "Yes. You have. You said you would, and you have." Closing her eyes again she relaxed against his chest, leaving Adam puzzled yet strangely content to merely sit holding her in his arms.

When Ray reached the doorway he saw Adam struggle to his feet, his niece in his arms; he saw the tender look in the younger man's eyes and nodded to himself, he had a feeling that Grace had finally found a man to love her.

With no little difficulty, the two men managed to get Grace down the steep and narrow attic stairs and into her bedroom whereupon Adam lay her gently on the bed. She had remained silent and only partially conscious, up to this point but now she opened her eyes and, struggling to focus, looked up at Adam who merged into Guilhem and back again. She shook her head, still unsure of where and who she was until the familiar scents of clean linen, floor polish and the fragrance of the sweet peas on the dresser permeated her senses and brought her fully back to reality, HER reality, and she became aware that she was lying semi-naked on her bed with the concerned faces of her Uncle Ray and Adam looking down at her.

Seeing her realisation of her near nakedness, Uncle Ray hastily thrust her cotton robe at her and Grace pulled it on – grateful for his thoughtfulness.

"Now, young lady," Ray said, "what exactly has been going on?"

"And why the feck are you wearing rags?" Adam added.

Grace sat carefully up. "It's a long story," she sighed, "and one best told when you've fed me!"

Both men laughed. It appeared that whatever may have happened to her, her appetite had not been affected.

Over copious amounts of tea followed by the cottage pie Mrs Parkes had left the previous day, which, in Grace's absence Uncle Ray hadn't eaten, she began to tell them the story of her sojourn in the past. They listened intently, interrupting occasionally for clarification or explanation as she recounted the days she spent in Carcassonne. Somehow the fact that the fantastical story was being told by someone as practical as Grace made it eminently believable.

Epilogue

Daylight was giving way to the grey of an early winter's evening. Grace drew the heavy brocade curtains in the family sitting room, her life had changed dramatically in the ten years since she had experienced her strange slip in time, she hadn't thought it possible to be so happy. Her mind wandered back.

*****

When Adam had found her collapsed and barely conscious on the floor of the attic, in his words "wearing little more than rags," something had begun between them which resulted in their marriage four years later. She had completed her midwifery training in Manchester and for some years the two of them had based themselves in the North West. When they discovered that she was pregnant and told her Uncle Ray, he had insisted on signing the old house in the Cotswolds over to the two of them, it wasn't a hard decision to accept his offer and move.

The twins were born only a few weeks after the couple moved in and the house came alive as it finally welcomed a family within its old walls.

She had never managed to work out what had happened to her whilst she lay unconscious. It was clear she had lain there for only 24 hours, yet it had seemed as if she had lived for a month or so in the 13th century. The time she had spent there had left the same kind of indelible memories as her real life; the sounds, scents, sensations and feelings were as real to her as anything in the 21st century.

Once she had eaten and rested, Grace had begun to try and make sense of what had happened but there was no logical explanation. In the end, she had resorted to writing everything down, from finding the clothes in the chest, to waking in Carcassonne and everything that had happened there. She shared all of this with Adam and her uncle; at first it was clear they thought she had simply had a very lucid dream but, as Adam, in true researcher mode, had begun to investigate he discovered that she did indeed seem to be recounting actual events. There had been a Guilhem in 1209 who was associated with Minerve, the massacre at Beziers had occurred, Carcassonne was besieged and did ultimately surrender, all this could be verified. She admitted she already knew the brief outline of the history so could perhaps have simply merged what she knew into a dream. However, it was her vivid descriptions of the characters of the individuals she said she had encountered; the food, the smells, the overcrowding in the Ciutat and general living conditions which were the most convincing. None of them could say for sure that Grace had definitely experienced the events she recounted but neither was it possible to deny that she felt she had.

To further underline her story, Adam had returned to the attic and retrieved the gold and ruby ring which Grace had claimed belonged to Guilhem, the clothes she had described in such detail were little more than faded scraps of fabric but evidence of the braided trims was still apparent and a silver headband was discovered in the far reaches of the old chest. He called in a specialist in

Medieval artefacts who confirmed the age of both the ring and the remnants of fabric and provided them with sketches of how the robes may have appeared when intact. Grace described how the dresses were loosened or tightened with the side lacings and the specialist concurred.

Adam and Ray had continued research into the Minter family line, but records were hard to come by. They did speculate that Grace's Ysabella and Guilhem may have escaped Minerve when it itself was attacked and overrun by the Crusaders exactly one year after the fall of Carcassonne, as it would be unlikely that they would wish to remain in what is now known as France. It seemed entirely possible that, exactly as they had discussed, they crossed into the territory of Peter, King of Aragon, who as Count of Barcelona held jurisdiction over Carcassonne and may have offered sanctuary. From there and over the ensuing two centuries the family could have made their way through what is now recognised as Spain and then finally back into northern France where the Breton trader with the Occitan name was found by his possibly antecedent.

As for the surname Minter, Grace wondered if maybe the descendants of Guilhem and Ysabella had, at some point after they crossed to England, taken the name of Guilhem's home -Minerve, in remembrance and that had been corrupted to Minter in the following centuries.

Whatever the whys and wherefores of her unexplained, real or otherwise, sojourn in the past, Grace and Adam both knew that history had brought them together and that from the beginning they had felt a bond which could not be rationally explained. Grace chose to believe that perhaps, just perhaps, she and Adam were the 21st Century Ysabella and Guilhem and that this time around they had a chance for a long, happy and trouble-free life. She wasn't sure if it was reincarnation or genetic history but to her it didn't matter.

*****

A sudden commotion disturbed her reverie as two small bodies simultaneously burst through the door and hurtled towards her; a curly haired girl and a black-haired boy launched themselves at her, giggling in unison as their father followed them into the room chanting, "Fee fi fo fum! I smell the blood of an Englishman. Be he 'live, or be he dead, I'll grind his bones to make my bread," and stomping his feet loudly.

The twins shrieked as he got nearer and nearer, burying their faces in Grace's neck as she knelt on the floor with them, laughing herself as they squirmed and giggled. When he reached the group, Adam knelt and began to tickle the children unmercifully, reducing them to tears of laughter before turning his attention to Grace.

"Right then, kids, I think it's Mummy's turn now. Don't you?" The children agreed with alacrity and Grace found herself under onslaught from all angles.

"Enough! Enough!" she pleaded, to no avail. Only the sound of the front door being opened and Uncle Ray entering the room interrupted her torture by tickling. Uncle Ray had changed little in the intervening years, maybe a little bonier perhaps, but his hair was still thick and permanently tousled and he still sported his trademark corduroy trousers and cardigans. He stood for a moment at the doorway, drinking in the sight of his beloved niece laughing helplessly amongst the tangle of her family. A broad grin split his face, this was what this house had always needed, strange that it had taken the ancient past to bring it about.

"Will! Izzy!" he shouted. "Leave your poor mummy alone". Hearing his voice the twins sprang to their feet and ran towards 'Uncy Ray' – they loved the older man and he adored them.

Adam hauled Grace to her feet and they stood, his arm draped around her shoulder; the past had led to a very happy present.

A Word From The Author

Although this is a work of fiction, the events at Carcassonne and the wider Occitan area did happen. Vescomtat Raimond Rogier and his wife Agnes were real, as was their son Raimond. The daughter, Alais, whose birth features in this novel, is fictitious (insofar as we know!). I needed a reason for Grace/Ysabella to be more closely linked to Lady Agnes than a regular lady in waiting and, given her modern day midwifery, this seemed an ideal plot strategy.

There WAS a Guilhelm linked to Minerve (something I only discovered AFTER I 'invented' him) but Ysabella is purely fictional.

Finally, if anyone is interested, there are some excellent websites out there about the area and history of Carcassonne and the wider Occitan, including what we now refer to as 'the Cathar' religion. In the time itself, it is doubtful that the followers of this type of Christianity referred to themselves by any kind of name - I chose to use Bon Crestian - the Occitan words for Good Christian.

ABOUT THE AUTHOR

Born and raised in Sheffield, Laura now lives in the Peak District with her partner. A writer from childhood it has taken her until her 6th decade to take the leap of faith into bringing her work into the public gaze.

With a passion for ancient history, 'A Time for Grace' is actually something of a departure in style but, 'Grace got into her head and wouldn't shut up until the story was told'.

Expect future works to embrace her more esoteric side, with a planned trilogy encompassing the possible alien seeding of humanity and how we 'may not be alone'.

Other Authors With Green Cat Books

Lisa J Rivers –

Why I have So Many Cats

Winding Down

Searching

Luna Felis –

Life Well Lived

Gabriel Eziorobo –

Words Of My Mouth

The Brain Behind Freelance Writing

Mike Herring –

Nature Boy

Glyn Roberts & David Smith –

Prince Porrig And The Calamitous Carbuncle

Peach Berry –

A Bag Of Souls

Michelle DuVal -

The Coach

Sean Gaughan –

And God For His Own

Elijah Barns –

The Witch and Jet Splinters:

Part 1. A Bustle In The Hedgerow

Part 2: The Shadow Cutters

David Rollins –

Haiku From The Asylum

Horsey

The Monster In The Fridge

Brian N Sigauke –

The Power Of Collectivity

Bridgette Hamilton –

The Break The Crave System…7 Steps to Effortless Lifelong Weight Loss

Michael Keene –

For The Love Of Tom

The Other Life

Richard Tyndall -

The Aldwark Tales

Steve P Lee -

The Oblivion Trilogy:

   Oblivion

   The Department 44 Files

   Assault On Charlestown

Truth C Matters -

I Rest My Case

Deborah Carnelley -

Milo

Dinky The Mermaid

Tianna

Zapher Iqbal -

Lucy At The Snake Sanctuary

Jon Carvell -

Chaos In Camelot

Amber Purnell -

The Plug Monster

Daddy, Daddy, What's That Sound?

Shirley Cawte -

Fine Wine From Chipped Cups

Jennifer L Rothwell -

The Firelighters

     Book One: A Spark Of Fire

Betty Valentine -

A Twist Of Starlight

Diana Hardy -

A Dog Is For Life

Victoria McDonald -

Billy's Red Ball Saves Christmas

Timea Ashraf -

Bibi And The Butterfly King

James McCann -

Fairy Unfairly

Daniel J Hainey -

The Adventures Of Maddie And Liv

ARE YOU A WRITER?

We are looking for writers to send in their manuscripts.

If you would like to submit your work, please send a small sample to

books@green-cat.co

GREEN CAT BOOKS

www.green-cat.co

Printed in Great Britain
by Amazon